D0783617

NONE SHALL SLEEP TONIGHT

HUGH MCCUTCHEON's first full-length novel, *The Angel of Light*, was acknowledged as an *uncommonly good thriller*, and in *None Shall Sleep Tonight* the author has written another swift-paced and exciting story which must be read at a sitting.

Philip Latimer came to Shellbridge as Town Planning Consultant and, while exploring the town, walked out on the pier. It was a foggy November night and he expected the pier to be deserted, until he saw the girl in the mink coat—just before she went over the edge into the English Channel.

He did not realize where her rescue was to take him until she told him she had not fallen or jumped but had been pushed, until he learned that she was the beautiful and wealthy Ruth Mannering and that all the wolves weren't in the forest.

Ruth introduced Philip to her American fiancé, the mysterious Johnny Kingdom and, later, Philip met Johnny again. But this time Johnny wasn't talking, for there was a knife in his back. Philip, unable to sleep because of his fears for Ruth became more and more involved trying to discover which of her rapacious friends was trying to murder her and why. Was it for her money? For her 'Spanish Nude'? Or was there some other reason? Who resurrected the body of Johnny Kingdom after Philip had buried it among the lonely sand dunes? Who fixed the booby trap in Johnny's London flat? Who used the deadly fer-de-lance as an instrument of murder?

Look for the answers in the pages of this action-packed thriller and—none shall sleep tonight.

None Shall Sleep Tonight

By

HUGH McCUTCHEON

RICH AND COWAN

London   New York   Toronto   Melbourne   Sydney   Cape Town

First Published 1953

1104

Made and Printed in Great Britain at GREYCAINES
(Taylor Garnett Evans & Co. Ltd.), Watford, Herts.
for
RICH & COWAN
Eclipse Press Service Ltd.
London, W.1

CONTENTS

CHAPTER ONE

DARK MEETING

At dusk, the fog rolled in from the sea and I thought Shellbridge the most dismal town I had ever struck. Tomorrow, subject to a satisfactory interview with the Town Council, it would be my duty to Town Plan the place and, having disposed of what passed for dinner in the draughty Ocean Hotel, I went out to see what I could see.

The fog was not too thick to keep me from forming an impression of the general layout, which was like that of any other large seaside town in the south of England. A long, straight main street, choc-a-bloc with hotels, shops, picture palaces, and amusement arcades; a hinterland of slums; a promenade that seemed to stretch for miles and, of course, a top-heavy amusement pier, sticking out like a sore thumb over the black water.

If there is one thing I detest in these seaside resorts, it is the amusement piers. To me a pier is a place for steamers to tie up at—nothing more—and if I were going to prepare an Advisory Plan for Shellbridge, it might not be a bad idea to start with the pier.

I crossed the street in front of a single-decker tram-car rattling its empty way through the fog like a mechanical ghost. The driver clanged his bell, and a lorry, lumbering along from the other direction, pulled up just in time with a protesting screech of brakes. I reached the promenade in safety, however, and, passing through the unattended turnstiles, stepped on to the pier.

At once I found myself in the midst of desolation. In the height of the summer season the pier would no doubt present a very different scene but now, in November, with the fog rolling in thicker than ever, it was the world's end. It was more like a miniature town than a pier but everything was closed and shuttered. A theatre with a ghastly, gilded dome, torn posters advertising the last summer show still adhering to its walls; a couple of pretentious cafés, all glass and lurid paintwork; a shooting gallery; a row of automatic gambling machines and peep-shows; ice cream kiosks; winkle and shrimp stalls; the usual conglomeration of inanity. It was a wonder the pier didn't sag in the middle with all this top-hamper.

The planks echoed dull and hollow under my feet. I could hear the water slapping and gurgling at the wooden piles and everywhere was the smell of old wood, creosote, seaweed, and general decay. Somewhere out to sea the fog-horn on the lightship kept up a mournful accompaniment to my footsteps, hoo-hoo, hoo-hoo, like an owl with a sore throat.

All at once I realized I could no longer see the end of the pier. The fog had closed in, thick, wet, chilling and in spite of my heavy ulster I began to shiver. If I went much farther I might quite easily step off the edge of the pier into the English Channel and it was scarcely the Channel swimming season.

I paused and was about to retrace my footsteps when the fog lifted momentarily, allowing me a glimpse of the end of the pier, a semi-circular café, and a girl in a fur coat standing quite still, like a silhouette cut from paper. She was dangerously close to the edge and I just managed to choke down a cry of warning. After all, if she chose to take the air at the end of a pier on a foggy November night, it was none of my business. Presumably she knew what she was doing.

The fog shut down again and I began to walk back. What on earth could the girl be doing there? A secret assignation? A lovers' meeting? Or did she mean to——? Surely not that! I halted as the dreadful thought crossed my mind and at the same moment a wild cry rang out, followed by a heavy splash.

She's done it, I thought, and began to run. At the edge of the pier I threw off my coat and dived straight in and it was only when I hit the water that I realized what I'd let myself in for.

I came up spluttering, apprehensive, chilled to the bone, enveloped in fog and darkness and a deep, frightening silence. The tide was going out and I could feel the current pulling at my legs, nudging me out to sea.

"Where are you?" I yelled. Silence. I called out again, the hollow sound of my voice mocked me and then, from somewhere on my left, not far away, I heard a faint cry. So you don't like drowning after all, I thought. You want to be rescued. Pity you hadn't thought it over a bit more before you jumped in. I began to swim towards the sound and after I had covered a short distance, I called again. The cry was repeated, close at hand and, a few seconds later, my left hand touched something soft and wet that slithered away from me. It was the girl's fur coat and, thank goodness, she was still inside it.

I turned on my back, grabbed her under the arms and, after a struggle, got the coat off her. I could tell it was a beautiful coat, it felt soft as mink, so that whatever anguish of mind had made her jump off the pier, it wasn't money. Some man, probably. The coat floated away or sank and the girl fought her way out of my arms.

I felt her go down, caught her by the hair just in time and shifted my grip to her arm-pits again. She flailed out wildly and a fist caught me in the left eye. "Stop it, you silly little fool!" I spluttered. "You'll drown us both."

She went limp and I thought she had lost consciousness. My teeth were chattering, my legs felt unbearably heavy, I had no idea now in which direction the shore lay and that infernal foghorn kept hoo-hooing at me as if in mockery.

I began to swim on my back, taking her weight on my chest, feeling the current pluck once more at my legs. I struggled against it but I had no idea if I was making any progress until my head struck something hard with a force that almost sent me under. I threw out an arm, felt woodwork slippery with seaweed, hooked my arm around it and hung on, holding the girl in the crook of the other arm. It was one of the uprights of the pier and feeling about with my legs, I found a cross-section and sat on it, pulling the girl up beside me. We were still sitting in about six inches of water, my head throbbed painfully and I was so cold I could have wept. Instead I swore, very satisfyingly and very loudly.

I felt the girl's head move against my shoulder, then she said in a tight, haughty voice, "Mind your language, please."

Now there was cheek for you if you like, after I had fished her out of the water at the risk of my life. I swallowed hard, hot words rushing to my lips, but all I said was, "Sorry, I thought you were unconscious."

"Well I'm not, so you can let me go now."

"And have you slide back into the water! Not likely. What

did you want to go and jump off the pier for, you silly little fool?"

"I didn't jump off the pier. I was pushed."

"Pushed! Do you mean to tell me someone deliberately pushed you into the water?"

"Yes."

"Who?"

"I've no idea. It might have been you for all I know."

"So's I could make your acquaintance by saving your life I suppose?"

"It's been done."

"I'm not as desperate for feminine society as all that. In fact, if you want to know the truth, I'm not desperate for it at all."

"You talk as if it was my fault."

"My apologies again. If you were really pushed, that makes a difference."

"Of course I was pushed. I was standing at least three feet from the edge when I felt a vicious shove in the back and I went right over."

"That's pretty serious," I said. "That's attempted murder. Can you think of anyone who'd want to murder you?"

"No, I can't. Whoever it was must have been mad."

"Well, mad or not, it's high time he was behind bars."

I felt her shiver against me and she said plaintively, "I'm so cold and we're sitting in water."

"There must be a way up to the pier somewhere," I said. "They usually have ladders fixed so that repairs can be carried out to the woodwork underneath, but with this pier nothing would surprise me."

"My grandfather built this pier."

"Then God rest his soul. Can you hang on here for a bit while I go and prospect?"

"Y-yes. You won't go far?"

"I hope I won't have to."

I wriggled past her and, crawling along the plank, soon found myself clear of the water and against another upright. I pulled myself to my feet, felt my way past the upright and almost at once my outstretched hand touched cold, wet iron. A ladder.

I called out to the girl and heard her scrambling and slithering along the plank towards me. Then she caught my hand and I pulled her against the ladder. "Up you go," I exhorted, my arm round her waist. "I'll hold you steady." Wet and shivering as she was, she was undoubtedly a cuddlesome morsel and I began to feel that out of evil might come good.

She hung back, however, and I could hear her teeth chattering. "Suppose—suppose whoever pushed me over is waiting up there?"

"He probably cleared off quick," I said, "but perhaps I'd better go first, just in case." I began to mount the ladder, forcing my chilled hands to grip the rungs and I heard her climbing beneath me.

"Think you can make it?" I called.

"If you can."

I went right on up after that, hoisted myself on to the pier and reached down a hand for the girl. The fog was as thick as ever and I couldn't see a thing. "I don't think there's anyone about," I reported.

She was standing beside me now and we both listened but the only sound was the mournful hooting of the foghorn. The pier was deserted. "Let's go," I said. "If you don't get these wet clothes off soon you'll catch pneumonia. I hope your coat was insured."

"I hope so too. My lawyer sees to things like that."

"Little Miss Moneybags, eh?"

"You needn't be impertinent just because you saved my life. I'm Ruth Mannering, by the way."

She said it as if it ought to mean something to me but it didn't. "I couldn't care less if you were the Queen of Spain," I said. "Come on."

As I took a step forward, I stumbled over my overcoat and picking it up, draped it about the girl's shoulders. She protested but I insisted, and taking her hand we began to run.

"Have you far to go?" I asked.

"Not far. What about you?"

"I'm staying at the Ocean Hotel."

"But that's at the other end of the town! You'd better come home with me. My chauffeur will give you a change of clothes."

"You really are rich, then?"

"I have enough."

"Very rich?"

"I'm afraid so."

"And yet you don't know anyone who might prefer you dead?"

She was silent. Then she said, "You'd better save your breath till we get home."

Something's registered, I thought. Aloud I said, "If I had to rescue someone from drowning I'm glad it was a millionairess."

"I'll see that you're properly recompensed."

"Perhaps your lawyer will send me a cheque."

"I'll instruct him in the morning."

"If he does I'll tear it up. Can't you take a joke?"

"When I see one."

"I wouldn't take a penny from you. Why do we have to snap at each other like this? Can't we be friends?"

"You started it."

I took thought. "You're quite right," I admitted. "It's because I'm so cold and this place has got me down. I'm not usually short tempered."

"You've every right to be in the circumstances. I've caused you a lot of trouble."

"You couldn't help that. Is it much farther?"

"Round the next corner."

We had crossed the fog-bound promenade and the deserted main street and were running up a steepish slope that led to the residential quarter above the town. We turned a corner, passed through an imposing gateway into an asphalt drive and came presently to the front door of a house. All I could see of the house was that it was massive and of Georgian architecture.

"I'd better introduce myself," I said. "I'm Philip Latimer."

"I couldn't care less if you were the King of Siam."

We were off again and when she rang the bell I said, "Don't they trust you with a latch-key?"

"The key was in the pocket of my fur coat."

Before I could say anything more the door was opened by a formidable-looking butler. He had a conical, completely bald head, three chins and a stomach to match and for a long moment he stared at us in an awestruck silence. Then he said, "Cor stone the bleeding crows, Miss Ruth! What you been up to now?"

Ruth advanced upon him and he retreated before her a wide and lofty hall. "Romney," she said, "how often h told you not to use that vulgar expression? I fell into the and this gentleman pulled me out. Get him some dry clotnes, will you? Blake's should fit him." She turned to me. "You'd better have a bath."

"After you," I said.

"We have more than one bathroom."

"This must be Buckingham Palace."

We stood looking at each other in the brightly-lighted hall and I caught my breath. She was a beauty all right. Dark, raven hair, smouldering blue eyes, a straight nose, a proud little head. There was quality in every line and curve of her delicately moulded figure and, pale and bedraggled though she was, she would have graced any company.

The arrogant tilt of the head, the fire in the blue eyes told me I was staring and I said, " 'She walks in beauty like the night of cloudless climes and starry skies.' "

"You look quite ridiculous," she said, "dripping with water and spouting Byron. Romney will show you to the bathroom."

I followed Romney up a wide, richly-carpeted staircase to the first floor and along to the end of a corridor panelled in light oak. The Turkey red carpet was fitted, there were wall lights on wrought-iron brackets and a handsome oil painting of an English landscape that I recognized as an early Constable. Romney threw open the last door in the corridor and, with a regal flourish of his arm, ushered me into the bathroom.

"There you are, cock," he said, "it's all yours."

"This isn't a bathroom," I said, seeing myself in about six different mirrors, "it's Aladdin's Palace."

"It's Her Ladyship's own bathroom, cock, so you oughter consider yourself honoured."

"Don't tell me she's a Peeress, too!"

Romney shook his head. "No, that's just me way of talking. She's just plain Miss." He dug me in the ribs with a horribly sharp forefinger and winked a mischievous eye. "Only she ain't so plain, eh?"

"I'm as democratic as most men these days," I said, "but I object to being addressed as 'Cock' by a comic opera butler. My name is Latimer."

"O.K., Latimer. Anything to oblige."

"Mister Latimer."

Romney gave a musical but wicked chuckle. "You'll do," he said. "You and Miss Ruth. As haughty a pair as you could hope to meet. Like flint and tinder you'll be together. I'll fetch you up some duds."

When he had gone I surveyed the bathroom with an architectural eye and decided I couldn't have designed it better myself. The walls and ceiling had been painted oyster pink over embossed paper and there was a curved recess fitted with a mirrored wall and a glass, built-in table top. Beneath the table top was a circular dressing stool and down each side of the recess was a row of built-in drawers. There was a sunk bath, fitted with a shower curtain to match the pale green window curtains and surrounded by shiny black tiles, recessed lighting, a wall heater, pale green rubber flooring and a circular black rug. Altogether it was quite a bathroom.

I turned on the hot tap and was proceeding to undress when Romney returned with an armful of clothing. "I'll just wait and take your wet things away, Mr. Latimer, sir," he said cheerfully.

"Miss Mannering could afford a real butler," I said, "so why does she keep you?"

"She's got a kind heart," said Romney. "Fine set of muscles you got there. Keep yourself fit, dontcher?"

"Who is Miss Mannering, anyway?" I said. "Is she someone special?"

"Sure, she's *the* Ruth Mannering. Strums on the old pianner." Romney, having gathered up my wet clothes, went out and I stepped thoughtfully into the bath. Ruth Mannering, the composer! I knew her now. The only child of wealthy parents who had died in a London blitz; the darling of the musical world. Her latest composition, *Arabesque*, had been featured in a recent promenade concert and she had played the piano accompaniment herself. I had heard it on the wireless and it had thrilled me to a state of wild excitement. It had everything; colour, tone, a stirring melody. I remembered the thunderous, never-ending applause that had greeted the final chord and noticed that my heart was beating faster at the recollection.

The chauffeur's tweed sports jacket and flannels fitted

reasonably well but the shirt was rather tight at the neck and the shoes too big. When I went downstairs Romney showed me into a tastefully furnished drawing-room, handed me an evening paper and intimated that Miss Ruth would be down shortly.

He paused in the doorway, looked me up and down as if he were taking an inventory of my features and said, "Anything more I can do for your lordship?"

"You could answer a few questions."

"Answering questions ain't a strong point with me, cock."

"Have you been in all evening?"

"Why?"

"Just put it down to natural curiosity, Romney."

"Unnatural curiosity, I'd say. I went down to the local about eight after Miss Ruth had finished dinner and I stayed there till nearly nine."

"The local being?"

"Bill Gates's pub in Royal Street."

"Talk to anybody there?"

"Just Bill Gates. If I'd known I was goin' to need an alibi, I'd have talked to a few more, but I didn't know, cock. I was just going about me lawful occasions, minding me own business same as I wish you'd do."

"If I'd minded my own business, Miss Ruth would have been drowned."

"How'd she come to fall in?"

"I'll let her tell you that herself if she has a mind to."

"She won't have a mind to. Keeps herself to herself, Miss Ruth does."

"A practice I also pursue," I said, "so that will be all, Romney."

The look he gave me was unfathomable but he withdrew without further speech. I wondered about him. He had been out of the house during the vital time but on the face of it there was no reason why he should try to drown his employer. Unless he had been bought.

The room was gay with flowers, there was a roaring fire in the grate and I was standing in front of it, warming myself and surveying the L-shaped room when Ruth made her entrance.

If she had been beautiful before she was supremely lovely now with her blue-black hair curled and waved and her lips

B

bright with colour. She was wearing a flame-coloured cocktail frock with a low-cut, square neckline, black suède shoes with diamond buckles and a diamond necklace that caught the light and turned it to rainbow fire. My eyes drank her in and a flush stained the ivory of her cheeks. "Feeling warmer?" she asked.

"Much," I said. "I thought I'd never be warm again but this is heaven!" I made room for her and we stood side by side, our backs to the fire. The top of her head reached no higher than my chin, but I am a tall man.

"You must forgive me for being so churlish," she said. "You saved my life and I can never thank you enough. If I was rude, it must have been due to the shock."

"I was rude too," I admitted. "Cold water isn't good for my morale."

"It was terribly brave of you to jump in like that. In that fog, not knowing where the shore was, you might easily have drowned."

"I didn't think of that till I was in the water."

"You mustn't be so modest. Would you like some brandy?"

"It would complete the cure."

She pressed a bell-push in the wall and, as if he had been awaiting the signal, Romney entered with a crystal decanter of brandy and two balloon glasses on a silver tray. He poured us each a generous measure, winked at me and silently withdrew. We raised the glasses to each other and drank.

"To Shellbridge Pier," I said.

"I thought you didn't like the pier."

"It led me to you. Have you phoned the police?"

"No."

"Are you going to?"

"No."

"Why not?"

"I don't want any publicity."

"Have you thought who it might be yet?"

"I think I can handle it, Mr. Latimer."

"Who's your next of kin?"

"Please don't bother about it. I'm terribly in your debt already but I'd be still more in your debt if you'd just drop it."

"Consider it dropped."

"How can I thank you?"

I nodded towards the cream-coloured grand piano in the angle of the room. "By playing me *Arabesque*."

She blushed again and her lips trembled. She had a lovely mouth, mobile and sweetly curved. "Oh! You know who I am then?"

"Romney told me."

She set down her brandy glass, walked with grace to the piano, sat down on the piano stool and began to play. The rich, barbaric cadences of *Arabesque* rippled across the room and I sank into a deep easy-chair and listened with enchantment. It was wonderful music. She must have passion and fire in her to pour out music like that, I thought. It stirred primitive emotions and made the blood drum in my veins.

I rose and walked over to the piano, irresistibly drawn towards her and it was then, as her supple fingers flashed over the keys, that I saw the engagement ring. The last wild notes of *Arabesque* died away into silence and she sat back and looked up at me, smiling shyly. Then she saw the direction of my gaze and her hands dropped to her lap.

"Thank you," I said. "I am too well rewarded."

She rose, still smiling and then I heard a telephone ring in the hall. The smile vanished and I saw her body go tense. There was a cream-coloured telephone on a cream wrought-iron table to the right of the fire-place and I saw her eyes flick anxiously towards it. A second later it rang and, collapsing into a chair, she picked up the receiver with a nervous, snatching movement.

"Oh it's you, Diana!" There was relief in her voice. This was not the person she had been expecting. "Of course I'm all right. Why shouldn't I be. . . . Oh, you just wondered because you hadn't heard from me!" I knew she was repeating the other person's conversation for my benefit and pricked up my ears. "I've been busy on a new concerto. . . . No, I haven't thought of a name for it yet. How's Peter? . . . Oh, I'm sorry to hear that. Is it a bad cold? . . . In bed is he? What a shame. How long has he been in bed? . . . Just today? You won't have been out then, if you've got to look after him. . . . Of course, darling, we must meet soon. I've someone with me just now but I'll ring you back." I saw her blush. "What a wicked mind you've got, Diana, it's nothing like that. Good-bye."

She replaced the receiver quickly and looked at me under long, veiling lashes. "You asked about my next of kin, Mr. Latimer. That was one of them—my cousin, Diana Randall. She lives with her brother Peter in a cottage in the next road to this one and if anything should happen to me, Peter and she will get everything I own between them."

"Lucky people," I commented.

"Peter's upstairs in his bed with a cold and neither he nor Diana have been out all evening."

"You've only Diana's word for that."

"They have a housekeeper, a motherly body called Mrs. Emmett. She would know if either of them went out tonight. I've only to ask her."

"What about your household here?"

"There are only Romney and his wife and daughter. Mrs. Romney does the cooking and Hilda helps with the housework. They're all three devoted to me."

"That I can believe," I said. "Anyone else in the town who might wish you ill? A rival composer, for instance, or a jealous lover?"

She lowered her eyes and I saw the beginning of a frown mar the smoothness of her forehead. "There's Henry Crane," she said. "He did threaten to kill me once."

"Why?"

She smiled. "He's the jealous lover. He's an important industrialist in this town and it was when he heard of my engagement. He said he'd rather see me dead than married to another man." She paused. "He wasn't entirely sober at the time."

"The world doesn't seem to have heard of your engagement," I said.

"We haven't announced it yet. Johnny—that is—we felt we'd like to keep it to ourselves for a bit."

"But your immediate friends know?"

"Of course."

"Is your fiancé famous too?"

"No. His name is Johnny Kingdom and he's an American."

"Have you known him long?"

"No, it was what the newspapers would call a whirlwind romance—another reason why we haven't announced it."

"Do you love him very much?"

I saw the frown again. "That's rather a personal question, Mr. Latimer."

"After saving you from a watery grave, I feel a personal interest. Is he musical?"

"No, Johnny doesn't care much for music."

"You don't sound exactly like soul mates. Has he money?"

"He says so. Don't you think it possible that a man might want to marry me for other reasons than my money?"

"Looking at you now," I said meaningly, "I should think it more than possible."

"Believe me, Mr. Latimer, I've had my share of fortune hunters."

Her voice and manner had gone cold and I said, "Include me out."

"Aren't you interested in money?"

"I prefer to earn it the hard way, though I admit it would be very pleasant to have enough to buy all the things one wanted. A new car, for instance. You should just see the car I'm driving now. It's fifteen years old and looks every day of it. It would be nice to hand a cheque to a dealer and say, 'I'll take the Bentley in the window.' "

"And you don't earn enough for Bentleys?"

"Hardly. I'm an Architect and Town Planning Consultant. In fact, that's why I'm here. The Town Council advertised for a Town Planning Consultant to prepare an Advisory Plan for Shellbridge and I'm meeting them tomorrow evening. If we can come to terms I expect I'll be staying in Shellbridge for quite a time."

"So that's who you are. I've heard of you."

"I'm not famous."

"Nonsense. You have an international reputation. Didn't you plan a new town in the Syrian Desert and several towns in South Africa?"

"Yes, but——"

"And didn't you design the new Church of St. Seramena in Florence?"

"How do you know all this?"

She smiled. "You'd be surprised." The smile made her eyes dance and for a moment she looked like a bright, mischievous little girl. She had personality. It was in the steady, blue eyes

and the firm, up-tilted chin. And she had charm. I was deeply
aware of her and of her disturbing effect on my emotions. I had
never met anyone like her.

There was a long pause in the conversation then she said
lightly, "You're not married, Mr. Latimer?"

I shook my head. "I'm a bachelor gay."

"You haven't found the right girl yet?"

"I always find the things I want too late."

She coloured at that and I said, "It's high time I was going,
but I would like to ask you just one more question, if I may."

"Ask it."

"What were you doing on the pier?"

I could feel the silence. It throbbed in my ear-drums and
then she said quietly, "I prefer not to answer that, Mr. Latimer."

I shrugged my shoulders. "Very well," I said, "I won't
press you but I wish you'd reconsider about calling in the police.
Whoever tried to kill you will try again."

"I can look after myself."

"Famous last words."

Tension was rising between us again and then the phone
bell shattered it. She fairly snatched up the receiver. "Johnny!"
This was the call she had been expecting all right. "When did
you get in? . . . Of course, come over. Come right away. There's
someone here I'd like you to meet."

She replaced the receiver and gave me a most winning
smile. "You must stay and meet my fiancé," she invited. "He's
just arrived at the Ocean Hotel from London and he'll be here
in twenty minutes. He'll want to thank you, too, for saving my
life."

To hell with him, I thought. Fortune hunting swine. Still,
I'd better take a look at him. He arrived well inside the twenty
minutes and came bouncing into the room as full of energy as a
performing flea. He was short and dapper with black, sleek hair
and a blue jowl. His nose and chin were sharp, his glittering
black eyes were everywhere at once and there was a nervous
force about him that was as disturbing as a charge of electricity.

He made a point of kissing Ruth in front of me, his eyes
mocking me over her shoulder, then he said in a brittle, metallic
voice, "Who's the guy?"

"Philip Latimer," said Ruth. "The famous Town Planner.

Johnny Kingdom." We looked at each other, disliking what we saw. "Mud in your eye," said Johnny.

"Same to you," I answered. "In spades."

"Staying in this dump?"

"At the Ocean Hotel."

"Gettin' kinda late, ain't it?"

"I was just going." Romney stuck his conical head round the door, whispered to Ruth and she went off with him to attend to some domestic detail. Johnny grinned a savage grin. "What's your racket?"

"Miss Mannering just told you."

"I mean with my girl?"

"I've only just met your girl. She's in danger."

"I can see that. Your eyes just about ate her."

"I'm serious, Kingdom. Get her to tell you what happened tonight."

"She'll tell me all right. After you've gone."

Ruth came back and I said, "I really must be going." She looked at me, saw that I meant it and went with me to the door. "Sure you'll be all right?" I asked.

She nodded, not meeting my gaze and, taking her hand, I squeezed it impulsively. She returned the pressure. "Blake will call for his clothes tomorrow," she said, "and bring yours. Good night."

"Angels guard," I said, and then the closed door was between us.

I hung around for a bit but Johnny didn't come out and at last I walked down through the fog to the main street. On the wall of a building at the corner I saw the words 'Royal Street' faintly illumined by a street lamp and, just beyond, a man was locking up a public house. He was a short, rotund man, his pub was the nearest to Ruth Mannering's house and as he turned away from the door I stopped and, acting on impulse said, "Bill Gates, by any chance?"

He stood under the street lamp, looking up at me, his manner wary and, after a prolonged scrutiny, he said, "You a copper?"

"Do I look like a copper?" I snapped.

"You're big enough for one. Supposing I am Bill Gates, what is it to you?"

"Mr. Romney asked me to tell you he wouldn't be down

tonight, but I got held up and didn't manage in to let you know."

"There must be some mistake. Romney was here as usual. Came in about eight and stayed near an hour."

"Oh, he must have changed his mind, then."

"Changed his mind nothing! There was no call for him to send word he'd be in or he'd not be. I keep open house and it doesn't matter a row of beans in hell if Romney drinks my beer or someone else's. I don't get this."

"You don't have to get it, Mr. Gates," I said. "Good night to you."

I left him standing stock still under the street lamp and I could feel him gazing after me as I walked away. It looked as if Romney, at least, was in the clear.

No one took any notice of me when I arrived back at my hotel and I soon went up to bed—but not to sleep. I couldn't get Ruth Mannering out of my head. The way she looked; the soft notes of her voice; her fingers flying over the piano keys as if endowed with a life of their own; the barbaric, haunting melody of *Arabesque*. I lived over again the hectic moments of the rescue.

Peter and Diana Randall, next of kin; Henry Crane, jealous lover; Johnny Kingdom, possessive fiancé. One of them had tried to murder her and would almost certainly try again. I must get to know them all. Must watch them. Must find out which of them had done it so that I could keep her safe. She was sweet, sweet—I slept.

Johnny wasn't down for breakfast next morning and though I stayed in the hotel for quite a time, I didn't see him. I had a look at the hotel register and his name was there all right. 'J. Kingdom, London', in flowing handwriting.

After lunch I couldn't stand it any longer and, looking up Ruth in the telephone book rang the house. Romney answered. "Miss Mannering is out."

"Where is she?"

"I wouldn't know. She ain't been in all morning."

Fear clawed at my heart. "It's Mr. Latimer calling. Ask her to ring me at the Ocean Hotel whenever she comes in."

"Righto, Your Highness," said Romney, and rang off.

I had had Blake's clothes parcelled up and had put on my

best suit for the interview with the Town Council. I was just
wondering whether to ring Ruth again when a page boy called
my name and, following him down to the foyer, I found a tall
man in blue chauffeur's uniform with a parcel under his arm.
"I'm Blake, sir," he explained. "I've brought your clothes."

I gave him his for mine, thanked him for the use of them and
then he said, "Your car's outside, sir."

I gaped at him. "My car's in the hotel garage or ought to be.
What do you mean?"

"This will explain it, sir." He thrust a long envelope into my
hand and walked off before I could detain him. I ran out but he
had vanished in the fog and then I saw something that took my
breath away. Standing at the kerb, opposite the hotel entrance,
was the most beautiful Bentley I had ever seen. It was black
and shining, a sports saloon with knife-edge styling and gorgeous
tan leather upholstery. It was a lyric poem of a car brand new
and, with shaking fingers, I ripped open the envelope Blake had
given me. It contained a car registration book made out in my
name (my London address too), an insurance certificate, two
car keys, and a letter.

Dear Mr. Latimer,
   I value my life much higher than the cost of this Bentley.
Please accept it with my heartfelt gratitude in memory of the girl
whose life you saved at the risk of your own. May you have many
happy times with it and God bless you.

                                        Ruth Mannering.
P.S. I drove it back from London this forenoon. It goes like a
dream.

There was a choky feeling in my throat and then it gave
place to burning rage. How dared she! How dared she! Did
she think I wanted even her gratitude for saving her life? She
must have bribed half the motor trade of England to get a car
like that on immediate delivery. Did she think her money
could do anything in the world?

I was shaking with anger. It would serve her right if I accepted
it, but I could never accept it. Never. One Bentley in return
for one heart! As soon as I could get into the driving-seat I
would drive it right back to her and she could do what she liked
with it. She could give it to Johnny.

Then, with burning cheeks, I remembered talking to her about how nice it would be to be able to buy a Bentley just like that. Perhaps she had thought I had been hinting but nothing had been further from my mind. I had only been making conversation.

I went down the steps, unlocked the door at the driver's side and looked in. It was a honey of a car all right. It had everything. Radio, heater, cigarette lighter, the whole works. I glanced along its graceful, flowing lines and my eye was caught by the luggage boot. Now there was something like a boot.

The boot of my own car was a constant source of irritation to me. It wouldn't even hold a small suit-case and my golf clubs comfortably, but a boot like this would hold everything I owned in the world. There would be no harm in just looking at it.

I went round to the back of the car and tried the handle but it was locked. One of the keys fitted, however, and, lifting down the lid of the boot, I looked into its black, capacious depths; into the dead, staring eyes of Johnny Kingdom.

CHAPTER TWO

DARK BURIAL

I SLAMMED the lid of the boot shut and stood shaking in the fog. My brain seemed to be in a fog too and for a moment I could not bring myself to believe the evidence of my own eyes. There was no one in sight, but diagonally across the road from me I could make out the dim outline of a parked car. It was impossible to tell if there was anyone in the car or not but if so, he would not have been able to see inside the boot of the Bentley.

Slowly, with a hand that trembled violently, I pulled the lid open again, half expecting to find the nightmare vision no more than a trick of imagination. But the body was still there, the face paper white, the teeth tightly clenched, the arrogant look that had enraged me so gone for ever.

I leaned closer and then I saw the gleaming handle of a knife protruding from between Johnny's shoulder-blades. I put out a hand to touch it only to draw it quickly back. Finger-prints! I mustn't put my finger-prints on it and, even as the thought crossed my mind, I recognized the knife. It was a silver handled paper-knife and I had last seen it on an escritoire in Ruth Mannering's drawing-room.

I closed the boot again and tried to collect my thoughts. I am a law abiding citizen. I pay my income-tax and I knew that I should telephone the police, but I hesitated and was lost. What would Ruth want me to do? Last night an attempt had been made to murder her yet she had refused to tell the police and now her fiancé had been murdered with her paper-knife. The Bentley had probably been standing in her drive and the body placed in its boot to embarrass her, not me. The murderer couldn't have known the car was intended for me. Or could he?

I went back into the hotel and phoned Ruth's house only to come up against the imperturbable Romney, who informed me blandly that she was out.

"Out where?" I demanded.

"I'm only her butler, cock, not her keeper."

I expressed my feelings in a forceful epithet and Romney said, "You can get jailed for cussing over the telephone. If the Postmaster-General was to hear you——"

"Oh shut up, you fat baboon!" I snapped, and slammed down the receiver.

I went up to my room and put on coat, hat, and gloves, then went out to the Bentley. I knew what I was going to do but not why I was going to do it. It couldn't be that I was in love with Ruth. Love at first sight is a madness of Spring and there should be no such madness in November. All the same, I was going to hide the body.

I had come into Shellbridge by the coast road and, remembering the massive sand dunes that flanked the road, headed the Bentley westwards out of the town. The big car glided along with effortless grace, the engine almost inaudible. When I pressed the accelerator the response was instant and impressive and I was aware of a pang of regret that my acquaintance with the car was likely to be short.

The fog was an opaque yellow veil in front of me and I slowed the Bentley to a crawl. Even so, I had the narrowest of escapes, for a lorry, lumbering towards me and hugging the crown of the road, missed my offside front wing by a hair's breadth.

I swerved violently, leaned through the window to swear at the lorry driver and received a vituperative broadside in return. The incident tore at my nerves, making my hands shake as they wrenched at the wheel. If we had collided and the police had appeared on the scene—as they have a habit of doing when not wanted—and if one of them had gone nosing round to the back of the Bentley and opened the boot! My mind shrank from the thought and I drove on at a snail's pace, peering through the windscreen till my eyes ached.

Fortunately, however, the road was quiet and when I had proceeded about two miles beyond the town, I saw the outline of the dunes on my right and, taking a chance, swung the Bentley across the road on to the grass, switched off the fog lamps and pulled up.

I could hear the fog-horn blowing out to sea, faint and far away, like the horns of elfland, but there was no other sound. It took all my resolution to force me to leave the driver's seat and, as I stepped down to the grass, a car went by on the road.

It had come from the direction of Shellbridge and for a horror-filled moment I thought the driver was going to stop. The car certainly slowed for a second then passed on into the fog and I breathed again. The driver must have seen me standing there but he would not have been able to make out my features.

The stiff, wiry grass of the dunes whispered under my feet, seagulls mewed invisibly overhead, and just in front a carpet of yellow sand stretched away into the gloom. The tide must be out for I could not see the sea although I could hear the slow waves breaking with a sad, hollow sound that was infinitely eerie. A faint breeze, fitful as a sigh, stirred the fog, left the taste of salt on my lips and was gone. I stood there for a long time, listening, then I went back for Johnny.

He was limp and heavy and when I dragged him clear of the boot, his arms and legs seemed to get in the way as if deliberately trying to impede my movements. I laid him down on the sand in a hollow between two overhanging dunes, drew Ruth's knife from his back, cleaned the blade by plunging it into the sand and put it in the inside pocket of my coat. Then, nerving myself for the task, I began to search his pockets.

They yielded a wallet not very full of notes, which I replaced, an identity card which I pocketed, a few keys on a ring, which I also pocketed and some odds and ends which I left alone. Then, just as I thought I had seen the lot, my probing fingers encountered something small, hard, and round. I drew it out and found myself staring at Ruth's engagement ring.

The blood began to pound in my head. So they had had a row last night and she had given him back his ring! I remembered her tension when the phone rang, the strained look on her face. She had not been looking forward to meeting Johnny and now he was dead, killed by her paper-knife. I had waited outside her house for a considerable time but Johnny hadn't come out. Of course he hadn't come out. The dead don't walk.

Mechanically, I slipped the ring into my pocket. What to do? An insidious voice in my mind urged me to get back in the Bentley and drive on out, out of Shellbridge, out of Ruth Mannering's life. It wasn't as if I needed the Town Planning job that Shellbridge had to offer. There were more Town Planning jobs than there were trained Planning Consultants and, so far, I had done pretty well out of Shellbridge. I had got a fine new

Bentley, incomparably finer than any car I had ever owned, so why should I not take what the Gods had given me and skip? There was nothing to connect me with Johnny, not once I had him safely under the sand.

I began to scoop out a narrow grave with both hands and when it was deep enough, I rolled Johnny into it and covered him with sand, working at feverish speed, till I was almost sobbing with the effort. It had to be done quickly if it were to be done at all and when at last I straightened up, I was pouring with sweat.

No nice new Bentley for Johnny. Only a knife in the back and a lonely grave. Not even a prayer for I was too overwrought to think of one. The beach would be unfrequented until the summer and there was little likelihood of untimely discovery. At least, so I thought.

At the moment it was obvious that the sand had been disturbed, but in a day or two new sand would drift over the spot and leave no trace. Meantime, whoever had murdered Johnny would be wondering what had become of him, which was all to the good.

I retraced my steps to the Bentley, started the engine and prepared to drive off. But in which direction? Northwards to London and out of it all or southwards to Shellbridge and danger? Perhaps the Bentley had been more than a reward for saving Ruth's life. Perhaps it had been a bribe. "Here's a nice new, expensive car. Just get rid of what's in the boot for me and it's all yours." But why would she have stabbed Johnny? Because she suspected him of having tried to drown her and had taken the surest way of preventing him from trying it again? I was half-way back to Shellbridge before I realized that I had made my choice.

I parked the Bentley outside the Ocean Hotel and hurried inside to the bar. I wanted to wash the fog out of my throat, Johnny out of my mind and Ruth Mannering out of my life, but the bar was closed. In England they do not cater for men who bury bodies in secret graves.

Locking myself in my bedroom, I ranged the exhibits on the dressing-table. Ruth's silver-handled paper-knife, Ruth's engagement ring, Johnny's identity card, Johnny's keys. Four clues to murder. I glanced at the mirror, half expecting to find that my hair had gone white, but outwardly I was the same, dark-haired, lean-faced Philip Latimer. Inwardly, however, I would never be the same again.

The identity card revealed Johnny's address as 24 King Arthur's Mansions, Holborn, a district I knew well, as I had a flat not far away. One of the keys would no doubt fit his door and I promised myself an early look inside, provided I was going on with it. But was I going on with it?

I went down to the phone. Romney again, very much on his dignity. "Still out?" I asked.

"Sticks and stones will break my bones but names will never hurt me," intoned Romney.

"What's that got to do with Miss Mannering's whereabouts?"

"You called me a fat baboon."

"I was wrong," I said. "A baboon is an intelligent animal."

Romney hung up on me and I went back up to my room to brood. There was still time to clear out if only I could make up my mind. I knew that up to now I had acted like a lunatic, that I had made myself accessory to murder, but somehow I seemed to have been driven to do what I had done.

Perhaps that was the way fate intended it and then I remembered that my interview with Shellbridge Town Planning Committee was timed for 7.15 p.m. I thought, I'll turn up for the interview, as planned, and cheek them a bit, tell them what I think of their town, charge them a thumping fee for my services and if, in spite of that, they give me the job, I'll know I'm meant to be mixed up in it. If they turn me down, I'll leave the Bentley at her door and go.

I had an early meal and, fortified by a couple of drinks, drove the Bentley through the persistent fog to the Town Hall. The Town Hall was quite a building, a marble and sandstone palace lit up like a Christmas tree. It dominated its squalid surroundings, as well it might, for after all, it was the town's show window but, as for the architect who had designed it, hell gaped for him. The Council Officer, resplendent in a green uniform with gold facings, conducted me to an ante-room to await a summons to the presence. "Alderman Crane's the Planning Convenor," he told me; "it's him as'll ask you the questions."

He'll get some damn' funny answers, I thought. Aloud I said, "Is that Henry Crane the industrialist?"

"That's him. He's a big man in this town."

Ruth had mentioned Henry Crane as having threatened to kill her rather than see her married to another man and I was certainly anxious to have a look at him. I had not long to wait, for in a few minutes the Council Officer returned and bade me follow him. He showed me into a walnut-panelled committee room in which about a dozen councillors sat round a long, oval table, gave me a seat opposite the Chairman and departed on silent feet.

"Good evening, Mr. Latimer," said Alderman Crane. "Please make yourself comfortable."

I leaned back in my chair, looked casually round the room and had to bite my lip to stifle a gasp of surprise. At the far end of the table, looking very young and pure in a trim little black suit with a white piqué collar, sat Ruth Mannering.

She was looking everywhere but at me and when I made an effort to catch her eye, she frowned and ruffled the agenda papers in front of her. No wonder she had known my London address and the details of my career for, as a member of the Council, she would have been furnished with a copy of my application.

I wondered what the reaction would have been if I had said, "Hallo, Toots, I've just been burying Johnny." It was almost worth saying it if only to see her face, but at that moment Crane cleared his throat and the interview began.

Crane had an easy manner and took me rapidly through the preliminary details of my qualifications and experience. He was a big man, broadly built, fortyish, and greying attractively at the temples. In spite of his quiet voice, he conveyed a sense of power and I could see that he had his committee well under control.

When he had turned me outside in to his satisfaction, he smiled grimly and invited the other councillors to question me. Then he leaned back in his chair and sat tapping his strong white teeth with the end of a silver pencil.

I gazed at the councillors and the councillors gazed at me. They looked a hard-bitten lot of money-grabbers, all except Councillor Mannering, who still sat with downcast eyes and an air of conscious rectitude. Then a young, slightly-built man with a discontented face and a hacking cough opened fire.

"Mr. Latimer," he said, in a high-pitched, ultra-refined voice, "what is your opinion of Shellbridge?"

"Councillor Randall," intimated the Chairman with, I thought, a slight air of distaste and I looked at the young man with greater interest. So this was Ruth's cousin, Peter Randall, joint heir with his sister, Diana, to Ruth's fortune; the man who had been so providentially in bed with a cold when Ruth was being pushed off the pier. He had a cold all right and seemed to be taking great pains to let everyone know it.

"From what I've seen of Shellbridge," I said, "the services of a Planning Consultant are long overdue."

Randall raised supercilious eyebrows. "So you don't like our town, Mr. Latimer? We have many fine buildings, you know."

"Too many," I said.

"Perhaps you will be more explicit."

"If you appoint me your Planning Consultant, I'll be as explicit as you like."

"I see. So you give nothing for nothing. Just what fee would you charge?"

I told him and there was a moment of awed silence, then he said, "I'm sure we could get a Planner for less than that."

I shrugged my shoulders to show I couldn't care less and Alderman Crane, trying to smooth things over, said, "We're most interested in Town Planning in Shellbridge."

"Nothing I have so far seen would lead me to think so," I said. "Is it not the case that the Planning Act obliged local authorities to submit a development plan to the Ministry by a certain date so you are really having Planning thrust upon you?"

"You're very outspoken, Mr. Latimer." It looked as if I was on the way out and then a quiet voice from the other end said, "Not a bad thing in the circumstances, Mr. Chairman. At least we must give Mr. Latimer credit for his honesty."

All eyes swivelled towards Councillor Mannering, who bore the concerted gaze with fortitude, and I saw the faces of the councillors change. They had been looking offended and angry, but if Councillor Mannering were pleased with me, they were prepared to overlook my conduct. Councillor Mannering was a woman and pretty. She was also very rich. She could do no wrong.

C

"If I were appointed," I said, seeking to undo the good she had tried to do, "I would advocate many changes."

"That would be your duty but we would be under no obligation to agree to them." She had me there and before I could speak again, she said quietly, "Mr. Latimer has the courage of his convictions and I'm sure that any Report he would make to us would be sincere. I therefore move, Mr. Chairman, that he be offered the appointment of Planning Consultant at the fee he has stated."

Peter Randall didn't like it but there was no amendment and I found myself leaving the Town Hall in a bemused state, committed to calling on the Town Clerk in the morning and to whatever Fate had in store for me regarding the murder of Johnny Kingdom.

It seemed that Ruth had another meeting, the Watching Committee this time, so I arranged for the Council Officer to phone me when the meeting was over and returned to the Ocean Hotel to wait. I sat in the lounge for some time, trying to concentrate on the local newspaper, then sought relief for my overwrought nerves in the bar.

The bar had obviously been designed by a disciple of Picasso and combined all the worst features of this modern age, black tiling, coloured mirror glass, chromium plate, and scarlet Chinese dragons. At least, I thought they were dragons but they might as easily have been the creatures of an artist's nightmare. The only occupant was a mournful-looking man with a small, sandy moustache and sparse, lustreless hair, who was sitting at a table near the counter with his nose in a tankard.

He raised his head as I approached and watched me inscrutably with unexpectedly bright blue eyes. His linen was none too clean and his rough brown tweeds looked as if he slept in them.

I ordered a double whisky from a slightly voluptuous blonde and, as I turned away to find a table, the man with the sandy moustache said, "Where's your bow tie?"

I paused, gave him a cold, interrogative eye and he added. "You're the Planner, aren't you?"

"Not that kind of Planner."

"Have they taken you on?"

"I'm afraid so."

He raised his tankard to me and drank. "My respectful sympathy," he said. "If you care to join me, I'll be your window on the town."

His name, it appeared, was Leslie Turner, he taught Higher English at the Shellbridge Grammar School and when he had talked about himself for a solid ten minutes, he broke off abruptly and said, "But you'll want to know all about Shellbridge. Well, it's full of rapacious landladies, astute business men, retired Indian Army Colonels—curry snobs—and decayed gentlewomen who sit all day behind their window curtains, sharpening their claws.

"In summer, the beach is invaded by shop girls in two-piece swim suits and pimply clerks with a passion for fish and chips and, when they have spent all their money and gone their ways, Shellbridge, glutted with their gold, sinks into its winter sleep."

"Sounds charming," I commented.

"Then there are the people who run the place, Henry Crane, who owns about half of it and Ruth Mannering, who owns the other half. I hate all women with money."

"I'm with you there," I murmured, thinking of the Bentley.

"There she sits in that big, draughty house with her dim-witted butler, endowing hospitals and scattering alms but never a hand-out to her starving cousins."

"The Randalls?" I asked.

"Yes, Peter and Diana. I'm engaged to Diana, by the way, hence my bitterness. Teachers aren't millionaires and I'd like my wife to have a dowry."

I looked at him more closely. So he, too, had a motive for murdering Ruth. He looked just the type who would enjoy living on his wife's money. He would probably give up his teaching and write highbrow novels that no publisher would buy.

"I take it that short of Ruth Mannering's death your hopes are likely to be blasted?" I asked.

He nodded. "Yes, and Ruth's disgustingly healthy. However, I'm not the only sufferer. There's Molly Piggott."

"Who's Molly Piggott?"

"The girl you bought your drinks from, a blonde by choice because gentlemen prefer them. Her motto used to be 'Every man for myself', but now she's narrowed it down to one—Peter Randall."

I raised my eyes to the dragon-ornamented mirror on the opposite wall. Molly Piggott was sitting in the far corner behind her counter, smoking a cigarette and knitting. I had not really noticed her before but I saw now that she was pretty, with fluffy, soft hair, green, candid eyes—at least, they looked candid —round, pink cheeks and a full, pouting mouth.

"Flying pretty high, isn't she?"

"In a town like Shellbridge it's just about her only chance to get out from behind the counter, but she's an intelligent girl, fit for any company. Talk to her on any subject under the sun and she'll know something about it. Hi, Molly, fill these up, will you?"

Molly came over and took our glasses. "Scandalmongering again," she said. "You really ought to know better, Mr. Turner."

"This is Mr. Latimer, Molly," said Turner. "He's Shell-bridge's new Planning Consultant. He juggles buildings about and alters whole districts regardless of cost. Why should he worry? He doesn't have to pay it."

Molly gave me a pleasant smile. "Please don't shift the bus station," she said, "it's so handy for my home." She had a nice voice and a lively, intelligent manner and I began to think that Peter Randall might do worse.

As if in answer to my thought, Turner said, "Seen Peter lately?"

"He was in yesterday at lunch time," said Molly, and I pricked up my ears. Peter was supposed to have been in bed with a cold yesterday and I wondered if Molly Piggott knew anything about the attempt on Ruth's life. After all, she had the same motive as Turner.

"Popped the question yet?" pursued Turner.

The girl surveyed him with a blank, level gaze and for a second her eyebrows drew together in something like a frown. "Nosy, aren't you?" she said. "Mr. Randall has not asked me to marry him and if he did I'm not sure I'd accept him."

"You'd be a fool if you didn't, considering he and his sister are the joint heirs of Lady Bountiful."

"Lady Bountiful's younger than either of them."

"But no less mortal, my dear. She may not make old bones."

"There's nothing wrong with her health that I know of."

"Not yet," said Turner, "but life is full of pitfalls, particularly for those with too much money."

"Any interest I have in Peter Randall has nothing to do with any interest he may have in his cousin's money."

"Oh, hasn't it indeed!" Turner's voice was derisive and thick with too much alcohol. "Tell that to the Marines, Molly."

"He's always been a perfect gentleman to me which is more than can be said for some that infest my bar and what's more, Mr. Turner, you know what they say about people in glass houses."

Turner's grin was infinitely mocking. "*Touché*," he said. "We're a pair, you and I. We'd make a good team."

"The trouble with you, Mr. Turner, is that you're too good at judging others by yourself." She turned to me. "I'm terribly interested in Town Planning, Mr. Latimer. You must be frightfully clever."

"Don't waste your time, Molly," said Turner. "There's not a great deal of money in it."

Molly flushed. "You've had too much to drink as usual," she accused. "I don't know how you can teach children with a mind like you've got. I really don't."

"I don't know how I can teach them with the surroundings I've got. They built the school next the gas works, Latimer. What do you think of that for planning?"

"What would you prefer me to do," I said, "shift the gas works or the school?"

"Both," said Turner. "The school's obsolete. There's not enough window space for one thing. We have to use artificial light much more than we should and the heating installation's hopeless. You must come and see it."

"I'll be very glad to have a look at it," I said. "I've had some practical experience of designing schools and if I can improve yours I'd be only too pleased."

"I think children should have the best there is," said Molly. "I went to that school myself, before Mr. Turner's time, fortunately, and it's a terrible place. Draughty, too. Many a cold I caught in that school."

"I bet you catch a whacking cold off Peter," said Randall, "when he kisses you good night. You are on kissing terms, at least, aren't you?"

"I don't know what you mean by 'at least'."

"Never mind. To the pure all things are pure. How about looking the school over tomorrow, Latimer? Come at three and listen to my English class murdering *Macbeth*. Then I'll take you to the Headmaster and he'll show you round."

"I'll come if I can make it," I said.

"Good show. Ask the janitor to bring you to my class-room."

At that moment I was called to the phone and, not without relief, took my leave of the embittered teacher and the ambitious barmaid. It was the Council Officer to say that Councillor Mannering had left the Town Hall ten minutes ago and, hurrying out to the Bentley, I headed it towards her house. The fog was still thick and I lost my way twice but at length I arrived at the grey Georgian mansion and rang the bell.

A few seconds passed, then Romney bulked forbiddingly in the doorway. "Miss Ruth's got company," he said loftily. "She can't see no one."

"All right," I said. "I unreservedly withdraw the expression 'fat baboon'. So now will you behave?"

His fat face creased in a smile. It was like the sun coming out. "Handsomely said, cock," he acknowledged. "I'll see what I can do."

He went away and presently Ruth came into the hall. She looked flustered. "Romney tells me you wish to speak to me, Mr. Latimer," she said, trying to be formal and distant, "but I'm afraid it's not very convenient. My cousin, Miss Randall, is with me."

"Get rid of her," I said.

Her mouth opened and she stared at me, her eyes frosting over, then two pink spots glowed in her cheeks. "How dare you speak to me like that!" she burst out.

"I brought your car back," I said. "It was exceedingly kind of you but I already have a car."

"There's no need for you to take it like that."

"There's no need for me to take it at all."

"Then leave it and go. I hope you won't find the walk back to your hotel too fatiguing."

"I also brought you this," I said, and opened my hand. Her ring glittered in my palm and she took a step backwards, staring at it as if it were some loathsome insect. The colour in her face was noticeably less and it was some time before she could master her voice. Then, "Where did you get that?" she demanded.

"Get rid of your cousin and we'll talk." She hesitated and I said, "I'm in deadly earnest."

"Very well. I'd—better introduce you. She'll be—curious."

She led me to the drawing-room where a tall, striking-looking young woman was standing in front of the fire-place, smoking a cigarette in a long ebony holder. Her straight, dark hair was cut as if someone had put a pudding basin over her head and cut round it. An urchin cut, I believe they call it and, though she seemed a trifle old for it, it suited her so well one couldn't imagine it being cut in any other way. Perhaps it was because of her long, willowy neck.

"This is Mr. Latimer, Diana," said Ruth. "Our new Planning Consultant. He wants to have a word with me about his work."

"Shouldn't he go to Henry?"

"I already know Miss Mannering slightly," I explained, "and thought I'd like to have a preliminary consultation with her. I've just left your fiancé, by the way."

"Leslie? Was he very down in the mouth?"

"I've met happier men."

"He writes plays, you know, but no one will back them. So frustrating." She looked meaningly at Ruth. "You can't get a play on in the West End these days without financial backing."

"Or good dialogue and an outstanding plot," I said. So she'd been trying to get Ruth to back Turner's plays!

She had very expressive-looking dark eyes, I noticed, with room to think between them and she was thinking now, for the creamy whiteness of her forehead was marred by a tiny frown. She had a full figure and wore a brick-red frock and a good deal of probably synthetic jewellery. The shape of her mouth was disguised by too much lipstick but it looked a hard mouth. She could be cruel.

At that moment the door-bell rang. I heard the lumbering footsteps of Romney, what sounded like an altercation at the door and then Romney was in the room, his attitude eloquent of disapproval. "There's a policeman at the door, Miss Ruth," he announced, "and he won't go away till he's had a word with you."

Ruth looked at me, her eyes widening, but I did not move a

muscle of my face. Diana was watching us both and I was determined that she would get no reaction, but I could feel my heart pounding. Had Johnny been found already?

Romney stood waiting, eyebrows raised, hands clasped in front of him, a solemn, caricature of the perfect butler. "Shall I let him in?" he inquired.

I smiled at Ruth. "He probably wants you to buy tickets for a policeman's ball."

I saw the tension go out of her, the tightness about her mouth relax. "Show him into the library," she ordered. "I'll see him shortly."

Romney went out. Diana removed the cigarette end from her ebony holder, threw it into the fire and immediately inserted another cigarette. I snapped my lighter for her and she blew smoke into my face, her wide-set eyes regarding me coolly the while. "Good looking," she said at last.

"Through leading a blameless life," I said.

She gave me a slow, challenging smile. "It won't last in Shellbridge."

"There are certainly temptations."

Diana turned to Ruth. "Sure of himself, isn't he?" she commented. "Watch yourself with this one, dear, he's dangerous." She threw a fur cape carelessly about her shoulders, picked up a lizard skin handbag and pulled open the french windows that gave to the garden. Dark eddies of fog swirled gratefully into the room.

"Ugh," she said with a realistic shudder. "I hate crossing your garden in the dark." She looked at me and the invitation in her eyes was unmistakable. I resisted it but she was not to be denied. "Perhaps Mr. Latimer would escort me while you talk to the policeman."

"Of course," I agreed, seeing no help for it. As I passed Ruth I said out of the side of my mouth, "Don't go near that copper till I come back."

The garden was a mass of shrubbery and twisty little paths that would have been confusing even in ordinary darkness. In the fog they were a perfect maze and Diana seized the opportunity to slip her arm through mine. She was humming a little tune, no doubt pleased with herself at the ease with which she had abstracted me from Ruth.

"Our cottage is just on the other side of the he
foot of the garden," she explained. "There's a gap i
that Peter and I use when we want to visit Ruth.
distance to go round by road."

"Very convenient," I said, thinking that it was too convenient; much too convenient if Peter or she were bent on
mischief.

"You must come to tea some afternoon."

"Will your brother be there?"

"Afraid?"

"No; just cautious."

"What are you after with Ruth?"

"What are you?"

"Ruth's my cousin. We're very good friends."

"That's nice," I said.

We negotiated the last bush and reached the gap in the
hedge. Diana, not without reluctance, released my arm. "I
wonder if Ruth's got rid of the policeman yet." Her tone was
provocative. "Perhaps you'd better give her a few minutes
more."

"I mustn't keep you standing in the fog," I answered.

"Your consideration does you credit." She couldn't keep a
touch of malice out of her voice and as I stepped back, she
put out a quick hand to detain me. Her perfume had a heady
fragrance, she must have steeped herself in it and her fingers
clung to my arm like talons. Chill, damp air surrounded us, she
was no more than a vague outline in the fog, yet I could feel the
power that seemed to radiate from her; the age old, incalculable
power of feminine mystery.

"You don't want to catch cold, do you?" I said.

"If I was going to catch cold, I'd have caught it from Peter.
I'm interested in Planners. What makes them take up such an
unpopular trade? What gets into them? And why, when they
start planning, does it get such a hold on them? Such a hold
that they just run riot, trying to plan every bit of our lives
from the womb to the tomb."

"I wouldn't know," I said, "but I think you're confusing
economic planning with physical planning."

"Are you planning anything physical at the moment?"

"I'm not a Planner in the wider sense, Miss Randall, I'm a

own Planner, interested in the proper construction and layout of towns and cities. A beautiful building can move me as much as a beautiful woman."

"And suppose there's only a beautiful woman around and no beautiful building?"

"As now for instance?"

"So you think me beautiful, or are you just being polite?"

"I think you're a bit of a man-eater if you must know."

"It would be easy to find out."

"Too easy," I said. "Good night, Miss Randall."

I heard her gasp as I turned away and half-way down the path I looked back but she had disappeared through the gap in the hedge into her own garden.

CHAPTER THREE

DARK THOUGHTS

I STEPPED into Ruth's drawing-room, closed the french windows and turned to face her. She was standing quite still in front of the fire-place, watching me, her face calm but her eyes shadowed with apprehension. She was still wearing the little black suit and looked very young and lovely and defenceless.

"Fascinating dish, your cousin," I observed.

"She thinks so. Would you like a drink?" She was trying to speak lightly but her voice had a betraying tremor.

"No thanks, I've been drinking all evening which is not my habit, but have one yourself and make it a strong one. You're going to need it."

"I'd rather not. Where did you get my engagement ring?"

"You left it in Johnny's pocket which was rather foolish and you left this in his back which was even more foolish."

I took the paper-knife from my coat pocket, held it up by the point so that she could have a good look at it and placed it on the escritoire where I had seen it lying the night before. "This is where it goes, isn't it?" I said. "Don't worry, I've cleaned it."

When I looked at her again she was white to the lips and her eyes seemed suddenly to have grown to twice their normal size. "Mr. Latimer, what are you trying to tell me?"

"Nothing you don't already know."

"I don't understand you. You said you'd been drinking——"

"What I've done tonight would drive any man to drink."

"What have you done?"

"I've buried Johnny."

She swayed a little and caught at the mantelpiece to steady herself. I stared into her eyes, trying to fathom their deep blue, troubled depths. There was fear there but was it guilty fear? I had to know, even if it made her hate me for life. "I buried him in the sand a mile or two out of town," I said, "and brought back your engagement ring, your paper-knife, and your car. If that was what you meant me to do, I've done it, but I can't keep the car. I don't want any part of it—or of you."

She moved suddenly and I thought she was going to faint, but she was only seeking the support of a chair. "Have you—killed Johnny?" Her voice was barely audible.

I relaxed. Her eyes were wide with horror but there was no guilt there. Unless she was a magnificent actress she was innocent of Johnny's death and deep inside me something started singing. "I'm sorry to break it to you this way," I said, "but I used shock tactics for a purpose. I didn't kill Johnny but someone did—with your paper-knife. His body was in the boot of the Bentley."

"In the boot! But how—how——?"

"I've no idea. Until a moment ago I thought you might know something about it but I'm sure now that you don't."

"And you—buried him?"

"Not very deeply, I'm afraid."

"Why didn't you go to the police?"

"Why are you so breathtakingly lovely?"

"Are you trying to suggest you did it because of me?"

"I probably did it because I'm a quixotic fool. I didn't stop to think why I did it. I just did it and now the police may have found him. I didn't want this policeman to spring it on you."

"He couldn't spring it on me any more brutally than you did."

"I wanted to read your face."

"How dare you think I would do a ghastly thing like that!"

"I don't think it any more."

"I should hope not, indeed. What am I to tell the policeman?"

"That's up to you. His patience will be wearing thin."

"Yes, I'd better see him now. Shall I get him in here?"

I nodded and she rang the bell for Romney. The policeman turned out to be Sergeant Fitch of the local constabulary. He was plump, red-faced, and jovial and he carried a bedraggled mink coat over his arm. I caught Ruth's eye, thinking she might have trouble explaining away the coat, but her face showed only relief. "Why, Sergeant!" she exclaimed, "where did you get my coat?"

"It was washed in by the tide, Miss. I found it myself on the beach and seeing it had your name on the tab, I brought it straight here."

"That was terribly good of you. I lost it in an awfully silly way. You see, I took a notion to walk out on the pier last night and I had the coat slung loosely over my shoulders, with the sleeves hanging down empty. In the fog I went too near the edge and only saved myself from going over by clutching at a bollard. The sudden movement caused my coat to slip from my shoulders and it fell into the water before I could catch it."

"I see, Miss." The Sergeant noted Ruth's explanation in his official black note-book but he seemed quite unsuspicious. The explanation was glib and she had put it over well. She had acting ability all right and I began to wonder if I hadn't been rather premature in absolving her from Johnny's murder. Perhaps, however, she had realized that the coat might be washed in and had thought up a plausible story in advance.

The policeman, having accepted a drink and Ruth's profuse thanks, went on his way rejoicing. Romney sniffed disapprovingly at the empty glass. "Feeding good liquor to bluebottles," he grumbled. "Might just as well 'ave chucked it in the ocean." He took Ruth's coat and threw it carelessly over his arm. "Fine goings on," he said. "If I 'ad a coat worth a thousand quid, I wouldn't go for a swim in it."

"That will do, Romney," said Ruth, and the butler went out, shaking his head. We were sitting opposite each other now, with the fire blinking between us, and I said, "Why did you lie to him?"

"What else could I do? He'd wonder why I hadn't gone to him last night with the truth."

"I'm wondering that, too."

Ruth sighed. "I'm wondering myself. Once you start lying you can't stop. It's like a snowball, getting bigger and bigger until——" She paused.

"Until it gets out of control," I supplied.

She nodded. "You see, I thought it might have been Johnny."

"Johnny! Why should your fiancé want to drown you?"

"I don't know."

"You know more than you're telling." I paused expectantly but she remained obstinately silent. "What took you to the pier

on a foggy November night?" I pursued. "You wouldn't tell m
last night. Don't you think you'd better tell me now?"

She was gazing into the heart of the fire and whatever sh
saw there disturbed her mind, for she clenched her hands ti
the knuckles showed white. "Why should I tell you?"

"Because I saved your life and because, however wrongly or
foolishly I may have acted since, I have tried to help you. I'm
told the Chinese believe that if you save a person's life, you're
responsible for that person ever afterwards."

"Fortunately I'm not Chinese but you have helped me, Mr.
Latimer, and I can never be sufficiently grateful. I went to the
pier because of an anonymous letter." She rose wearily, crossed
to the escritoire, unlocked a drawer and held out a single sheet
of plain white note-paper. I stood up to take it from her hand
and remained standing while I read it.

The letter was printed lightly in pencil and ran:

*What makes you think Johnny Kingdom is in love with you?
All he wants is your two million quid. Whenever he visits Shellbridge he spends a lot of time with Molly Piggott before he comes
near you. Tomorrow night he's meeting her outside the café at the
far end of the pier, as usual. If you don't believe me, be there at
half-past eight and see for yourself.*

Well Wisher.

"So you've got two million quid," I said.

"That was what my father left but there were heavy death
duties and——"

"Poor little rich girl."

She stepped forward from the escritoire and slapped my face
all in one movement. It was a hefty slap and the sting of it made
me gasp. I took an involuntary step backwards, the chair caught
the back of my legs and I sat down with a thump. She stood
over me, white with anger, her eyes hard as sapphires and I
glared up at her, every bit as angry. "Leave my house," she
snapped, and then the telephone rang in the hall, followed
almost immediately by the sharper ring of the extension in the
room.

She snatched up the receiver and sank into her chair. "Oh,
hallo Diana—— Yes, the—the policeman's gone. It wasn't

anything, really. He'd found something of mine I thought I'd lost—— No, Mr. Latimer's still here but he's just leaving." Her voice, now that she had mastered it, was dangerously crisp and as she continued making small talk with Diana, I felt my anger ebb gradually away and I began to think.

After all, I had asked for it. The girl had been in distress and I had stung her with a bitter and uncalled for gibe. What had made me speak to her roughly like that, when every instinct prompted me to comfort and protect her? Was it because her fortune was a barrier I felt I could not cross? Because I wanted the unattainable? If I left now I knew it would be for ever. I would write the Town Clerk in the morning declining the appointment and never set foot in Shellbridge again as long as I lived. There was a Planning job going on the Gold Coast and I had liked Africa. Yes, it would be exciting to visit Africa again. The farther away from Shellbridge the better.

She replaced the receiver and looked at me as if she were seeing me through a mist. The anger had died out of her eyes but not the unhappiness, and I smiled at her with all the reassurance I could muster. "You don't have to believe it," I said, "but I'm sorry. I don't bury discarded fiancés every day and my nerves are all on edge."

"I'm sorry too," her voice was flat, infinitely tired, "but you aren't the only one whose nerves are on edge."

"Shall we call it quits and start afresh?"

"Please."

"All right. This anonymous letter: was it posted?"

"Yes, and the postmark was local."

"Any idea who might have written it?"

"No."

"Quite sure you have no idea?"

"Quite sure. That's what makes it so—hateful."

"You realize now that the writer's intention was to lure you out to the end of the pier at a certain time, lie in wait for you and—murder you by drowning?"

"I know that now."

"Molly Piggott is supposed to be interested in your cousin Peter."

"So I've heard."

"And as Johnny was staying at the Ocean Hotel, where she

is the barmaid, he wouldn't have needed to make an assignation on the pier if he'd wanted to meet her."

"That did occur to me but I had to know. So I went to the pier."

"And when you were pushed over the edge, you thought Johnny might have been waiting for Molly, seen you arrive and in a fit of rage at your spying on him, attacked you?"

She nodded. "I thought that might have been it. I tackled Johnny about it after you left last night but he denied it strenuously. Then we had a blazing row and I gave him back his ring."

I tried to remember what the end of the pier had looked like. There had been a semi-circular café with a glass dome, a single-storey building, situated to the left, quite close to the edge. Someone could have been lurking behind the far wall of the café waiting for Ruth to appear, someone with a vicious, twisted, covetous mind, bent on murder.

Up till now I had met five people who might have been capable of murder, and passed them in review through my mind. First, there was handsome Henry Crane, the industrialist and Chairman of the Planning Committee, who had certainly looked as if he could be bitterly jealous and who had told Ruth he would rather see her dead than married to another man. Then came Peter Randall, thin of face and weak about the mouth, probably a heavy spender, living on his expectations. Then the sandy-haired schoolmaster, Leslie Turner, who wrote plays that no one would back, and Molly Piggott, the plump and pouting barmaid with social ambitions. I knew, none better, how stern a master ambition can be. Lastly, there was Diana Randall, of the cool gaze and wide-set eyes, a hard type if ever there was one. A near nymphomaniac who could be had for the asking. At least that was how I saw her.

Up till now they were no more to me than five strange faces but all of them would have fared better with Ruth dead, except perhaps Henry Crane, of whose mental stability I was in doubt. I would have to get behind those five faces, into the hidden depths of their minds and time was running out. When Johnny was found, Sergeant Fitch was going to remember that coat.

Ruth was watching me, her face impassive, her lovely,

expressive eyes deeply shadowed. "What are you thinking?"
she asked.

"Dark thoughts," I admitted. "Had you any reason to
doubt Johnny's devotion?"

She had one of those ridiculously tiny handkerchiefs that
women carry and she was twisting it savagely and unknowingly
with both hands. "No reason," she said, "just instinct and I
couldn't trust my instinct. You get that way when men are after
your money."

She rose and began to pace the room. "When you called me
poor little rich girl, you spoke more truly than you knew. That's
why I was stung into losing my temper. A woman wants to be
loved and cherished, to have a home and children and I'm
no different to the rest. Having money hasn't changed me but
it's changed the men. I've had proposals, a lot of them, but few
of them sincere. All the wolves aren't in the forest and I had
grown pretty disillusioned about men when I met Johnny.

"It was three months ago at a dance in a hotel on the London
road. A party of us went together. Peter and Diana, Henry
Crane, Leslie Turner, one or two more. It was rather a boring
dance and I was sitting out on a little balcony overlooking the
car park. Most of our party were dancing, Peter had gone to
fetch me a drink and for the moment I was quite alone.

"I saw a car drive into the park and a man get out, speak to
the attendant and walk towards the hotel entrance. Then, a
piece of paper fluttered down from his clothes and I stood up,
leaned over the balcony rail and called out, 'Excuse me, but I
think you've dropped your parking ticket.'

"He spun round—I remember thinking how quick and light
on his feet he seemed—and stood staring up at me. He stared
for a long time then he said, 'Oh speak again, bright angel.' "

"Probably the only Shakespearean line he knew," I
commented.

"Perhaps, but *Romeo and Juliet*'s my favourite play and I
was intrigued. Then he said, 'Stay right there, beautiful, I'm
coming up,' and before I could answer he was climbing the
drain-pipe as nimbly as a monkey, tails, white tie and all.

"When he swung himself over the balcony rail, I said, 'You
might have broken your neck,' and he said, 'Lady, the risk was
worth it.' I knew I was looking as nice as I would ever look, I

D

was wearing a white satin evening dress that Christian Dior himself had designed for me and a diamond necklace that had belonged to my mother. There was a full moon shining, making the diamonds glitter and the sequins on my dress, and he said, 'My name's Johnny Kingdom, my old man's in real estate back in New York and he's got stacks of dough, so how about you and me getting married?'

"I said, 'You don't even know my name,' and he laughed— he had a gay, careless laugh—and answered, 'What's your name matter? I'm gonna change it, anyway. You've got the loveliest eyes in the world and the sweetest voice and when I saw you standing on the balcony like a fairy queen, I felt something come over me. I'm like that; romantic.' "

"It was romantic all right," I conceded. "So that's how you met?"

"Yes," her voice trembled; "that's how we met."

"And how did you part?"

She went back to her chair and sat down. She had twisted the handkerchief into a limp rag and looked pretty limp herself. "In bitterness and disillusionment," she said, and the tremble in her voice increased till it took all her resolution to keep from bursting into tears. "At first I thought him wonderful. He was so different with his quick-fire American speech, his nervous energy, and his romantic way of wooing. He gave me no peace till in the end I agreed to marry him and when I told him I had lots of money too, he said I could give mine away as he had more than enough for both of us. I think what attracted me most was the belief that it was me he wanted, not my money, that he hadn't even known my name, much less my circumstances. Then, slowly, I began to doubt."

"What made you doubt?"

"Money again. He was always talking about money, about how rich his father was, yet when we became engaged, he wouldn't let me write to his father, said he wanted to break the news himself when he went back to New York. I never even knew his father's address. He suggested flying to the Riviera for our honeymoon and when I agreed to that he said that we should each make a will before going on the plane. He said he had a friend who was killed in a plane crash and there was a lot of trouble about his estate because he had died intestate."

"I suppose the idea was that you should leave him your money and he would leave you his?"

"Yes, but while I knew how much I had to leave, I had only his word that he was rich. I told him we would probably both be killed if the plane crashed but he kept harping on it and then I got the anonymous letter."

"I think I know how you must have felt," I murmured.

She tooked a cigarette from a silver box and lit it unknowingly. "Last night I told him about the attempt to drown me, confronted him with the anonymous letter and demanded an explanation. He was indignant. He said he hardly knew Molly Piggott and that if he had wanted to drown me he'd have waited till I'd made that will. He harped on about the will again until I snapped at him. By this time he was white with rage and I was just as angry. I told him I knew nothing about him, where he lived in America, why he was in England, where his money came from. I said I wouldn't marry him unless he was frank with me and he called me a horrible name. So I threw his ring on the table and told him to take it and go."

"And did he go quietly?"

"Not at first. He tried to argue with me but I wouldn't listen. Then he began to plead and that disgusted me. Finally he went. His last words were that he had a darned good idea who had tried to drown me and that he was the only one who could see I stayed alive."

"That's interesting," I said. "It gives us a strong motive for his murder." Her cigarette went into the fire, half smoked, and I stood up. "One thing I've just thought of," I said. "When they miss him at the hotel, they'll go to the police and the hunt will be up. I wonder if I can fix that too."

"How?"

"I'll work something out but I'd better get busy right away. I'll phone you how it goes."

"Mr. Latimer, I really don't know why I've told you all this and I don't want to sound ungrateful but, after all——"

"It's none of my business?"

"Please, don't take it like that. What I meant was you're under no obligation to run any risks for me. We—we don't really know each other and——"

"I know that you're Queen Cophetua and that I'm the beggar man."

"That isn't what I'm getting at at all and it's not very fair of you to suggest it. I'm terribly, terribly grateful to you for what you've done for me, but I don't want you to get into trouble over me. Oh dear, I'm not doing this very well."

"I understand you perfectly," I said. "You're refusing all further offers of assistance."

Her face was twisted with embarrassment and her eyes implored me so desperately that I had to relent. "I've got to protect myself too, now," I explained. "I burned my boats when I buried Johnny and I must try to cover my tracks as well as I can. You see that, don't you?"

"Yes, I see it, but——"

"So I'm really helping myself, not you." I gave her my most reassuring smile and, after a momentary hesitation, she smiled back.

When I left a thin rain was falling, laying the fog, and I was half-way back to the hotel before I realized I was still driving the Bentley. I had meant to leave it in her drive but it was too late now. I would just have to keep it till tomorrow.

The hotel garage was open but there was no one about and I parked the Bentley alongside my own battered old car which seemed to me to exude an air of reproach. Then, using the greatest caution, I peeped into the hall-way of the hotel.

There was a light above the reception desk and the night porter was sitting there with his nose in a book. He looked incredibly ancient, with his thin, bowed shoulders, his steel-rimmed glasses, drooping mouth and scraggy, wrinkled neck. His lips moved soundlessly as he read aloud and I felt compassion stir in my heart, but as he continued to sit there as if turned to stone, compassion gave way to irritation.

Then a buzzer somewhere above his head rasped an imperious summons. He looked up at the buzzer and made a wry grimace then, with painful deliberation, he struggled up from his seat, placed his spectacles carefully on top of his book and, muttering to himself, began to climb the stairs. His shadow, bent and grotesque, went before him on the wall until he vanished round the bend of the staircase. The hall was empty now and, tiptoeing in, I crossed to the desk and took a quick look at the register.

Johnny's room number was seventy-seven, three doors away

from mine on the opposite side of the corridor and his room key was hanging on a hook close to my own. I took both keys then I noticed the call book lying open on the desk beside the porter's novel and wrote in it, 'Call 77, 8 a.m.', to establish the belief that Johnny had returned to the hotel. I had had a good look at his signature in the register, his flowing writing was easy to copy and I have a draughtsman's gift for forgery.

I was listening all the time for the returning footsteps of the porter, then, just to my right I heard a door open and stepped quickly away from the desk. Two figures emerged from the bar and stood facing me in the fog-dimmed hall. They were Molly Piggott and Peter Randall and they looked like children caught robbing the pantry.

They must have been alone in the bar for some time, for it closed to the public at ten o'clock and it was now twenty to twelve. Molly's hair was like a jackdaw's nest and there was a smear of lipstick at the corner of Randall's mouth.

"Ah, good evening, Latimer," he said in his high, affected voice. "Molly was just giving me something for my cold."

"I didn't know lipstick was good for it," I said.

"What? Oh!" He pulled out a handkerchief, wiped his mouth, looked at the handkerchief and swore under his breath. Molly giggled and Randall swayed a little as he tucked the handkerchief back into his pocket. He was strongly redolent of whisky and looked as if he had imbibed enough to cure a dozen colds.

"I'm glad to see you have a sense of humour," he commented. "I thought Planners were all very serious people, inflated with their own importance."

"Some of us are almost human," I said.

"Well, try not to be too human, there's a good chap. We want you to do a good job here and not take too much time over it. We like to get on with things in Shellbridge."

"You appear to have been putting your principles into practice," I said.

Molly giggled again. "You won't get much change out of Mr. Latimer, Peter," she prophesied. "I'm sure he's clever. He's got an awfully clever face. I think I'm going to like him."

"The fact that you like him," said Randall, "will of course endear him to me for ever. Good night, Latimer."

"Good night," I acknowledged. "I hope your cold will be better in the morning. I'm sure it won't be Molly's fault if it isn't."

They went out arm-in-arm and as I climbed the stairs I heard the whine of a self-starter and the purr of a well-tuned engine. Above me I heard the slow, dragging steps of the returning porter, but I was out of sight round the bend of the first floor corridor before he reached my level. I stood still against the wall until he reached the ground floor then I went straight to Johnny's room and let myself in.

His bed had been turned down for the night, his pyjamas lay on the counterpane, his brushes on the dressing-table. A shirt hung over a chair and his suit-case stood in a corner next the wardrobe. It had only been partly unpacked and, gathering up the rest of his things, I bundled them into the case.

I laid three pounds notes on the dressing-table, tore a leaf from my note-book and, still copying Johnny's writing, wrote, *Sorry to sneak away, but there's a guy here I don't want to meet. This should cover the bill. J. Kingdom.* I laid the note on top of the money and, leaving the key in the door, carried his suit-case back to my own room.

The problem now was to get rid of the suit-case. A few feet below my window was the flat roof of an outhouse and just beyond that again, on a slightly lower level, the roof of the garage, also flat, and I decided to try and get the suit-case out that way, lock it in the boot of the Bentley for the night and return by the front door as if I had just come in.

There was no one to be seen in the courtyard and, throwing the suit-case down on the outhouse roof, I dropped after it, threw it across to the garage roof and jumped the intervening space, landing lightly on the garage roof. I was about to proceed further when I heard someone whistling below.

I lay flat on the roof, the suit-case beside me, and listened. The whistling grew louder and then I heard someone come out of the garage and walk across the courtyard. It was probably the garage attendant and I wondered if he had heard the thump of my arrival on the roof. He did not appear to have any suspicion, however, and it was probable he had been at the far end of the garage out of earshot.

I risked a peep over the edge and saw a blurred figure in a

peaked cap standing outside the tradesman's entrance. Then the door opened, letting out a flood of light, and I saw that it was the garage attendant, all right. He went inside, the door closed, I heard a momentary rumble of voices, a girl's high-pitched laugh, then all was still again.

I waited a couple of minutes, wondering if the attendant had gone off duty for the night or if he would be back, then I dropped the suit-case to the ground and, hanging by my hands from the edge of the garage roof, let myself go.

The drop was longer than I had thought and the stinging pain in the soles of my feet brought the water into my eyes. I limped into the deserted garage, unlocked the boot of the Bentley, pulled open the lid and made to throw the suit-case in. Then horror swept over me like a cold, stifling wave and I stood gaping in fear and unbelief. The body of Johnny Kingdom, the body I had buried with my own hands that same afternoon, was back in the boot.

CHAPTER FOUR

REPEAT PERFORMANCE

I DON'T know how long I stood there staring at the body but it must have been a considerable time. The whole thing savoured of witchcraft but I knew there must be a logical explanation, and then I was seized with a shuddering fit that shook my whole body. Somewhere in Shellbridge a malignant and perverted mind was gloating over this macabre joke and I clenched my hands in a sudden onset of rage. Whoever he was, I would hunt him down. Henceforth there would be no quarter between him and me.

I remembered the car that had been parked across the street the first time I had discovered the body. Someone had been in that car, watching. When I had stepped out of the Bentley in the sand dunes, a car had slowed up then passed on and I knew now that it must have been the same car. It must have stopped farther on, round the bend, and the occupant had crept back, watched me at my grisly work, removed the body after I had left the scene, concealed it in his own car and waited for an opportunity of putting it back in the Bentley.

I tried to think back over all the places the Bentley had been that day. It had stood for some hours outside the hotel just off the fog-bound street, then it had been parked in the Town Hall courtyard, then in Ruth's drive, and lastly in the hotel garage.

I could feel malignance in the very air. It was all around me in the dim and silent garage like an invisible mist. The head-lamps of the rows of cars were like dark, goggling eyes and the thought sprang to my mind, suppose there was someone lurking in one of those cars now, enjoying my discomfiture, gloating in sadistic glee at my confusion and dismay.

I put Johnny's suit-case in the boot beside his body, armed myself with a spanner from the tool-kit and went grimly from car to car. At the far end of the garage a single light fought a losing battle with the fog but I did not want to put on the rest of the lights in case I attracted some member of the hotel staff. The garage attendant was probably still in the vicinity and might return at any moment. Or did he make a habit of leaving the garage doors open when he went off duty?

There was no one hiding in any of the cars, no one anywhere in the garage, but the atmosphere of malevolence lingered and all at once the anger that possessed me burst its bounds. I slid into the driving-seat of the Bentley, started the engine and drove out into the street. The clock on the dashboard told me that it was after midnight but I couldn't have cared less.

The fog was thinning, driven back by the persistent rain, and I could see for quite a distance. There was no longer a need for cautious driving and the Bentley pierced the night like an arrow, straight to Ruth's mansion. For the first time I saw it clearly, huge and cumbersome in its Georgian solidity. The windows were dark.

I rang the bell. Nothing happened. I rang again, keeping my finger on the button. I could hear its strident clamour going on and on unceasingly then slow, unhurried footsteps and the door was jerked open. Light sprang up in the hall and Romney peered out, bulging formidably in a scarlet dressing-gown. "Get Miss Ruth," I said.

"She's in bed, cock."

"Get her out of bed."

"She's asleep."

"Then wake her. There'll be no sleep for her tonight, none for me and probably none for you. None shall sleep tonight, Romney. Get cracking."

"You gone nuts?"

"It wouldn't be surprising if I had. Are you going to wake Miss Ruth or shall I?"

"There's something I gotta know," said Romney, planting himself firmly in the doorway and looking as stubborn as Horatio guarding the bridge. "Miss Ruth's in some kind of trouble, it don't take brains to tell that, but I don't want to know what trouble 'less she chooses to tell me. What I do want to know is, whose side are you on?"

"Hers."

"Is that the straight griffin?"

"Cross my heart, Romney."

"You ain't got a heart, knocking folks up this time o' night, but I'll wake Miss Ruth for you, cock, and the rest's up to you."

"What is it, Romney?" I heard Ruth's voice in the background, and Romney stood aside to disclose her standing very straight and dignified at the bend of the staircase. The light spilled richly over her night-black hair, over her clinging house-coat of crimson velvet. She had never looked so beautiful.

"Push off," I said to Romney, and stepped into the hall. Her colour fled at sight of me and she came slowly down the stairs, her eyes looking an agonized question. Romney was still hovering in the background and she pushed open the drawing-room door. "In here," she invited.

The fire was embers, the room had settled for the night and seemed, to my fevered fancy, to resent the intrusion. "Johnny's back," I said.

"Back where?"

"Where I first found him. Someone must have watched me bury him then scratched him up and put him back in the Bentley."

"No! Oh no! It can't be true."

"I only wish it weren't."

She sat down, abruptly, in the nearest chair, huddling up in the house-coat and holding out her hands to the dying fire. One of her quilted slippers fell off and I was quite startled by the almost transparent whiteness of her foot and its delicate tracery of blue veins. It stirred primitive emotions, a feeling of almost savage tenderness, but when she saw the look in my eyes her foot dived into the slipper like a mouse seeking sanctuary and she tucked both feet out of sight under the hem of her gown. "What are we going to do?" she asked, and her voice died on a sigh.

I noted the 'we' with a fierce, triumphant joy. "Bury him again," I said, "and his suit-case with him, but this time I can't go through with it alone. Someone's got to keep watch to see that I'm not disturbed."

She rose at once. "I'll put some clothes on and come down." I lit a cigarette but before it was half smoked she was back, wearing a camel coat over her black suit and a turquoise scarf at her neck. She hadn't bothered with a hat but had run a comb hurriedly through her hair, creating a disarray that was wholly delightful.

Romney waylaid us in the hall. "Want me to wait up?" he demanded.

Ruth shook her head. "No, I don't think so, Romney. And, Romney, none of this has happened."

"The three wise monkeys 've got nothing on me," assured Romney, and opened the door for us with a dignified flourish.

As she made to step into the Bentley, Ruth paused. "Will you need a spade?"

"It would make a quicker job."

"The tool-house is to the right of the flagged courtyard round the back. The key will be in the door. Here's a torch."

She took the torch from a pocket of her coat and I said, "That was thoughtful. You're a born conspirator." She sped me on my way with a perfunctory smile and when I came back with the spade she was sitting quietly in the Bentley, waiting.

Rain was still falling steadily, thin, minute drops that made no sound. Stray tendrils of fog curled away before us and the road unfolded like a ribbon of wet, black paper.

"Better not pick the same spot," advised Ruth.

"No," I agreed. "We'll go farther out."

About four miles beyond the town I spotted a likely stretch of dunes and swung the Bentley off the road, backing it almost to the edge of the sand. We both got out and Ruth said, her voice quiet and steady, "Will you need help with him?"

"No. He's no sight for you."

"I drove an ambulance during the raids on London. I've helped to carry the dead many times."

"I can manage. I'd rather you watched the road." She nodded and went over to the roadside, standing with her back to me, her hands in the pockets of her coat.

I chose a spot between two sheltering dunes and got to work with the spade. Then, when the hole was large enough, I lugged out Johnny. This time he was stiff as concrete and twice as heavy, but I managed to drag him over to where I wanted him. Then I went back for the suit-case.

When the grisly business was finished, I threw the spade in the boot and called to Ruth. She joined me in the car, produced a flask from her pocket and held it out. "Brandy," she said, "in case you're feeling faint."

"Ministering angel," I commented, and drank. The tide was coming in; I could see the white flash of the wavelets breaking on the sand. If only there had been a boat I might have been more venturesome in getting rid of Johnny but there was no boat, nothing but the crouching dunes, the desolate beach, the faintly muttering sea and, beyond, the vague outline of the lightship, its foghorn silent now.

"You saw no one?"

Ruth shook her head. "There's no one within miles; of that I'm certain. Can't you just feel the loneliness?"

"I'll always feel it," I said, "waking or sleeping. Let's go."

As I started the engine she asked, "Where now?"

"Back home for you," I told her, "London for me. I'm going to have a look inside Johnny's flat."

"At this time of night! Why?"

"Because I feel that I can't rest till I get the swine that killed him."

"None shall sleep tonight," she murmured. "Yes, I heard you say that to Romney and I see what you mean. Take me with you."

"I'm going to commit burglary."

"Then you'll need a watcher again. Please let me come. I couldn't sleep either."

For answer, I turned the Bentley to the right, towards London, and Ruth snuggled back in her seat, lit two cigarettes and passed one to me. I put my foot hard down on the accelerator and the Bentley drank the road. For several minutes there was silence between us then she said, "Ought you to drive a new car so hard?"

Remembrance of the gulf between us flooded my mind with sudden bitterness. "I should worry," I growled, "it isn't my car."

The silence could be felt after that and when I could stand it no longer I said, "You don't need to run-in a car like this in the same way as an ordinary car. The engine is run in first on the bench."

"I see."

"So I'm not harming your property."

"I don't care what you do with it."

Slowly, the resentment in my mind gave place to remorse. "I'm being a boor again," I admitted. "Please forgive me."

"You can't help your temperament."

"But it isn't my temperament. I don't know what's come over me lately. Perhaps it's just nerves."

She gave me a sidelong glance and I saw her smile. "Poor Mr. Latimer. You have walked into a mess. It's a wonder you didn't run away from Shellbridge when you found Johnny the first time."

"I meant to make the Town Planning Committee turn me down so's I could leave with honour but you put your foot on that. Another thing I've got to thank you for. My nice job."

"Now don't start that again. I wanted you to have the job because I think you're the right man for it. Shellbridge needs someone honest and someone with vision. I'm sure you're an idealist, Mr. Latimer."

"I'm an accessory to murder," I said savagely. "If that's what idealism does for one, you can have it."

For a long time after that she was silent then she said. "Mr. Latimer, how do you think Johnny's body got into the boot?"

"The first or second time?"

"Both times."

"When did you bring the Bentley back from London?"

"About midday. I parked it at the back of the house opposite the drawing-room windows and it stood there till Blake drove it over to your hotel."

"Could Blake have had anything to do with it, or is he devoted to you like Romney?"

"Blake wouldn't have done it, he's absolutely trustworthy."

"It was opposite the french windows?"

"Yes."

"And were they open?"

"They weren't locked."

"Do me a favour and keep them locked from now on. The cottage of your charming cousins is too close. By the way, they have a car, haven't they?"

"Yes."

"Another of your munificent gifts?"

"As it happens, yes, though I don't see what it's got to do with you."

"And when they want to visit you they come through the gap in the hedge, cross the garden and then go round to the front door?"

"Mostly, yes."

"I'd have that gap closed if I were you and let them drive round if they're too lazy to walk. Have they ever come in through the french windows without being announced?"

"Frequently. I don't stand on ceremony with my relations—or my friends."

"Don't ever let them do that again."

She gave a sad little sigh. "Do you really think it might have been Peter or Diana?"

"Would you say that either one of them was capable of it?"

For a long moment she sat silent, with bowed head, then she said, so quietly I could barely hear, "Yes."

"What other windows of your house overlook the spot where you parked the Bentley?"

"None. The drawing-room was an addition to the house, built on by my grandfather."

"The car must have stood there for over three hours," I said. "So it was probably done then. But there's just a chance it was done when Blake left it outside the hotel and came in to give me my clothes. The car would be unattended for about five minutes, the fog was thick and when I found Johnny there was another car standing across the street. I think the owner of that car followed me, dug up Johnny after I'd gone and waited his chance to put him back in the boot. He could have done that at almost any time during the rest of the day."

"It's horrible. I can't believe that anyone would be so vicious, so utterly evil."

"As you said yourself earlier," I reminded her, "all the wolves aren't in the forest."

She was silent again and the Bentley rushed on through the night. The constant purring of the windscreen wipers seared my nerves but I kept the speedometer needle well above the sixty mark, for I had a feeling that there was urgent need for haste. I had no idea how long Johnny would lie in his grave undisturbed but I knew it wouldn't be for ever.

The rain eased slightly as we reached the outskirts of London and I took the Bentley through the quiet streets with scarcel lessened speed. Once an angry policeman blew a shrill blast on his whistle but I paid no attention. I was going too fast for him to have got my number.

Ruth had been quiet for so long that I thought she had fallen asleep but all at once she said, "This isn't the way to Johnny's flat."

"So you've been to Johnny's flat!"

"I met him outside it once but I never entered it. Not that it's any of your business."

"Sorry."

"Where are you taking me?"

"I want to pick up something at my flat first. It isn't far from Johnny's."

A minute later I pulled up outside the communal entrance to my flat. "Come up with me, please," I invited. "There's something I want you to see."

"Etchings?"

"If that's what you think, you can wait in the car." I stepped out of the Bentley and she at once stepped out on the other side. "Lead on, Sir Galahad," she said. "After all, I can always scream."

We went up to the second floor in silence. I unlocked the door, followed her in and switched on the light in the lounge. "Oh!" she exclaimed. "What a lovely room!"

"Furnished regardless of expense," I said. "Look at that carpet; real Persian, and that radiogram; real walnut."

"It must have cost you an awful lot of money."

"It didn't cost me a penny." I turned to face her. "Up till now," I said, "I've been a man with one ambition, to make a way for myself in the world and to pay as I go but it seems I'm not to be allowed to do that. One woman gives me a Bentley and a job, another furnishes my flat. I never even saw the stuff until it was in."

"You must have some strange power over women."

"This was an elderly one," I explained. "She loved my father once but he married someone else. I was the son she might have had. She has a house agent's business and it was through her I took the flat. When I had signed the missive I spent several blissful days going round the second-hand furniture shops, picking out some delightful pieces at throw-away prices.

Then I collected the keys of the flat and went in to do some measuring. I found it as you see it now, completely furnished. Being a man of delicacy, I won't show you the bedroom, but the Shah of Persia wouldn't be ashamed of it."

"Knowing you, I expect you were furious."

"I was indeed, but what could I do? She had loved my father. She was rich and she wanted his son to be happy. I hadn't the heart to make her take the stuff back so I'm stuck with it, but I can never feel that this is my home."

"Poor Mr. Latimer."

"So now you know why I was so angry about the Bentley."

"The Bentley was different. I like being alive but I never realized how precious life was to me till I thought I was going to lose it. But for you I would have lost it and I'll always remember you with heartfelt gratitude."

"I'll always remember you, too," I said. "I haven't many happy memories but you will be one of them."

Her eyes fell before mine and she stood nervously pulling at one of her gloves. Neither of us could think of anything more to say and, crossing to the sumptuous bureau in the window space, I unlocked the top drawer. I heard her gasp as she saw the revolver in my hand.

"So that's what you came here for! What are you going to do with it?"

"There's a murderer in Shellbridge," I said, "and I'm going to smoke him out. When I do, he'll be dangerous and, like you, I like being alive." I dropped the gun in my pocket and relocked the bureau drawer.

"Where did you get it?"

"A relic of my army service."

"Oughtn't you to have turned it in?"

"I kept it as a souvenir as many ex-officers did. It's quite a human failing."

"I didn't think you had a human failing."

"Let's get out of here," I urged, "before I demonstrate that I have others."

On the way to the door she stopped and gazed at a coloured photograph on the wall. "Is this the church you designed in Florence? What a lovely building! I've never seen anything so wonderful."

"Thank you."

"I mean it. It's so—so delicate. You know at once that it's a holy place." Then she spotted a photograph of me in boxing kit that stood on a table to the left of the door. "Oh, I didn't know you boxed!"

"I don't now."

"Did you box for your university?"

"No, I boxed so that I could afford to go to a university. I was a professional."

"A professional?"

"Not a very good one. I never got beyond fighting in fair-grounds under flaring naphtha lamps and giving displays in small and dismal towns."

"I'd no idea you'd had such a romantic life. What made you go in for Town Planning?"

"Slums."

"Oh!"

"I was born in one. My father died three months before I was born and my mother had no money. She had a pretty hard time of it and died a few days after I left school. I've had to fend for myself ever since."

"You've fended amazingly well. You're quite famous already and I'm sure you're going right to the top of your profession. You love it, don't you?"

"I'm doing what I like to do and getting paid for it so I ought to be a very happy man. You realize, of course, that there are slums in Shellbridge?"

"There are slums in most towns."

"But Shellbridge is a veritable whited sepulchre. All those fine buildings along the front, built to hide some of the worst slums I've ever seen."

"But you'll change all that. How much will it cost?"

"About two million pounds. The same amount as your fortune."

"Please try to forget about my fortune."

We stood looking at each other steadily and I was conscious of rising tension. "To me your fortune is your least attractive attribute," I said, "and if you've quite finished extracting the story of my life, let's get on with the business in hand, which is searching Johnny's flat."

E

Her sudden gurgle of laughter was tantalizing but enchanting. It seemed to emphasize her youth and desirableness and, opening the door quickly, I almost pushed her out. On the way downstairs she said, "I've learned more about you in two minutes than in all the time I've known you."

"You've known me a very short time."

"It doesn't seem short."

I smiled at her and she said, "You should smile more often, Mr. Latimer, it makes you look quite human."

I let that one go. She seemed to be in a teasing mood but I had weightier things on my mind. "We'll leave the Bentley here if you don't mind," I suggested. "It will attract less attention than outside Johnny's flat and it isn't far to walk."

The streets of Holborn were deserted save for an occasional cat in search of amorous adventure. Once, at a crossing, I saw lamplight fall on the rain-soaked cape of a policeman and, taking Ruth's arm, urged her hurriedly across the road and round two more corners to 24 King Arthur's Mansions.

It was an impressive red-brick building, half surrounding a stone-flagged courtyard with the main entrance in the central block. There was no lift and the stairs were in darkness, but Ruth shone her torch on each door as we ascended and, on the fourth floor, a white card to the left of a plain, dark-painted door, displayed Johnny's name.

The second of Johnny's keys fitted, the door swung open and I instinctively recoiled, tramping on Ruth's toes in my excitement. There was a light on in the hall. "Careful," I whispered. "I think someone's forestalled us," and on the last word the light went out.

It was the eeriest, most uncanny thing I had ever experienced for the hall had been empty. I had been able to see right into it and there had been nobody to touch the light switch. Yet the light had gone out suddenly and silently, leaving us in a tunnel of darkness.

I heard Ruth gasp behind me and at the same moment I realized what must have happened. Someone in another part of the flat had heard the door being opened and had turned off the lights at the main. There was someone in the flat now, waiting and listening in the darkness for the next move.

"The torch," I whispered.

Ruth pushed it into my left hand and I switched it on. The hall was still empty and I stood on the threshold with the torch in one hand and my gun in the other, listening to the silence. No sound. No movement.

In my own flat the electric light meter was fixed to the wall of a cupboard in the kitchenette. It would probably be the same here, and, moving on tiptoe, I crossed the hall and opened the nearest door. The living-room, empty, with another door beyond, leading almost certainly to the kitchenette.

"Stay here," I whispered to Ruth, and going forward to the other door, put my ear close to it. I caught the sound of a stealthy movement from within and tried the handle. The door was locked.

"Open the door and come out with your hands up," I called. "I've got a gun."

Silence. I flicked the safety catch off. "You've got ten seconds," I said, "then I shoot through the door."

I heard a movement at my side and whipped round. It was Ruth. "You can't shoot," she said. "Someone will hear."

"When that door opens, someone's going to get hurt," I said, "and it isn't going to be me." If ever there was a sentence to tempt providence, that was it.

The silence continued and, stepping back a couple of paces, I charged full tilt against the door. It gave before my weight with a protesting crack of splintering woodwork and I went on in, blundered against a length of string stretched taut across the room and, the next second, a heavy cooking pot fell from a high shelf and crashed full on the top of my head, beating me to my knees. I rose sick with pain, sparks flashing before my eyes and then I felt Ruth's arms supporting me. By some providential dispensation, the gun in my hand didn't go off but it must have been a very near thing.

The kitchenette was empty. In front of me the window gaped open to the night and, looking out, I saw the spidery framework of a fire-escape a few feet to my right. It seemed to spiral down to a dark, narrow alley and, as my eyes raked the darkness, I heard a car engine start up at the end of the alley, followed by the crunch of a mis-timed gear change. The engine note died away into silence and the kitchenette flowered into light. Ruth had found the meter switch.

"What kind of car did you present Cousin Peter with?" I asked.

"An Armstrong Siddeley."

"With a preselector gear change?"

"Yes."

"Then that wasn't it. That car had the usual syncromesh gear-box."

"Who could it have been?"

"Your guess is as good as mine—probably better." I put a hand to my aching head, felt a sizeable lump and winced. "Pretty cool customer, whoever he was. He took the time to rig up a neat little booby-trap and I walked right into it."

"It must have been a burglar and we disturbed him."

"I'll bet it was no ordinary burglar. It was someone connected with Johnny's murder and he broke in here to look for something. Let's see if we scared him off before he found it."

We went through to the living-room and it was obvious at once that the intruder had indeed been looking for something, for the top drawer of a table-desk in the window had been pulled out and its contents strewn on the floor. I went over and raked through the scattered papers but there was nothing that gave any clue to Johnny's activities or his origin. The remaining drawers of the desk yielded nothing either and I was about to turn my attention elsewhere when my eye was caught by a small red book lying on top of the desk beside the telephone.

It was an engagement diary and it was scrawled all over with telephone numbers, initials and meaningless little notes in Johnny's now familiar writing. None of them seemed to make any sense then, all at once, a sentence stood out that made me draw in my breath. Looking up, I saw Ruth watching me, a little frown marring the whiteness of her forehead. "Found something?" she asked.

"Can you remember the date of the dance where you met Johnny?"

"Yes, it was the twenty-seventh of August."

"And the name of the hotel?"

"The Caravan Hotel. What is it?"

"This," I said, "under the date twenty-sixth August. 'Meeting R. M. tomorrow night. Caravan Hotel,' and then under twenty-seventh August, 'Met R. M. according to plan. She fell for it.'"

"Oh!" The stricken look on Ruth's face went to my heart. "Then—he knew who I was—all the time?"

"Yes," I confirmed. "He knew all the time. He went to that dance on purpose to meet you but the meeting didn't go quite according to plan. You spoke to him from the balcony as he was about to enter the hotel and he recognized you and went into his act. He must have been shown your photograph or seen you before and if he hadn't met you in the way he did, he'd have fixed something else. Perhaps a member of your party would have introduced him to you. In fact, the more I think of it the more I'm sure that's the way it was meant to happen."

"I'll never trust a man again as long as I live."

"You mustn't take it like that. We're not all treacherous. When we get back to Shellbridge, will you give me a note of the names and addresses of all who were in your party at the dance?"

"You think one of them murdered Johnny?"

"And tried to murder you. Johnny was part of some plot against you. What part he was intended to play I don't know but he didn't play it properly and so—he died."

She had been amazingly self-possessed since the moment she had agreed to help me bury Johnny again. She had been cool and rock steady, she had had the forethought to provide the torch and the brandy and to suggest the spade and I had been proud of her. But now she had had just about as much as she could take and she stood with bowed head and a dispirited droop to her shoulders. She was just beginning to realize the full extent of Johnny's perfidy and the moment of revelation must have been bitter.

"What have I done?" she said in a small, lost voice.

"You haven't done anything," I said. "You just happen to have too much of the root of all evil, that's all."

My arms ached to gather her close to my heart, but I made no move. Only a few inches separated us but we were worlds apart. She raised her head and I saw that her eyes sparkled with unshed tears. She blinked them away and then, all at once, she seemed to straighten, to take on strength and poise. "All right," she said, "so Johnny was after my money. I suspected it, anyway, but who set him on to me and why?"

"Someone in Shellbridge," I said. "Someone made a plan

with Johnny, a plan that went wrong. That someone came here tonight to see if there was any evidence that might link him with Johnny. He meant to destroy that evidence but we interrupted him before he could complete his search." I held up the red engagement diary. "This book was the sort of thing he was looking for and it was right under his nose. I expect that's why he missed it."

I put the diary into my pocket and Ruth said, "You keep saying 'he' but couldn't it have been a woman?"

"Quite easily," I agreed, "but you can't keep on saying he or she or you get mixed up with your grammar. The male embraces the female."

"You would put it that way," she said, with the ghost of a smile.

I almost suited the action to the word then but caution held me in check. "What we have to do," I said, "is to trace the connection between Johnny and this mysterious he or she. If it's a she, it's either your cousin Diana or Peter's ambitious girl friend, Molly Piggott, but I don't suppose Molly has a car?"

"Her father has. He's a hairdresser in Shellbridge and he owns an ancient Morris that Molly has the use of whenever she wants it."

I looked round the room. "Well, we'd better carry on with the search although I doubt if we'll find anything."

During the next fifteen minutes we turned Johnny's flat upside-down but, as I had feared, we found nothing. "Where do we go from here?" asked Ruth, pushing back a stray tendril of hair and, at that moment, the telephone rang.

We both jumped and then I glanced at my wrist-watch. Who could be calling Johnny Kingdom at half-past two in the morning? I heard Ruth gasp as I lifted the receiver and then a voice that was the merest whisper said in my ear, "That you, Johnny?"

"Yeah," I said, trying to remember Johnny's clipped way of speaking.

"Spike here."

"So?" I asked.

"So keep away from the Mermaid Club. Tyler ain't too pleased with you for running out on him. His boys are trying to find you right now so if I was you I'd scram out of town."

"O.K.," I said. "Thanks."

I replaced the receiver and turned to Ruth. "Ever hear of the Mermaid Club?" She shook her head and I picked up the telephone directory that hung from a hook on the wall. The Mermaid Club was listed all right, a night club in one of the little back streets off Piccadilly. Probably it would still be open.

"If the Mermaid Club was one of Johnny's haunts, we might get a lead there," I suggested. "Let's go and see."

Ruth hid a yawn with the back of her hand. "None shall sleep tonight," she said. "You meant it when you said that, didn't you?"

"I never meant anything so much," I said. "Shall we go?"

CHAPTER FIVE

ORDEAL AT THE MERMAID CLUB

A GLASS mermaid glowing with a pale green light and fixed to a wall bracket revealed to us the whereabouts of the Mermaid Club. It was at the end of a cul-de-sac and I parked the Bentley alongside the kerb between a Rolls-Royce and a Daimler. A flight of steps led down to a dark basement and a black-painted door with a small glass panel. Behind the panel were more green lights and a doorman who was dressed like a commissionaire and built like a chucker-out.

He barred our way effectively until I told him we were friends of Johnny Kingdom and slipped five bob into his ready palm. Then, still with an air of suspicion, he permitted us to enter.

We found a table for two close to the small square of dance-floor and I ordered champagne cocktails which seemed to be 'the speciality of the house'. The price was special, too, special to millionaires. There were only a few couples dancing and they looked as tired of life as the dispirited dance-band that kept thumping out 'blues' numbers on a rostrum at the far end. A few more couples sat at tables and on couches set in alcoves, whispering intimately in the half-darkness, for the room swam in the same pale green, unearthly light.

Painted mermaids frolicked in and out of painted fronds of seaweed on the walls and Ruth, surveying them with a tolerant eye, said, "Pretty ladies."

"I can't stand women with tails," I growled.

"You seem in a very ungracious mood."

"I've got a very sore head and I'm out to get the blighter that caused it."

"I'd hate it if you weren't on my side," observed Ruth. "You are on my side, aren't you?"

"Now and forever." The waiter loomed up with the cocktails and I said, "Johnny Kingdom been in tonight?"

He paused longer than I thought necessary then he said, "I'll inquire," and drifted away through the gloom. He spoke in a soft whisper very like the whisper I had heard over the telephone and I wondered if he could be the person called Spike who had warned Johnny of danger.

The slow thud thud of the music seemed to intensify the ache in my head and I looked round the room, trying to make out the different faces. The light was too dim, however, and even those nearest me were no more than blurs.

Some of the lighting came from imitation conch shells, some from globes made to look like divers' helmets. The alcoves were painted like submarine grottoes and at the opposite end from the band was an aquarium stocked with various kinds of fish. The fish were the liveliest things in the room and in a moment of revulsion at this submarine nightmare world, I said, "Let's dance."

Ruth nodded indifferently and we took the floor. She was feather-light in my arms but there was no life in her dancing. She fell in with my steps like an automaton, but her eyes were half-closed and her mind obviously far away, far away down the dark labyrinth of murder that had led us from Shellbridge to the Mermaid Club.

She didn't seem to be hearing the music which was perhaps just as well for its slow, laboured beat drugged the senses like an opiate. A huge negro, black face shiny with perspiration, gyrated across our path, a slim, startlingly blonde girl held so tightly against him they might have been glued together. His teeth flashed like a piano keyboard and he looked as if the music were right up his jungle street. So there was no colour bar at the Mermaid Club, I thought, and wondered if anything was barred at all.

We spoke no word while the dance lasted and when we returned to our table the waiter was standing beside it. "Johnny Kingdom ain't here," he said in his toneless whisper. "He ain't been near the club in a long time."

"Perhaps Tyler could tell me where to find him," I suggested. "Is Tyler around?"

The waiter hesitated. "Tyler Clay?" he asked.

I took a chance and nodded. "I can always ask him," said the waiter, and glided away on silent feet. I watched him leave the hall through a swing door to the right of the band, then Ruth said, "I don't like that man."

"I don't like any of them," I decided. "The band, the people, the place. They're all unhealthy."

"Like creatures from Dante's *Inferno*?"

"Like creatures from the under side of a flat stone," I said viciously. The band vocalist began to intone a number called 'Black is the colour of my True Love's Hair' and I looked at Ruth's raven tresses shining in the dim light. How different it could have been if only the dead, grinning face of Johnny Kingdom would not insist on thrusting itself between us. I thought of her in Johnny's arms, as she must have been many times, and clenched my hands under the table. Then I looked up into the expressionless eyes of the waiter.

"Tyler would like a word with you," he announced. "Just follow me."

We rose and followed him through the swing door, along a straight corridor to another door at the far end. I slipped my hand into my jacket pocket and flicked off the safety catch of my gun, then I produced a ten-shilling note and offered it to the waiter.

He looked at it, then at me and shook his head. "Keep it," he said. "There's some things I don't do." He gave me a sudden shove over the threshold and I staggered into a sickening thunderburst of pain and a whirlpool of blackness.

. . . . . .

When I opened my eyes I flinched back from the hard, white light that struck my eyeballs. I was in a small, square room with bare walls, scantily furnished and almost as comfortless as a prison cell. Heavy hammer-strokes of pain throbbed in my skull and when I turned my head I almost fainted again.

I was tied to a chair in the middle of the room and opposite me sat a giant of a man with my own gun in his hand. Behind him another man, a thin, gangling creature, leaned against the door, watching me dispassionately with dull, heavy-lidded eyes. He was chewing on the stub of a cigarette that had gone out and looked slightly less intelligent than an inferior species of slug.

The big man holding my gun looked as if he had suffered some rough handling, for he had a cauliflower ear and a flattened nose. But his eyes were keen and bright and his mouth firm giving the face an alert look. His double-breasted dinner-jacket was well cut, his linen reasonably white and he looked like an unsuccessful boxer who had become a successful business executive.

When he saw that my eyes were open, he grinned a fierce grin and said, "Feeling better, chum?"

I realized then that Ruth was not in the room, that I was alone with these two thugs and my heart began to beat sickeningly fast. "Where's my wife?" I asked.

The big man sniggered. "Who're you kiddin'? She ain't anybody's wife. No wedding-ring. I suppose you thought we'd treat her more gentle if we thought she was married, but you can make your mind easy, chum. She ain't been hurt."

"Where is she?"

"In the next room. I understand you want to talk to me about Johnny Kingdom?"

"You're Tyler Clay?"

He shook his head. "Tyler Morgan, chum. There ain't no Tyler Clay. Spike just put in the Clay to test you. Sorry I had to slug you but when a bloke comes looking for Johnny Kingdom, then asks for Tyler without knowing who Tyler is, I gotta take precautions. Did Johnny send you?"

I shook my head and immediately wished I hadn't for the wave of pain brought a momentary darkness. "Did you have to hit so hard?" I complained.

"It'll pass," said Tyler Morgan. "Tell me about Johnny."

"What do you want to know?"

"Where I can find him."

"I don't know that."

"You're lying." Tyler's voice was suddenly fierce and his eyes blazed. I saw the veins stand out on his forehead and then, slowly, he calmed down.

"Mustn't lose me temper," he said. "Bad for me blood-pressure, but I gotta know about Johnny. I want him bad. I done a lot for Johnny and he's let me down. I don't stand for that."

"I don't know anything about him," I persisted, "and if I did the way you've treated me would hardly induce me to talk."

"I'll induce you to talk all right, chum, don't you worry

about that." He looked significantly at the gun in his hand and I said, "That gun makes a frightful noise."

"*You* wouldn't hear it," pointed out Tyler, "but you don't have to worry. I ain't gonna shoot you—yet."

He got up heavily, pocketed the gun, stood in front of me and, clenching a huge fist, held it under my nose. "I was a heavy-weight boxer once," he said. "Used to fight around the fair-grounds till I got me a more profitable racket. I still have a batter at the old punch-ball now and then, just to keep meself fit."

I looked at him more closely then but failed to recognize him. I had done a fair spell of fighting around fair-grounds myself but Tyler must have been before my time. He grinned an anticipatory grin. "I feel the urge for a bit o' practise right now," he said, "but I ain't got a punch-ball." He paused. "I just got you."

"Cut me loose," I suggested, "and I'll be your sparring partner."

That seemed to amuse him for he uttered a short, harsh laugh. "You don't scare easy, chum, I'll give you that. Now, where's Johnny hiding out?"

"I don't know."

"I'll ask you again, chum, just once more."

"You'll get the same answer."

I didn't see the punch coming till the last second, then his fist looked as big a ham. It exploded on the point of my jaw, with all his weight behind it and as the chair crashed over, taking me with it, a dark curtain came down and engulfed me.

Then I was aware of a roaring in my ears and renewed pain. As the mists receded, I found I was lying on the floor with the chair on top of me and all I could see of Tyler was his outsize black shoes. "Set him up again, Joe," I heard him say, and the thin man who had been lounging against the door came over and replaced the chair so that I was once more facing Tyler. My head lolled on my shoulders and I saw him dimly through a sea of pain.

"Like that, chum?" he asked.

I straightened up, looked him full in the face and called him a name. He grinned tigerishly, rubbing his knuckles and flexing his thick fingers. "This guy's got guts, Joe," he said to his silent companion. "I could like him if only he'd co-operate. He's got a hard jaw, too." He looked ruefully at his knuckles and his eyes narrowed. "Why should I break my hands on you, chum? Mebbe I got a better idea. You ever go to the flicks?"

"Frequently," I said. "I've seen characters like you on the flicks. They always get it in the neck in the end." I must have bitten my lip when he punched me for I could feel a trickle of blood making its slow way down my chin.

"You ever see that film *Odette*? That was a hot scene where the Gestapo tortured Odette. Realistic that was." He turned to Joe who had taken up position again beside the door. "Joe, let's have the young lady in on this."

I saw then that there was a second door in the room, to my right and, crossing over to that door, Joe went out and came back in a few seconds pushing Ruth before him. She was pale but composed until she saw me bound in the chair, then she rushed over to my side. "Oh!" she exclaimed in a shaking voice. "What have they done to you?"

"Nothing that won't mend," I assured her, and managed to raise a smile.

Tyler took her by the arm, led her into the middle of the room, looked at her then at me. "Pretty, ain't she?" he said with a horrid significance.

"All right," I surrendered. "Let her go free now and I'll tell you everything you want to know."

Tyler chuckled, released Ruth's arm and turned to Joe. "I like this guy more and more," he said. "Let the girl go, he says, and I'll talk. Asks nothing for himself, you'll note. That's what they call chivalry. You ever met a gentleman before, Joe? Take a good look at him, they ain't so common."

Joe took a good look at me but his 'dead pan' expression didn't change. Tyler stood over me again. "O.K., chum," he said, "I'll play straight with you for you've earned my respect. Speak your piece and the girl goes free."

"She goes free first," I stipulated.

"We'll do it this way," suggested Tyler. "That door Joe's propping up leads right out to the alley behind the Mermaid Club. Joe'll bring your car round, facing out, make the girl sit in it and stand by." He turned to Ruth. "Can you drive, honey?"

Ruth nodded, watching him calmly and I envied her her gift of self-possession. "Right," went on Tyler. "You sit in the car under Joe's eye, your boy friend and me will have a cosy chat, then, if I'm satisfied, I gives Joe a wave through this window and he lets you drive away." He whipped round to me. "O.K. by you?"

"Provided you mean it."

"I mean it all right. I might even let you go with her if you was to give your word not to go to the police."

"I think when you hear what I've got to tell you," I said, "you'll realize I can't go to the police."

Tyler nodded. "Didn't think you'd want the police in, not when you come in here with a gun in your pocket. Mebbe you an' me'll understand each other yet."

"The beginning of a beautiful friendship," I said.

Tyler removed the keys of the Bentley from my pocket and handed them to Joe who went out by the door leading to the alley. There was a strained silence then Tyler said, "I see you got Johnny's identity card in your pocket. Nice job of work that was, you'd never think to look at it it wasn't genuine. I got it for Johnny meself when I took him into partnership, but he ain't used that address for weeks. I own the Mermaid Club, by the way."

"Then permit me to commiserate with you on the appalling bad taste of the *décor*."

Tyler looked hurt. "Me, I thought the *décor* pretty classy. What d'you know about *décor*, anyway?"

"I'm an architect."

"An architect, eh? A guy with a business on the level and you come after Johnny with a gun! You got some explaining to do, chum."

I heard the murmur of the Bentley's engine then Joe came in and jerked his head at Ruth. She followed him to the door, paused, looked at me. "Don't say anything," I counselled. "Just go quietly, sit in the car and—wait for me."

She nodded, gave me a last backward, unfathomable look and the door closed behind her. "What was Johnny's real name?" I said casually.

"King," answered Tyler. "He just added three letters and made it Kingdom. Neat, eh?"

"Thy Kingdom come," I murmured.

"Bit soon to start praying, chum."

"I was praying for Johnny. He's dead."

"Dead!" Tyler stood stock still, his eyes goggling, his mouth open like a harpooned shark. "How come?"

"Cut me loose and I'll tell you," I said. "I can't do you any harm. You've got my gun."

He hesitated, then shrugged his shoulders and proceeded to cut away the cords that bound me to the chair. I stood up shakily and leaned against the wall. Through the window I could see the roof of the Bentley and, moving farther over, I saw Ruth sitting next to the driver's seat and Joe lounging against the opposite wall, his hand significantly in his pocket. My jaw was stiff and numb and my head throbbed with a grinding, persistent pain.

Tyler gave me a cigarette and I began to talk. I told how I had met Johnny, how, later, I had found his body in the boot of the Bentley and buried him in the sand. I didn't reveal who Ruth was but explained that Johnny had been engaged to her and that I had buried him partly for her sake and partly for my own, because we hadn't wanted to be mixed up with murder. I didn't mention Johnny's resurrection and second burial nor the mysterious intruder in his flat, but I told him how we had gone to the flat to look for clues and how a mysterious voice on the telephone had warned me, thinking I was Johnny, to stay away from Tyler and the Mermaid Club.

Tyler's face was grim. "That would be Spike Murphy, the waiter," he said. "He was fond of Johnny."

I didn't reveal that the man had called himself Spike, for although he had delivered us into Tyler's hands, I was no Judas. It was obvious to me now that the Mermaid Club was the cover for a gang of crooks, that Johnny had been one of that gang and had committed the unforgivable sin of walking out on his associates.

Tyler confirmed this by saying, "So someone cooled off Johnny! Well, he had it coming. Looks as if he thought he'd found a good thing and wanted to keep it to himself, but all it got him was a knife in the back."

"Having told you all that," I said, "you'll admit I can hardly split to the police about you. You know too much now."

Tyler nodded. "I guess you can go," he said. He strode across to the window and waved his hand, then jerked his head towards the door. I went over and stood with my back to it. "Was Johnny really an American?" I asked.

Tyler nodded. "He was over here with the G.I.s in the war and I guess he got left behind."

"Deserted?"

"I guess so, chum."

"Had he a record in the States?"

"Looks like it or he'd have gone back, wouldn't he?" Tyler produced his cigarette-case. "One for the road, chum," he offered. "To show there's no ill feeling."

I took the cigarette with my left hand, clenched my right and hit him like lightning on the jaw. He went down like a falling tree and, stooping over him, I retrieved my gun from his pocket. Then I lit the cigarette and waited. After a few seconds Tyler opened his eyes and lay blinking at the ceiling, a dazed look on his face.

"I used to fight around the fair-grounds too, chum," I said, and left.

Ruth saw me at once as I reached the alley and I heard the Bentley's engine purr into life. Joe, his hand still in his pocket, backed warily round me and, jumping into the driver's seat, I put the car in gear and let in the clutch.

The Bentley slid smoothly away and, glancing in the driving mirror, I saw Joe step into the room I had left. "Duck!" I said to Ruth, changed gear and rammed the accelerator hard down. Looking into the driving mirror I saw Joe come tearing out, gun in hand, and tightened my lips. No shot came, however, and I swung sharply out of the alley, relief flooding my heart. Joe had been a fraction of a second too late.

CHAPTER SIX

SPANISH NUDE

THERE was no more trouble and, as the Bentley darted through Piccadilly, Ruth said, "Were you afraid Joe would try to shoot at us? Why?"

"Because he found Tyler on the floor. I knocked him cold and took my gun back."

"I'm glad." There was a note of savage exultation in her voice. "He must have hurt you terribly."

"I'll recover. What happened after I was knocked out?"

"I tried to scream but Joe put his hand over my mouth. Then Tyler said you would get it worse unless I kept quiet. They pushed me into the room next door and another man stayed to watch me."

"Did he touch you?"

"No, but he had horrible eyes. He kept staring at me and licking his lips."

"I'm sorry I let you in for that," I apologized. "I shouldn't have let you come."

"I'm glad you did. You were wonderful."

"It was a pity I had to tell him the truth about Johnny but I couldn't let him hurt you."

"I'll always remember how you made him let me go and asked nothing for yourself. Tyler was right when he said that's what they call chivalry."

"You won't give me another Bentley, will you?"

"Not if you promise to keep this one. Please keep it, Philip. It will make me look so silly if you insist on giving it back."

My heart was singing and I felt fiercely exultant. She had called me Philip and her voice had been infinitely soft and tender. I would have given her the last drop of my blood. "I'll keep it," I said. "I'll keep it forever. If I should starve in the gutter, I'll still keep it."

She gave my arm an impulsive squeeze. "I'm so glad, Philip." There it was again; Philip. It hadn't been a slip then. I should have stopped the car and swept her into my arms but I let the moment pass; a moment that might never come again.

She was silent till we had turned Hyde Park Corner, then she said, "What will Tyler do about Johnny?"

"Nothing, I hope," I said, but I had a feeling my hope was vain, that we had not heard the last of Tyler Morgan. "Johnny's real name was King," I told Ruth, "and he was a deserter from the American Forces after the war."

"I see." Her voice was dead. "He was nothing but a cheap criminal, then?"

"Looks that way. I'm sorry. Tyler's a crook all right and Johnny was his partner."

"I did make a fool of myself, didn't I?"

"You're not the first," I pointed out, "and you won't be the last."

The rain had ceased and the Bentley swept with its smooth glide through Upper Tooting, Merton, and Cheam. I did not feel up to driving full out and the soft purr of the powerful engine was almost inaudible. If there was such a thing as the perfect car then this was it and it was mine; mine! It would make Ruth unhappy if I spurned her gift and I could not bear for her to be unhappy. She had conquered my pride.

There had been a subtle change in our relationship since the night's adventure. Danger shared and overcome had drawn us closer together and henceforth we would be Philip and Ruth to each other. Ruth herself had initiated this new sense of comradeship by promoting me to Philip, but I had not yet ventured to call her Ruth. I couldn't wait to do so. I had to hear how it sounded.

"Ruth," I said. It sounded wonderful but there was no reply and, glancing to the left, I saw that her head was bowed in sleep, her body slumped forward in her seat. I reduced speed so as not to disturb her but, as I negotiated a sharp bend, she slid sideways till her head was resting against my shoulder.

On through the lonely night, through sleeping Reigate to the Crawley By-Pass until, south of Bolney Common, we met the fog again, stealing back after the rain. I switched to the fog-lamps and slowed the Bentley to a crawl. Ruth muttered in her sleep and her head moved against my shoulder but she did not waken.

I could feel her body shaking and knew that, even in sleep, she was unhappy, that she was alone and frightened in a world of nightmare. I drew her closer against me, uttering soothing sounds but she would not be comforted. Once she shuddered violently and gave a loud, despairing cry. Then she said, "Johnny! Johnny!" Her voice rising on a note of terror.

"If I hadn't been forestalled, I would have killed him for you," I said. The pain in my head was coming in ever increasing waves and I was conscious of a growing feeling of sickness.

Ruth straightened up in her seat, gave a little, weary sigh and said, "More fog! Where are we?"

"Coming near home," I told her. "Fog and Shellbridge seem to be inseparable."

"I must have been asleep for ages." The pale dashboard light intensified the whiteness of her face and I saw her giving me an intent look. "Philip, are you all right?"

"Yes," I lied.

"You look a wreck. I shouldn't have gone to sleep and left you alone. You're not fit to drive. Let me take over."

I shook my head and the pain tore at my nerves. "It isn't far now. I'll manage." It was quarter-past five in the morning and black as Egypt's night. I could smell the sea, salty and dank. We must be almost home and then, in spite of my failing senses, an idea flashed into my mind.

"Ruth," I said, thrilling inwardly to the use of her name, "whoever raided Johnny's flat can't have got back to Shellbridge more than an hour in front of us. The car he or she drove will be wet and the radiator will still be warm."

"I suppose so."

"You said Molly Piggott's father has a car she sometimes uses. Where does he keep it?"

"In a shed behind his shop."

"We'll go there first then. What about Henry Crane?"

"He has a garage at his house."

"And Leslie Turner?"

"He has an old two-seater he keeps in the Ocean Hotel Garage."

"We'll go round them all," I said.

"But, Philip, you're ill. You need sleep."

"None shall sleep tonight," I said. "Remember?"

"You're the most obstinate man! Even if you do find that one of the cars has been out, it won't prove anything."

"No, but it will be a useful pointer and if the person who drove the car can't explain where he or she drove it to, that will be enough for me. It's a great help to know your enemy."

We were in the main street of Shellbridge now, running parallel with the promenade and Ruth said that Piggott's shop was just round the next corner. I drew into the kerb, stopped the car and allowed Ruth to lead me through an entry between two shops into a cobbled courtyard.

At the far end of the courtyard was a long, open shed roofed with corrugated iron and in this shed stood Joe Piggott's car. It was covered with a tarpaulin, its radiator was stone cold and it had obviously not been out that night. It was unlocked and I rummaged in the dashboard cubby hole and the door pockets but found nothing of interest.

"There's nothing for us here," I said, and then Ruth grabbed my arm. "Listen!" she whispered.

I heard the ring of footsteps on the pavement outside and was suddenly conscious of my heartbeats. The footsteps came closer, a heavy, unhurried tread, and stopped just outside the entry. "Bobby," I whispered, and then the footsteps sounded again on the cobbles of the courtyard itself.

I jerked the car door open, pushed Ruth in, got in beside her, closed the door and gathered her quickly into my arms, "Keep your face out of sight," I whispered.

I felt her nod and then she snuggled close into my side, her face against my coat. The policeman stamped all round the courtyard, paused just outside the shed and for a long moment the world stood still.

We tried not to breathe and I could feel Ruth trembling against my heart. I braced myself for the inevitable, for the tarpaulin had been partly displaced, leaving half of the windscreen clear and I was certain the policeman's suspicions would be aroused. I was right.

The beam of a torch flashed on the windscreen, the door was pulled open and a deep voice said gloatingly, "O.K. The necking party's over. Out you come."

"Stay where you are," I whispered to Ruth, and scrambled

out of the car to face the largest and beefiest constable I had ever seen.

"All right, Mrs. Grundy," I said. "I didn't know there was a law against courting."

"There's courting and courting," said the policeman. "Who have you got in there?"

"Molly, of course," I said. "Who else would be using her old man's car? She's frightfully embarrassed and afraid to show her face."

"And no blooming wonder, either," growled the constable.

"Can't you be a sport, Officer, and forget you've seen us? Mr. Piggott won't half take it out of Molly and we weren't doing any harm."

He hesitated, looking doubtfully past me at the car. But he had switched off his torch and for once I was grateful for the fog. "Dunno," he said at length. "Half-past five in the morning ain't no time for canoodling in cars."

"But it's her father's car and we're on her father's land. What could you possibly charge us with? We've been to a dance in London and that's why we're up so late. Haven't you ever done any courting yourself?"

The policeman nodded gloomily. "Wouldn't be pounding this beat now if I hadn't. I'd of gone to sea and seen a bit of the world. Oh well, I guess I can look the other way for once, but if I was you I'd pack it up and cut off home. You don't want to go getting Molly into trouble."

"Nothing was further from my mind," I assured him, and with a grunt he stumped off. When the echo of his tread had died away Ruth emerged, somewhat shakily, from the car.

"Oh dear," she said. "What have you done to Molly's reputation?"

"Nothing Molly hasn't done herself," I said. "For from what I've heard, she's already got quite a reputation for fun and games. The policeman won't think anything of it, but if he'd found out it was you, he'd have thought plenty. He'd have run us both in for trespass and the scandal would have rocked Shellbridge from end to end."

"I know. Once again you've given me cause to be grateful. You're very resourceful."

"I got you into it so I had to get you out of it."

I heard Ruth chuckle. "I could hear your heart beating like a kettle-drum," she said.

"That wasn't just because of the policeman," I said meaningly. "Let's go."

The garage at the Ocean Hotel was dark but I soon found the light switch and Ruth pointed out Leslie Turner's shabby two-seater. It was plentifully bedaubed with rain and mud splashes and the radiator was quite warm.

"This car's been out all right," I said. "I wonder where." I was aware of a growing sensation of faintness and leaned for a moment against the side of the car. There was a ringing in my ears and the pain in my head seemed worse. Then the dizzy spell passed and we left the garage, Ruth switching off the lights.

Henry Crane's house, like Henry himself, was large and impressive. It stood in its own extensive grounds, on a hill-slope dominating the town and all the windows were dark. A wide, stone-built garage with roll-up doors stood at the back, but the doors were locked.

"There's a small door at the side," whispered Ruth. "Try that."

The small door was ajar and, slipping quickly inside, I switched on Ruth's torch and saw a massive black Buick about as big as a truck. I put my hand on the radiator and the heat made me jump. Then I saw the tell-tale rain splashes. The car had not only been out of the garage, it had been out of Shell-bridge for it had obviously been driven hard and Crane could scarcely have driven it like that within the fog-bound precincts of the town.

I rejoined Ruth, who was waiting in the drive. "Crane's been on a long journey tonight," I told her, "and he hasn't been back more than half an hour. I wonder if he's in bed yet."

As I spoke a dog set up a sudden clamour of barking inside the house and Ruth tugged at my sleeve. "Quick!" she urged. "His dog's a Great Dane and terribly fierce."

A yellow square of light blossomed in an upper window, I heard the window go up and saw the head and shoulders of a man in the opening. "Who's there?" came the voice of Henry Crane. "Stay where you are till I come down or I'll let the dog loose."

As we turned to run, I stumbled over a heap of bricks,

probably intended for bottoming a path, and almost fell. The pain jumped in my head, almost blinding me, and then I snatched up a brick and threw it. I heard the crash of glass, an oath from Crane and the window went dark. I grabbed Ruth's hand and we ran headlong down the drive and out of the gate. As the Bentley slid away into the fog, we heard the Great Dane snarling in the garden.

"You shouldn't have done that to Henry," reproved Ruth.

"No, I shouldn't, should I?" I said. "I love Henry like a brother. Like Cain loved Abel. He'd rather see you dead than married to another man, would he! How would you like to marry Henry and play mother to a Great Dane?"

"I don't know. He's very masterful. Where are you taking me now?"

"Home," I said. "Then I'll go through the hedge at the foot of your garden to Peter's garage and take a look at his car." I could hardly speak for the pain in my head and was so overcome by exhaustion that I could scarcely grip the wheel, but I gritted my teeth and carried on. Peter's garage was the last port of call and then I could sleep.

We parked the Bentley in the drive opposite Ruth's drawing-room window and she guided me down the garden path to the gap in the hedge. The door of Peter's garage was unlocked but his Armstrong Siddeley was covered by a dust-sheet, its radiator was cold and its paint-work dry.

"Looks as if your cousin's in the clear," I said. "Unless he drove some other car." I felt as though I were walking on air and leaned heavily on Ruth's arm. "Well," I said, as we reached the Bentley. "I'd better be getting back to my hotel. Altogether it's been quite a night."

I took her hand and then giddiness swamped me like a giant wave. "Ruth," I said, "I—I——" In desperation I clutched at her for support and the last thing I remembered was her startled cry.

* * * * * *

I awoke to music; rippling piano music that I could not identify. I was lying on my back in one of the softest beds I had ever known, gazing up at a lofty, cream-painted ceiling and gradually recalling the events of the night. The room was large, furnished in Jacobean oak and richly carpeted. It was full day but through the tall window I could see that the fog was still with us.

The music went on and on, infinitely soothing, and I realized that Ruth must be playing the piano in the drawing-room below. The pain in my head had subsided to a dull ache and, exploring with cautious fingers, I found two sizeable lumps, one on top of my head and another at the back near my right ear. I was wearing a suit of woollen pyjamas, the jacket of which fitted like a tent, and there was a hot-water bottle at my feet.

I yawned, stretched, looked lazily round the room and saw my clothes on a nearby chair. Then a picture on the opposite wall caught my eye. It was a seventeenth-century Dutch interior, like a Medici print but considerably larger and, from the serenity of the background and the distinctive manipulation of light, it looked like the work of Jan Vermeer of Delft.

Being interested in Art, I had studied the technique of the great painters and the more I looked at the picture the more I was convinced that it was no reproduction, but a genuine Vermeer. If so, it must be worth thousands, and then I remembered the Constable landscape in the first-floor corridor. I was indeed moving in exalted circles these days, mixing with people who could afford to have real Old Masters, even in the bedrooms.

On the wall close to the bed I caught sight of a bell-button and, just to see what would happen, I gave it a vigorous jab. For about three minutes there was no reaction and then a heavy tread in the corridor heralded the impressive entrance of Romney.

"That's right, cock," he encouraged. "Make yourself at home. I got nothing else to do but run up and downstairs answering bells."

"You never ran in your life," I said. "Who put me to bed?"

"Who the 'ell d'yer think put you to bed? Miss Ruth?"

"There's no need to be coarse."

"None shall sleep tonight, you said, an' you never spoke a truer word. I hadn't hardly closed me eyes before Miss Ruth was battering me door down to get me to carry you in. She wanted to fetch the doctor but I done some First Aid in me time an' I said no doctors. Doctors is too nosy."

"Your discretion was admirable," I commented.

"An' me best pyjamas, too. You take care of them, mind. How did you get the bash on the noggin?"

"Preserving your job."

"My job?"

"In other words, taking care of your employer. Who d'you think would employ you as a butler if anything happened to her?"

Romney rubbed his chin. "Mebbe you got something there, cock," he conceded. "Feel like getting up?"

"Yes," I said. "I'll get up right away and many thanks for your good offices."

"Think nothing of it, cock," said Romney. "I got a kind heart. I'll put a razor in the bathroom for you and after that you're on your own."

It did not take me long to shave and dress and as I came downstairs, the piano music stopped, the drawing-room door opened and Ruth came out, looking cool and fresh in a light grey sweater and skirt. For a moment we stood gazing at each other, then I said lightly, "That was wonderful music."

"Are you all right?" Her voice was as composed as her appearance.

"Yes; I must have been a frightful nuisance. I'm sorry."

"Don't be silly. After what you've done for me you could never be a nuisance. If I'd realized you'd been so badly hurt, I'd never have let you drive all the way home and I certainly wouldn't have let you chase round looking at those cars."

"I'm glad I did look at them," I said. "Two hadn't been out but two had. We've got to find out where."

"How do you propose to do that?"

"By judicious inquiry. I'd like to meet those people socially and see what I can get out of them. Could you throw a cocktail party for them tomorrow night, say, and invite me, too?"

"Yes, I think so. I could invite them to hear my Sicilian Scherzo. I've just finished it. Whom do you want?"

"Henry Crane, Leslie Turner, Peter and Diana, and anyone else you like to make weight. Oh, and Molly Piggott, unless that would be too democratic."

"I'm not a snob, Philip. I'll ask Peter to bring her. Eight o'clock tomorrow night and don't bother to dress."

"Fine," I said. "Now we're getting somewhere."

"There's some coffee in there." She nodded towards the drawing-room door. "I'll get Romney to bring another cup."

I hesitated and she said, "Just go in and wait; there's no one there. You'll find some magazines."

She went along the corridor towards the kitchen and I pushed open the drawing-room door then paused, staring. She had said there was no one there, but a man was standing near the fire-place beside the table that held the coffee-pot. He was a tall man with a slight stoop, greying hair, a tight, clean-shaven mouth, and a confident manner. "Hullo," he said. "Did I startle you?"

I came into the room, closing the door behind me. "You did, rather," I admitted. "I was told there was no one here."

"I've just arrived. I came in by the window." He nodded towards the french window on his right. "Most of Ruth's friends come in that way to avoid the ordeal by Romney. You've met Romney?"

"Yes," I said grimly. "I've met Romney."

"In his eyes Ruth's a celebrity who should only be seen by appointment. When any of her friends come to the front door he puts on an act. The haughty butler. 'I'll inquire if Miss Ruth is at home,' you know the sort of thing, so if we feel like dropping in for a chat, we just come in this way. Ruth doesn't mind, in fact I think she rather likes it. Gives her the feeling of running a sort of *salon*, a meeting place for art and music lovers."

"What if she should be out?"

"Then we ring for Romney and with fiendish glee he shows us the door. My name's Patrick Conway, by the way. I'm Ruth's lawyer."

"I'm Philip Latimer," I told him.

"The Town Planning chap?"

"Yes, and please, don't give me the joke about not shifting the railway station because it's convenient to your house. I've heard that one."

"My dear fellow, you can do whatever you like with the railway station. It's hideous."

All the time we were speaking my mind was racing. This man Conway was Ruth's lawyer. He probably had access to her money or some of it, at least. Suppose he'd been dipping his fingers in it? If so, he'd have every reason to kill her to keep her from finding out, and I had found him standing beside the coffee-pot. Suppose he had——?

I went forward to the table and lifted the coffee-pot. "Have some coffee?" I invited.

He shook his head. "No, thank you. Never touch coffee till after lunch and then I have it extra white. I have a duodenal ulcer." He smiled suddenly, quite a winning smile. "Looking after other people's troubles plays hell with your health."

I nodded without replying. Ruth mustn't drink that coffee, but how to stop her? I poured a little coffee into the cup and raised it to my lips. "I'll have some myself," I decided. "Ruth's fetching another cup." I pretended to taste the coffee and made a wry face. "It's almost cold," I said. "The incomparable Romney has let it lie too long."

I picked up the tray and without another word, walked out with it. The clatter of dishes led me to the kitchen and Ruth and the butler stared at me as I walked in.

"Let's have some fresh coffee, Romney," I said.

"Who gives the orders in this house, I'd like to know?" demanded Romney. "That coffee's just been poured."

"Quiet, Romney." Ruth's voice had an edge to it and Romney subsided. "What's the matter with you, Philip?"

"When I went into the drawing-room there was a man there, your lawyer, Patrick Conway. He'd just come in through the french window. I thought I asked you to keep that window locked?"

"I know. I just hadn't got around to it yet. What's Patrick got to do with the coffee?"

"He looks after your fortune, doesn't he?"

"Part of it. You don't think——? No, Patrick would never do that."

"He wouldn't drink any himself."

"He seldom does."

"All the same, let's have some fresh coffee. Romney can pour that lot into a bottle and I'll have it analysed later."

Romney grunted but under Ruth's compelling eye, he moved to obey. "Tell Patrick I'll be in shortly," she called after me as I went back to the drawing-room.

Conway, hands behind his back, a cigarette drooping from the right corner of his mouth, was gazing at a picture on the wall.

Up till now I had not paid much attention to the pictures in the drawing-room. There were only four, all woodland scenes by Corot and all unmistakably originals.

"The Mannering family have a pretty taste in pictures," observed Conway. "Ruth's grandfather bought most of them."

"They must have cost him plenty," I commented. "What with Constables in the corridors and Vermeers in the bedrooms."

"To say nothing of the Velasquez in the dining-room," said Conway. "You've seen the Velasquez, of course?"

"As a matter of fact, I haven't."

"Not seen the *pièce de résistance*? One of the greatest pictures ever painted, and worth a king's ransom. What was Ruth thinking of not to show you the Velasquez?"

"I expect she hasn't got around to it yet."

"Then come with me and see it now. I want another look at it, anyway. It's partly why I'm here."

I was struck by his obvious familiarity with the house as he led me to the dining-room. Ruth must be pretty trusting with her friends. Too trusting. He threw open the dining-room door with a flourish and I found myself gazing at a picture that took my breath away.

It showed the naked figure of a slim young girl, reclining on a couch against a red ochre background, her back to the viewer, and for a moment I thought I was looking at a copy of the famous 'Rokeby' Venus in the National Gallery. Then I realized that although the picture was different, the model was the same and remembered that Velasquez had frequently painted the same model. A small plate attached to the lower part of the heavy gilt frame bore the title, 'Spanish Nude, by Diego Velasquez, 1599–1660'.

"Wonderful, isn't it?" said Conway. "Look at the delicate shadows and the cool flesh tints. It was thought that the 'Rokeby' Venus was the only nude study by Velasquez in existence and then this was discovered in a Paris cellar. Ruth's grandfather paid twenty thousand pounds for it and I'm trying to buy it from Ruth for thirty thousand."

"For yourself?" I asked.

"No, for a client, Henry Crane."

"And Ruth won't sell?"

"No," came Ruth's voice from just behind us. "Ruth won't

sell. I love that picture and Henry won't get it so long as I'm alive."

Somewhere in my brain the words echoed, 'So long as I'm alive', and I felt my hands clench. The feeling of danger was in the room, thick and choking as the fog outside. I could feel it with every instinct I possessed.

The three of us stood gazing at the picture and then I said, "You're sure it's genuine?"

"Absolutely," declared Conway. "Crane got Ruth's permission to have it vetted by an expert who made photo-micrograph tests. See that drapery?" He pointed to a wisp of blue at the figure's narrow waist. "The expert said that was made up of a mixture of azurite and smalt. Smalt only came into use in 1600 and azurite wasn't used after 1650. Velasquez, as you can see from the title plate, died in 1660."

"Art dealers go by brushwork," I said. "That is the artist's real signature that no one can forge. Have you ever had an offer from a dealer, Ruth?"

"Several," said Ruth, "but I'm not selling. After all, it isn't as if I needed the money."

"You may not need the money," said Conway, "but Henry's ego needs the picture. Thirty thousand pounds is quite a sum, even to him, but he's prepared to pay it."

"If I remember rightly," I murmured, "the 'Rokeby' Venus, painted by Velasquez from the same model as this, was bought for the nation for forty-five thousand."

Conway gave me an acid smile. "I didn't know you were Ruth's agent," he sneered. He whipped round suddenly on Ruth. "Would you sell for forty-five thousand?"

"No."

The lawyer's mouth tightened. "I wish you'd see reason, Ruth. You know what Henry's like when he's thwarted. Positively murderous. He's quite capable of taking his business away from me if I'm unsuccessful and I can't afford that."

"You're forgetting that you're Ruth's solicitor as well as Crane's," I pointed out. "Ruth might have to take her business elsewhere if you put Crane's interests before hers. I don't think you could afford that either."

Just for a second, a spark of malignance glowed in Conway's eyes then the acid smile was back. "I don't think I'm going to like you, Latimer," he said silkily. "I don't think I'm going to like you a bit."

Ruth put her hand on his arm. "Don't worry about it, Patrick. I'll talk to Henry myself. He must learn to take no for an answer and not to be such a megalomaniac."

When Conway had left, I said, "There goes another man with a motive for your murder. You can see he's afraid of losing Crane's business over that picture and besides, he could make enough to retire on out of your estate."

"Patrick can be very ruthless but I doubt if he'd stoop to murder."

"I wonder if his car was out last night."

"He hasn't got a car. Says he can't afford it."

"He could afford it if you were dead."

Ruth shuddered. "I wish you'd stop talking about my death at this time of the morning. It makes me feel queer."

I went closer to the Velasquez. It was a wonderful painting. The girl reclining on the dark couch had been recreated by the touch of a master. She was young and vividly alive across three centuries of time and something about the tender line of her cheek, the narrowness of her waist, the slenderness of her limbs, reminded me of Ruth. For a moment the picture seemed to change and it was Ruth herself lying there amid the red and gold Spanish hangings, with the delicate shadows on her almost translucent flesh. It was a vision I would never forget.

"You seem quite fascinated by that picture," observed Ruth.

"It's one of the wonders of the world," I said. "I wonder how he got that authentic shade of gold in the leather hangings. Tinfoil, I suppose, varnished with sandarac and a mixture of saffron and aloes."

"You know about pictures, don't you? And you really like and appreciate them. I'd rather give you that picture for nothing than sell it to Henry for a fortune."

"I'll make do with the Bentley, thanks."

She laughed. "Romney says you can stay to lunch."

"That's extremely good of Romney."

"It is, you know. For some reason he seems to have taken a fancy to you. As a rule, he detests my friends."

"After meeting some of your friends, I can hardly blame him."

Ruth shrugged her slim shoulders. "You have to make your

friends where you live, but I often wonder how many real friends I'd have if I weren't rich and a celebrity in the musical world."

"You'd have me for one," I said.

She squeezed my arm and her eyes misted over but her only comment was, "Come and have some coffee."

After the coffee I was left to my own devices and amused myself by reading magazines and playing Ruth's gramophone records until lunch-time. Mrs. Romney was an excellent cook, the lunch more than adequate and when I rose to leave I was heavy-eyed and sleepy.

"You'll keep that french window locked, won't you?" I said.

Ruth promised and as Romney showed me out, he said, "You don't need to worry about that coffee, cock. It's O.K."

"Did you drink it?"

"Wot d'jer take me for? Tried it on the cat next door and it didn't turn a hair."

"I'm glad," I said. "It was just a chance but don't leave coffee in that room when it's empty unless the french window's bolted on the inside."

"You leave it to me, cock," promised Romney. "From now on I'm the guardian angel of this here establishment."

CHAPTER SEVEN

A LESSON FROM "MACBETH"

IT was almost quarter to three and I remembered I had half promised to visit Leslie Turner and look over his school. It was the last thing I felt like doing for my head was still painful, but as Turner was one of my suspects it was time I got to know him better.

Thick and clammy, the fog cut down visibility to a few yards and I had some difficulty in finding the school. I remembered, however, that it was near the gasworks and my nose reinforced my eyes in leading me aright.

Turner had not exaggerated in declaring the school to be obsolete. It was a hideous building of sooty yellow brick, more like a factory than a school, the playground surrounded by high, rusty iron railings. Lights were on in all the class-rooms, making yellow blotches in the fog, and the massive, green-painted retorts of the gasworks loomed in the background, ghastly monuments to the graceless soul of man.

The forlorn face of an urchin peeped out at me from the door of a ground-floor cloak-room. "Hallo," I said, memories of my own schooldays crowding in on me. "Have you been turfed out of class?"

The urchin nodded gloomily, watching me with suspicious eyes. "If it's a fair question," I said, "what had you been up to?"

"I put an empty beer bottle on Mr. Turner's desk and he came in an' caught me."

"Mr. Turner's!" Now that I looked at him I saw he was older than I had thought, fifteen or sixteen perhaps, but he was so small and undernourished he would have passed for several years younger. "So you're one of Mr. Turner's flock! Why did you afflict him with an empty beer bottle?"

"He drinks. Once he came to school tight and couldn't teach properly and the Head told him to go home. And last week Millie Roberts heard the Head tell him he'd have to cut out drinking and—and wenching."

"And the beer bottle was to add point to that excellent advice?"

"I just did it for fun."

"Well," I said, "it so happens that I'm looking for Mr. Turner's class-room and if you'll be so kind as to direct me to it, I'll put in a word for you."

"Second door on the right across the hall." He jerked a thumb in the direction indicated. "I gotta keep out of sight case the Head pops out and wants to know what I'm doing away from class."

"Then, I suppose, the fat would be in the fire?"

"You said it."

I paused outside Turner's door. I could hear his voice going on and on like the high, angry whine of a trapped hornet and when I knocked and went in the silence in the class-room could be felt. It was not the normal silence of a class attentive to a teacher. Such a silence would be broken by fidgets, coughs, the creaking of desks, but this was a stunned silence; a cowed, apprehensive silence.

"Am I interrupting?" I said.

The communal gasp that followed my words was one of unbearable relief. Young faces brightened, then the coughing and fidgeting started and everything was normal again. Turner, who had been pacing up and down the room as he talked, came forward to greet me, wearing a smile that had been switched on like a searchlight. He still looked as if he had slept in his clothes and his gown was crushed, one sleeve torn and the tab showing above the collar.

"Ah!" he said. "The punctual Planner. I took a bet with myself you'd be dead on time."

"Then pay yourself and show me round the school."

"When the class is over I'll be delighted, but first let me try and knock some appreciation of Shakespeare into these unreceptive heads. We're doing the Letter Scene from *Macbeth*."

He indicated a chair beside his desk and when I had seated myself facing the class, he said, "Boys and girls, this is Mr. Latimer, Shellbridge's new Town Planning expert. He's going to design a nice new school for us."

This information was received with a marked lack of enthusiasm and Turner continued, "But we mustn't let Mr. Latimer think his work will be wasted. We must show him how much we benefit from the blessings of a higher education, mustn't we?"

This was received with even less enthusiasm and as Turner's probing eye roved round the class the uneasy silence closed in again as palpable as the fog outside. His right forefinger stabbed out like a dagger. "You there, with the dirty finger-nails, Charles Hopkins, stand up."

A boy in the front row stood up sheepishly, rattling his seat in obvious embarrassment. "Let us hear in your most dulcet tones," said Turner, "the passage I gave you to learn last night."

The boy flushed, hung his head, then blurted out, "Please, sir, I didn't learn it."

Turner took two swift strides forward, towering over his now shrinking victim. "You didn't learn it!" he said in a terrible voice.

"No, sir. You see, sir, my mother's sick and my father's——"

"In jail."

The roar of laughter from the class was sycophantic rather than mirthful, an expression of relief that someone else was being put through it.

"No, sir," protested Hopkins. "Please, sir, he's a traveller and he's gone to Scotland for a week."

"I bet that's just what your mother told you." Again the burst of laughter, quickly suppressed when Turner held up his hand. "Why didn't you learn it?"

"Please, sir, my mother's sick."

"It was you I asked to learn the passage, not your mother. I suppose you think the late William Shakespeare a poor substitute for the late Peter Cheyney?"

"No, sir, but I had to look after her and——"

"All right, all right, don't stand there bleating like a mentally defective sheep. You'll learn it tonight and the next twenty lines or so to the end of the scene, and if you can't repeat the lot tomorrow, without a mistake, you'll wish your mother and father had never met. Is that understood?"

"Yes, sir."

"Then sit down and repent of your sins. Horace Trevor, let's hear from you."

A youth in the back seat, wearing large horn-rimmed spec-

tacles, stood up confidently and began. " 'The raven himself is
hoarse that——' " Turner stopped him with upraised hand.

"There's more than the raven hoarse. What's the matter with
your voice?"

"Please, sir, I've got a bad cold."

"Then you shouldn't be here, contaminating the rest of the
class. Go on, and put some expression in it. You're Lady Macbeth
contemplating murder, not Horace Trevor wondering when the
bell will ring."

The class tittered and Horace went on with his recital, but
his confidence was destroyed and he stumbled badly. Turner
put his head in his hands and moaned. "What an exhibition,"
he said. "If I believed in flattery, I would describe you as a cretin
and what Mr. Latimer thinks of it all I don't know."

"You wouldn't be flattered if I told you," I said out of the
side of my mouth, but he affected not to hear.

"I'm sure the girls can do better," he went on. "Mary Gordon,
let's hear from you. Start where Horace left off."

A pretty, dark-haired girl of sixteen or so stood up in her
place. She was blushing like a peony and seemed quite unable to
speak. "Go on, Mary," encouraged Turner, "don't be shy."

A copy of *Macbeth* lay open on Turner's desk and glancing at
it, I was horror-struck at the ordeal before Mary Gordon. The
next line read, 'Come to my woman's breasts, and take my milk
for gall, you murdering ministers', and, from Mary's own budding
shapeliness, she was only too well aware of the meaning of the
words.

She stood, still silent, big brown eyes imploring Turner to
have pity. To ask a shy, sensitive schoolgirl to repeat that line
aloud was to inflict acute mental torture, and to force her to
repeat it before a man who was a total stranger to her was a
refinement of cruelty that would have delighted Torquemada.

"Cat got your tongue?" asked Turner. There was a gloating
inflection in his voice that turned my stomach.

"Sorry to butt in," I said, "but I haven't got much time.
Couldn't you just show me round now?"

The girl turned her eyes on me, hope struggling with despair.
"The bell will ring in five minutes," said Turner, "then I'll be
free. Hurry up, Mary."

Hope died. It went out like a candle flame and in a low voice that was quite inaudible, Mary stammered the fatal line. Turner stopped her. "That will never do," he said. "If you were playing Lady Macbeth on the stage, they wouldn't hear you beyond the footlights. Start again, and speak up."

Once more Mary spoke the line, louder this time but in her haste to reach the next line she ran all the words together and again Turner stopped her. "For God's sake, Mary," he protested, "don't be so *gauche*. You're Lady Macbeth, you've just received a letter from your husband, telling you that the witches have prophesied that he'll be King of Scotland, and the news has excited you. You know that the King is to spend that night in Macbeth's castle and already the idea of persuading Macbeth to murder him is forming in your mind. You are invoking the powers of darkness to come to your aid, to harden your heart. You speak slowly, almost hesitantly, your mind filled with your fell purpose, your voice firm with resolve. Now try again."

Mary tried again and this time the words were audible but her voice was far from being firm with resolve. Turner was enjoying himself, stopping her again with sadistic glee before she could proceed to the second line. "That's better, Mary, but it's not right yet. The *tempo's* too quick. Each word must be distinct and separate, charged with emotion. Now, slowly, Mary, and *con espressione*."

But Mary had been goaded beyond human endurance. Her shoulders went back, her chin came up, her eyes glared defiance. Then she spoke the line, loudly and clearly, spitting out the words, pausing for a long time after each. "There," she said at the end of it. "Is that slow enough for you?" Then she wilted, burst into tears and sat down.

"Mary!" thundered Turner.

Mary's shoulders were shaking and she was sobbing into a handkerchief big enough to have been her father's. The class watched her, stunned. "Mary, leave the room at once! And report to me first thing in the morning when you've recovered your sanity."

Mary gathered up her books and fairly ran for the door. I could hear her crying in the corridor as if her heart would break.

"If I believed in flattery," I said quietly, "I would describe you as a filthy swine."

Turner only laughed. "Serve the little bitch right," he said.

"To quote dear Lady Macbeth, 'she looks like the innocent flower but is the serpent under it'. Last week I caught her pinning a piece of paper to the back of my jacket. Do you know what she'd written on it?"

"Nothing scathing enough," I said.

"She'd written, 'Don't shoot the Teacher, he's doing his best.' "

In spite of my disgust, I burst out laughing. "You can laugh," growled Turner, "but how the hell can I maintain discipline if I let them get away with tricks like that? Well, there's one thing certain; after today she'll never play a trick on me again as long as she lives."

"You know what you've done, of course," I said. "You've murdered Shakespeare for her as surely as Macbeth murdered Duncan. She'll never be able to read a line of Shakespeare without horror and loathing. You did that deliberately and you waited, just as deliberately, till I was present, so that the ordeal would be even worse for her."

"What does it matter?" he said. "I don't suppose she'd ever appreciate Shakespeare, anyway. She'll probably be married and have a kid before she's twenty and read nothing but these ghastly women's papers."

The bell rang shrilly and the class made a concerted rush for the door. "Gently!" bellowed Turner. "Where's the fire?" They trooped out, more slowly, and I saw a buxom, red-haired girl with pouting lips and a glorious complexion, give him a quick, sly, secretive smile as she passed. He smiled back, looked quickly at me to see if I had noticed then said, with an embarrassed titter, "Come on, and I'll introduce you to the Headmaster. He'll want to show you round himself."

The Headmaster's name was Fiske, a tall, spare man with thin, white hair and charming manners. He had almost reached the retiring age and, as far as a new school was concerned, he couldn't have cared less, but he showed me round pleasantly enough, pointing out features, obvious to my trained eye, that were obsolete or inconvenient.

I tried to ask intelligent questions but my mind was not on the school but on Leslie Turner as a possible murderer. He had just revealed himself as having a vicious and revengeful nature and Ruth had disparaged his play. That alone would have been enough to turn his spite against her but, more than that, she stood in the way of his fiancée, Diana Randall, becoming a rich woman, and he had just been reading *Macbeth*. Was there not a parallel between Macbeth's murder of Duncan to secure his own advancement and the attempted murder of Ruth? Turner would not be the first to turn his thoughts to murder after reading Shakespeare.

I took my leave of Mr. Fiske and Turner came with me to the door. "It was good of you to come," he said. "Now you can see what we're up against in education and accommodation."

I can see what I'm up against in you, I thought. He looked out at the fog and shuddered. "I hate fog," he declared. "Aren't you scared to drive that smashing Bentley in muck like this?"

"I'm being very careful," I said, "and it's not so bad really until darkness sets in. Didn't I see you out last night driving a two-seater?"

He stiffened. "Where? When?"

"On the London road, pretty late."

"No, couldn't have been me, old chap. Besides, how could you have recognized me in the fog?"

"I just thought it might be you."

"It was no night for a car to be out," he said, but he didn't say his car hadn't been out and I knew it had. Abruptly—too abruptly, he changed the subject. "The School Inspector's coming next week and I've thought of a brilliant wheeze to impress him. I've told the class that when I ask a question, everyone's to put a hand up. Those that know the answer put their right hand up, those that don't know it, the left. Then I pick someone with the right hand up and when the Inspector sees the forest of hands, he'll think I've got a keen, intelligent class and give me a good report. That's the way to get promotion."

"It's one way," I commented. "Well, I hope for your sake your Play will be a success. Teaching is so obviously not your vocation." With which parting shot I left him.

As I drove out of the playground I passed a girl walking towards the gates. She was walking with her head down, looking perfectly miserable, but she looked up as I passed and I recognized Mary Gordon. I stopped, opened the nearside front door and called out, "Can I give you a lift?"

She smiled uncertainly, took a tighter hold on her school books which she carried in a strap, looked at the car, then at the

open gates, then at the car again. The car won and she stepped
in, sat down carefully on the edge of the seat and pulled the door
shut after her.

"What a lovely car!" she exclaimed. "It's got almost as
many knobs on the dashboard as an aeroplane."

I showed her how the cigarette lighter worked and the
heater, then I turned on the radio and dance music came through,
clear and strong. She was enchanted and wriggled back in the
seat until she was comfortable. The Bentley slid away with its
smooth, silent purr and I asked her where she lived.

"Do you know Thomson Street?"

"I'm afraid not. Is it far?"

"It's quite a bit but I can get a bus, really I can."

"Don't worry," I said. "I'll have you there in a jiffy if you'll
just direct me."

She told me which way to turn, peering eagerly through the
fog and, toning down the radio, I said, "You had my sympathy
this afternoon."

"I made an awful fool of myself."

"Not without some assistance in that direction from Mr.
Turner."

"He can be awfully vicious sometimes and he had it in for
me."

"If I tell you how to get your own back without getting
into trouble, will you promise me something?"

"I'd promise almost anything for that."

"Then promise me you won't let him spoil Shakespeare for
you. There are some wonderful things in Shakespeare. He's
everybody's heritage and the English language and literature
are much richer because of his incomparable genius. If you
could see that Scene you were doing this afternoon—the Letter
Scene—on the stage with a really good actress as Lady Macbeth,
you couldn't fail to be thrilled by it.

"And there are other wonderful plays. Have you ever tried
to read *Romeo and Juliet*?"

"No, I've heard about it, of course."

"Then read the Balcony Scene sometime or better still, see
it acted. 'But, soft! What light through yonder window breaks?
It is the east, and Juliet is the sun! Arise fair sun and kill the
envious moon, who is already sick and pale with grief, that

thou her maid are far more fair than she. . . . It is my lady; O,
it is my love!' "

"It does sound lovely the way you say it. You've got a lovely
voice."

"Then you won't let Mr. Turner spoil Shakespeare for you?"

"I wouldn't be so silly."

"Good girl. I thought you looked sensible. He was telling
me about his dodge to fool the Inspector, about those who
know the answers putting up the right hand and those who
don't know them putting up the left hand."

"He's full of tricks like that."

"Do you think you could persuade the whole class to put
up the left hand the first question he asks?"

She looked at me, brown eyes wide with surprise, then she
began to giggle. "I say, that's rich," she said. "What a perfectly
marvellous idea. That will bring him down off his perch all right."

"Will they do it?"

"You bet they'll do it. They'll love it."

"If they all stick together there won't be much he can do
about it. I suppose you can trust them not to give away the fact
that you put them up to it?"

"I can trust them all right."

"When they were all leaving the class-room at the end of the
period there was a red-haired girl who smiled at him in rather a
knowing way. Who would that be?"

"Elizabeth Pollock. She sucks up to him all the time and he
seems to be a bit—you know—smitten with her. She can't do
grammar and he goes and sits beside her sometimes, pretending
to help her. He puts his arm round her waist, too, trying to be
funny and—and he takes her out in his car."

"He what!"

"He does, really he does, he's taken her out at least twice."

"Wouldn't she give away the plot then?"

"No, she wouldn't dare because she'll know she'll be jolly
well scragged if she does. She'll be scared to tell him."

"Look, Mary," I said, speaking in a serious tone. "Could you
find out if he took her out in his car last night?"

"I suppose I could. She doesn't wrap it up. I mean she's
proud he takes such notice of her and I'm sure she'll tell me if I
ask her."

"Then ask her."

"Why do you want to know? You're not a detective, are you?"

"No, but Mr. Turner's engaged to be married and he ought not to be making up to schoolgirls. It's got to be stopped and his fiancée's the one to stop it."

"You'll tell her?"

"If I have to. It's got to be stopped for this Elizabeth Pollock's sake too. She's very silly to encourage him and it could get both of them into serious trouble."

"I'll find out for you, really I will, but how can I get in touch with you?"

"I'm staying at the Ocean Hotel and you can telephone me there. Do you know how to use the telephone?"

"Of course I do. I'm sixteen past."

"That's settled then and you won't forget the left hand up business?"

"Not likely. I can't wait to tell the others. That's Thomson Street on the left."

I turned down a street of Council houses, each one exactly similar to the one before. "How do you know which is yours?" I asked.

She laughed. "There's a lamp-post at the gate. That one there. Thanks awfully. You've been terribly nice."

I opened the door for her and she skipped out like a spring lamb. It looked as if I had undone most of the harm that Turner had done and, feeling unusually virtuous, I drove at a snail's pace through the fog to the Town Hall.

After running the usual blockade of minor officials, I was shown in to the Town Clerk, John Wilmot, a man in the mid-forties with a florid face, bushy white hair and a worried look. Remembering my interview with the Town Planning Committee, I was not surprised that his hair had turned prematurely white.

His impressive mahogany desk was piled high with papers over which he surveyed me with world-weary blue eyes. His greeting was cordial enough and after a few preliminary pleasantries, we got down to business.

I explained what I required in the way of office accommodation, ordnance survey sheets, etc., and from time to time he nodded and pencilled a note on a pad. I soon found that he had a keen mind, knew exactly what I wanted and why and was prepared to co-operate. It was agreed that I would bring down two assistants from my London office and that he would second one of his typists, that two disused rooms in the Town Hall would be made available to me and telephone facilities provided.

Every few minutes the telephone on his desk would ring and he would snatch at the receiver with an exasperated air, deal crisply and efficiently with the various inquiries and slam the receiver down. "There are days when I could throw this dam' telephone through the window," he growled, "and this is one of them. A Town Clerk never gets any peace and never makes a fortune."

The phone rang again as if in derision and Wilmot sighed. "Here we go again," he said. "Yes, Mr. Wilmot speaking. Insurance? I've arranged all that. It's coming by road from London and should arrive some time tomorrow but I don't know when. You know what carrier services are these days. . . . It will be packed in a wooden box marked 'Livestock, with great care'. . . . Yes, there will be plenty of air holes. . . . Keep it warm? What do you want me to do, put a hot-water bottle in with it? . . . You do? But Great Scott, man, I'm not its nurse! . . . Very well, if you really mean it. I'll ask Carmichael to see to it at the London end. He knows how to handle reptiles and he'll be supervising the packing, anyway."

Wilmot replaced the receiver and sat for a moment staring into vacancy. "I'm everything in this dam' place," he said. "Legal Adviser, Chief Administrative Officer, Fuel Overseer, Entertainments Officer, Catering Manager and now I'm a snake's nursemaid."

"It must be an interesting life," I commented.

"Two years ago the Town Council fell heirs to a private Zoo," went on the Town Clerk, "and now every dam' one of them imagines he's a Fellow of the Zoological Society. The Zoo's their pet. We turned over half of the public park to it, but it's grown so fast we'll soon have no park left. That's something you'll have to provide for in your Advisory Plan, by the way, a new site for the Town Zoo."

"Would the bottom of the sea do?" I asked.

"The very place for it," said Wilmot. "There's a reptile house but as fast as we fill it with snakes, the snakes die on us. To show their dislike of captivity, they embark on a suicidal

ast and have to be forcibly fed. Ever try feeding a snake against
ts will?"

"My acquaintance with snakes is of the slightest," I said.

"Then pray that you don't make the acquaintance of the
brute that's coming tomorrow; a young fer-de-lance from
Martinique, one of the deadliest snakes known."

"Don't you have it de-venomed before it arrives?"

"No, they'll do that at the Zoo. Some of the experts there
want it intact so they can study its poison apparatus. They
want me to arrange for a hot-water bottle to be put in its case
before it leaves London, to keep it warm and sluggish. Apparently
its habits are nocturnal and if it arrives here at night it will be
wide awake and looking for trouble."

I heard the door open behind me, and, glancing round,
beheld the assured and arrogant figure of Henry Crane. He
hadn't troubled to knock or to have himself announced, for was
he not an Alderman, Chairman of the Town Planning Committee
and a power in the land? He was immaculately turned out but
his air of prosperous authority was slightly marred by a square
of sticking plaster on his forehead.

"Sorry to interrupt, Wilmot," he said, planting himself on a
chair. "But they told me Mr. Latimer was here and I thought
I should make his acquaintance. Getting down to work, Mr.
Latimer?"

"We were," I said.

"Anything you want just let me know and if it's reasonable
I'll see you get it."

"Mr. Wilmot is looking after me wonderfully well."

"I'm sure he is. Excellent man Wilmot but he hasn't quite
my influence, you know." He turned to Wilmot. "I was speaking
to Fredericks at the Zoo this morning and he's wondering when
he's going to get that snake."

"It will be here tomorrow," said Wilmot. "Hot-water bottle
and all."

"What time tomorrow?"

"In the evening, probably. Have you had an accident,
Alderman?"

Crane scowled. "Surprised someone prowling round my
garage in the early hours of the morning. He threw a brick at
me, smashed the window and I got a splinter of glass in the

forehead. I've just been round to see the Chief Constable about it. The police here need waking up."

"Do you think someone was trying to pinch your car?"

"Looked very like it but my dog scared him off."

"It wasn't much of a night for driving a car," I said. "What with the rain and the fog. Had your car been out at all?"

"No," said Crane, "my car wasn't out last night." He veiled his eyes from me but I was unable to keep a flash of awareness from mine. There it was; the lie! The damning and damnable lie! I knew, none better, that his car had been out last night and as he caught my fleeting expression of excitement, he knew that I knew. I saw the light of comprehension dawn on his face and from that moment enmity was born.

In an instant both our faces were expressionless again and everything seemed the same as it had been before. But we both knew that it wasn't the same, that it would never be the same again. Crane was drumming with his knuckles on the Town Clerk's desk, watching me and thinking hard. I wondered just what thoughts were passing through his active brain and then a clerk knocked, entered, addressed a few words to Wilmot and Wilmot left the room with him, explaining that he would be back in a minute. Crane and I gazed at each other like fencers seeking an opening and I wondered what form the attack would take. I did not have to wait long.

"You seem to know Miss Mannering very well," he began.

"We'd met before."

"When?"

"Oh, a long time ago."

"Conway tells me he met you at her house this morning."

"That's so."

"And that you interfered in a matter with which you had no concern."

"I'm not aware of it."

"I think you are. I'm referring to the Velasquez picture. I'm told you tried to abet Miss Mannering in putting up the price."

"I could see that Miss Mannering didn't want to sell so I gave her some support."

"I see. Currying favour, were you?"

"At least I'm not trying to curry favour with you."

"It would be a lost cause. If you want to retain your post as

Planning Consultant here, you'd better be careful. I could break you, you know."

"I don't break easily."

Wilmot came back and resumed his seat at his desk. If he noticed the tension between Crane and me, he didn't show it. Crane rose. "I needn't detain you longer," he said. "I think Latimer and I understand each other. You won't waste time on the job, will you, Latimer. The social life of Shellbridge is not for you."

"It's not for anyone," I said, "who has a better use for his time."

Crane went out without replying and Wilmot said, "Go easy with Henry. He runs this town."

"He doesn't run me."

"He'll run you out if you give him cause. Is there anything else I can do for you?"

I shook my head, thanked him for his co-operation and withdrew. Outside the Town Hall a newsboy thrust the early edition of a London evening paper into my hand and, tossing him a coin, I sought a quiet corner of the hotel lounge and began to race through the columns. Nothing about Johnny, nothing about the raid on his flat, nothing about the incident in Crane's garden. Evidently Johnny's body hadn't been found yet or, if it had, the police were keeping it quiet.

I was about to lay the paper down when a stop press item caught my eye:

NIGHT CLUB WAITER KILLED BY HIT-AND-RUN DRIVER

Early this morning the mangled body of James (Spike) Murphy, a waiter at the Mermaid Club, was found lying at the mouth of the alley leading from the Club's rear premises to Piccadilly. From the nature of his injuries it is surmised that he was killed by a hit-and-run driver.

I dropped the paper, feeling the blood begin to pound in my veins. Spike Murphy was the waiter who had wanted to warn Johnny against Tyler Morgan and now he was dead. I didn't believe for an instant in that hit-and-run driver. It was more likely that Spike had been knocked unconscious and deliberately run over, that Tyler had a short way with traitors.

CHAPTER EIGHT

A GAME OF HIDE AND SEEK

I WONDERED where Tyler Morgan was now and what he was doing. He wouldn't forget that parting punch I had given him and he knew the truth about Johnny. I was going to have trouble with Tyler, I could feel it in my bones and I realized that what I had started I would have to finish; that there was no going back. Even if it meant complete ruin, loss of reputation, liberty, even life, I would have to see it through.

I had a sudden insane desire to drive out past the spot where I had buried Johnny just to see that all was quiet, that no Tyler Morgan was prowling around, but I fought it down. That way madness lay. Perhaps Tyler had his hands full with his own concerns, perhaps he would leave us alone. I decided to calm myself by going for a haircut.

Piggott's shop was half empty and the thin, bald-headed, garrulous man who cut my hair confided that he was Tom Piggott himself, that he knew who I was and that his daughter Molly had a rare word of me. As my acquaintance with Molly had been of extremely short duration, I put that down to blarney and, by putting one or two seemingly artless questions, soon had Piggott talking about Shellbridge and its people.

Shellbridge, it seemed, thought the world of Miss Mannering, admired the business acumen of Henry Crane, despised Peter Randall for a spineless waster and thought his sister Diana something worse than a minx. Patrick Conway was a crafty type, Leslie Turner had a mean streak and Miss Mannering's butler, Romney, wasn't nearly so stupid as he pretended.

Piggott was a competent hairdresser and was exceedingly gentle in dealing with the lumps on my head. Of course he wanted to know how I had come by them but I put him off with a vague story of a fall. He wound up with a short lecture on Town Planning, about which he knew less than nothing, pocketed the coin I gave him, brushed me off and bowed me out into the fog.

Darkness had fallen on Shellbridge, the cold darkness of a winter's night, and the streets were almost deserted. At intervals, along the shore road bordering the promenade, yellow, sodium lights made futile circles of radiance in the fog and an occasional tramcar clanged dismally on its way. The foghorn on the light-ship kept up a fitful moaning and as I walked back to the hotel my feeling of uneasiness grew stronger.

Footsteps, magnified by the fog, had a sinister echo, making me start with alarm in the belief that I was being followed. Several times I halted to listen, only to learn that the footsteps belonged to innocent pedestrians and by the time I reached the hotel entrance, every nerve in my body was on edge.

Without Ruth I felt lost, as if my life had no meaning, no purpose. I had often been alone but never before had I been lonely and I wondered if I dare ring her up and invite her out for the evening. Would she regard it as presumption or would she be gracious and accept? If she did accept, where could we go? In the entrance hall I scanned brightly printed advertisements of cinema shows but none of them appealed.

I was conscious of a buzzing in my head—Piggot's scissors had not been light enough in spite of his care—and I knew that if I had any sense at all, I would take a couple of aspirins and go to bed but I decided to telephone Ruth anyway, if only to hear her voice, to satisfy myself that she was safe. Romney answered; indomitable and imperturbable as ever. "Miss Ruth's in her bath," he informed me loftily, as if he were the servant of royalty.

"Is she all right?"

"I ain't her lady's maid and the keyhole's blocked."

"Has anything happened since I left?"

"There was a bloke hangin' about outside half an hour ago. Looked as if he was watchin' the house. I went out to him but he breezed off."

"What was he like?"

"Just a shape in the fog, cock."

"All right. Keep your wits about you."

"Where else would I keep them?" growled Romney, and rang off.

Bright lights beckoned from the bar and I went in. There was only one customer, a burly man sitting on a stool at the counter, talking to Molly Piggott, and I was close up to him before I recognized him. He was Tyler Morgan.

He recognized me at the same moment, jumped off his stool and aimed a vicious right swing at my jaw. I ducked just in time and sent him staggering back with a straight punch to the mouth. Rage blazed up in me like a forest fire and I went after him, hitting him with both fists, time and time again. He was hitting me too but I was so angry I scarcely felt the blows, then he fell back into an arm-chair beside the fire-place.

I saw him dimly through a red mist of anger. He was panting heavily and blood was trickling down his chin from a corner of his mouth. "Turn it up, chum," he wheezed. "I gotta watch me blood pressure."

I stood over him, both fists clenched. "Get up," I said. "Come on, get up and fight. I'm going to take you apart bone by bone."

"Oh no you're not! Not in my bar." Molly Piggott thrust herself between us, her arms akimbo, sparks in her green eyes. "I'm surprised at you, Mr. Latimer, I really am. And you too, Mr. Morgan. You started it."

"I couldn't help taking a swing at him, kid," said Tyler. "Last time we met, he hit me when I wasn't looking."

"At least you weren't tied to a chair," I said.

"If you're going to fight, it won't be in here," insisted Molly, "or I'll get the police in, quick."

Tyler grinned up at her, a crooked grin that made him look, with the blood-marks on his chin, unbelievably sinister. "The fight's over, kid. It was just spontaneous combustion." He turned his grin on me and nodded at an adjacent chair. "Siddown, chum. I got things to say to you."

"I've got nothing to say to you," I said, "except this: Get out of Shellbridge while you can still walk." The red mist was subsiding and my brain was beginning to work again. This man was dangerous and, with the knowledge he possessed, he held most of the cards. As the thought crossed my mind, he said slyly, "Johnny been found yet?"

I smiled at the barmaid. "Sorry to have caused you any worry, Molly," I apologized. "It won't happen again."

Molly nodded. "That's O.K., Mr. Latimer. You know how it is." She retreated behind the bar and I sat down opposite Tyler

"How much?" I asked.

"Fifty thousand quid."

"For your silence?"

"That's right."

"I haven't got fifty thousand shillings."

Tyler stretched himself like a sleepy bulldog, wiped the blood from his chin and relaxed in his chair. "Mebbe not, chum," he conceded, "but the girl friend has." He leaned forward and tapped me confidentially on the knee. "Mebbe you thought I let you off pretty easy last night at the Mermaid Club and mebbe I did, too. But I had a reason. I smelled dough."

"I must do something about your sense of smell," I said, raising a warning fist. Tyler ignored it. "You see, chum, I recognized the dame. Ruth Mannering, the pianist, and a blinkin' millionairess, too. I seen her photo often and once I seen her play. I never forget a face."

"I can do something about that, too," I murmured.

"So when you told me what you done with Johnny, I smelled dough. Big dough. I let you go because I knew I could pick you both up any time and this morning I decided to pay Shellbridge a little visit. Can't say I appreciated the welcome."

"And suppose we won't play?" I said.

"Then a little note goes from me to the cops, anonymous, saying where they can find Johnny and who put him where he is."

"And a little note goes from me to the cops," I said. "Also anonymous, saying what really happened to Spike Murphy, that he was run over on purpose by order of Tyler Morgan. And why."

Tyler shook his head. "You couldn't make it stick, chum. There's no evidence. Whadda you think I am, an amachoor?"

"I think you're a blackmailer and a murderer," I said, "and if you aren't out of here by morning, I'll kill you, Tyler."

He threw back his head and laughed. "You kill me with laughing, chum. I know your type. You got a reputation, you got a career. You ain't gonna throw it away by killin' anyone."

"My career is already endangered," I said. "If what I've done comes out, I'll be ruined and I'll stop at nothing to see that t doesn't come out. I mean it, Tyler, every word of it. I'm not bluffing, and your death wouldn't trouble my conscience. You're already a murderer and your life is forfeit to the law."

H

"Only the law can't prove it."

"I can save them having to try. Johnny could do with company out there in the sand."

Tyler thought for a minute then he nodded. "I believe you do mean it," he said. "You got a desperate look in your eye. Mebbe I've gone about this the wrong way. I should have fixed you first, then done my business with this Ruth Mannering. Mebbe she'll listen to me."

"One word from you to her," I said, "and Johnny won't be alone much longer."

Tyler rose and I rose with him. "You must be pretty fond of that dame. Well, I guess I'll go do some thinking. We're getting nowhere fast."

"Do your thinking in London," I said. "It's the only place you'll be safe." For a long moment he looked straight into my eyes, then his gaze fell and he went out.

I sat down again to collect my racing thoughts. I had not been bluffing. I was in deep and in to the end. There was no way back. If Tyler menaced Ruth then Tyler must die. This was a fight to a finish with no quarter given or asked.

I went to the phone, rang up Romney, described Tyler and told him that on no account was Tyler to be allowed to speak to Ruth.

"Wrong 'un, is he?" asked Romney. "I'll fix him if he comes here. Just leave it to me, cock. Don't you worry."

But I worried all right. I worried all through my lonely dinner, not knowing nor caring what I ate, and afterwards I went out and walked quickly through the fog-shrouded streets to Ruth's home. Outside the gate I lingered, listening, and then I heard the scrape of a footstep on the other side of the road. Through swirls of fog I saw a figure standing under a street lamp and, taking out a cigarette, I crossed over and asked him for a light.

He struck a match and as it flared up I recognized Tyler's lieutenant, Joe, the lean and silent gunman who had brought the Bentley round to the alley behind the Mermaid Club, who had almost certainly been the instrument of Spike Murphy's dissolution. "Why, Joe!" I said. "How nice to see you again."

The gun was half out of his pocket before my fist sank into the pit of his stomach and, as he doubled up with a gasp, the gun clattered to the pavement and went off with a bang that seemed to split the night. The next second, a police whistle shrilled along the street, Joe turned and staggered away, bent double, his hands clutching his stomach and I heard the thud thud of heavy footsteps approaching at the run.

I sprinted across the street, in Ruth's gate and round to the back. Romney opened the door at my first knock and I pushed past him into the kitchen.

"Blow me down!" he exclaimed. "You came bustin' in here as if the police was after you."

I kicked the door shut and stood with my back against it. "You're a good guesser, Romney," I said. "They are."

I was standing in a large, comfortable kitchen and a large, comfortable woman was sitting in a rocking-chair by the fire. Her black, liquid eyes took me in impassively then, with a Gallic shrug, she looked away. She had been beautiful once and was still a handsome woman.

Romney spoke to her in fluent French then turned to me. "The wife don't speak much English," he explained, "and she minds her own business. Met her at Dinard on a holiday once, learned her lingo all next winter, went back next summer and popped the question in French. What you done now, cock?"

"Tackled a thug who was watching the house," I told him. "His gun went off by accident and a copper heard the bang."

"Did he hear you come in here?"

"He just might."

Romney stroked his huge expanse of jaw but before he could comment the door burst open and Ruth, a poem in arrested motion, stood framed in the entrance. Her eyes were blue sparks of fear but her voice was commendably calm. "Philip! What are you doing here? Did you fire that shot?"

"No," I said. "That was our old friend Joe."

I told her what had happened and as I finished there was an imperious ring at the front door. "That bluebottle smelling around," growled Romney. "Take Mr. Latimer into the drawing-room, Miss Ruth, and start banging the old panana. Bang it good."

"I always bang it good, Romney," said Ruth. Her eyes were still troubled but there were traces of a smile at the corners of her mouth.

"Bang it loud, I mean," amended Romney, taking my coat and hat. "You both been there all evening and you didn't hear no shot." He rounded on his wife. "You neither."

The Frenchwoman nodded and went on rocking herself placidly in her chair. The bell rang again and Ruth ran before me into the drawing-room, sat down at the piano and began to play the *Warsaw Concerto*. The notes rippled defiantly across the room and in the background I was faintly aware of Romney's voice expostulating at the front door.

I relaxed in an arm-chair by the fire, broke a cigarette in half, lit both halves and stubbed them out in the ash-tray on an adjacent table. Then I took out another cigarette, broke it also, threw one half in the fire and lit the other half. A half empty glass on the table would have helped also but there was no time for that.

Ruth had the loud pedal down, the ornaments in the room vibrated, then the door opened and Romney came in with a policeman. "This is Constable Craig, Miss Ruth," he announced. "I told him you was engaged but he insists on seeing you."

Ruth rose from the piano, calm and gracious, the perfect hostess. No one would have guessed that she was under a strain. The policeman was young and didn't know what to do with his hands, but if he was embarrassed he was also determined.

"Excuse me, Miss," he said, "but did you hear a shot a few minutes ago?"

Ruth arched her eyebrows in surprise, shook her head and looked inquiringly at me. I shook my head also, smiled at the policeman and said, "It would be an insult to the pianist to say that I heard a shot."

"Quite so, sir, only when the shot was fired the piano wasn't playing or I'd have heard it."

The silence seemed to shriek; the moment of tension was unbearable, then I said, "Perhaps not, but we weren't listening for shots." I gave Ruth an openly adoring look. "We had other things on our minds."

She lowered her head and I saw a blush spread over her cheek. Constable Craig saw it too, then his eyes took in the two cigarette stubs on the ash-tray. "You've been here for some time then, sir?" he asked.

"It doesn't seem long," I said, "but it must have been a

hour or two." I threw the cigarette I had been smoking into the fire and the constable's eyes followed it till it was lost in the flames. His brow furrowed slightly and I knew I had made a mistake. I should have stubbed it out in the ash-tray with the other two.

The constable brought his right hand from behind his back. Joe's gun was in it. "This wouldn't be yours, sir, by any chance?"

"No," I said. "Is it loaded?"

"All but one chamber, sir."

"Then for Pete's sake point it some other way. I've been scared of guns since childhood."

I was acutely conscious of the fact that I kept my own gun in the right-hand pocket of my jacket and hoped the constable would not notice the bulge. He seemed an observant type and I kept my elbow pressed close against the pocket. Then, with an inward start, I realized that I could not feel the gun. I pressed my elbow closer but there was nothing there. My gun was gone and for a moment my senses reeled and it took everything I had to keep my face expressionless. When and where had I lost it? Had it been in my coat pocket after all? No, I remembered only too clearly slipping it into the pocket of my jacket. I looked more closely at the gun in the constable's hand but it was not mine.

"Just after the shot," went on Constable Craig, "I had a feeling I heard this gate click."

"Whoever fired it might well have escaped this way," I said. "There's a path at the back that leads through a gap in the hedge to the Randalls' cottage."

"Indeed, sir, then perhaps I'd better ask at the Randalls'." He turned to Ruth. "Perhaps your butler would show me the way, Miss."

"It would be a labour of love," said Romney, who was still standing in the doorway. "This way, cock."

The door closed behind them and we relaxed. Ruth slumped down on the piano stool, took the cigarette I offered her and said in a breathless little voice. "Do you think he suspected anything?"

"Don't know," I said. "He's all there, that one." I hunted in vain through my pockets. "Funny thing, I seem to have lost my gun."

"How could you have lost it?"

"I wish I knew. I could swear it was in this pocket." The

door opened to admit Romney. He was bearing with tremendous dignity a silver salver and on the salver was my gun. He bent stiffly and proffered the salver with a regal gesture. "Better 'ave this back, cock," he said. "I took the liberty of abstracting it. Bluebottles have sharp eyes."

I took the gun with a surge of relief. "You grow on me, Romney," I admitted. "I might even end up by almost liking you."

"You must think this all very strange, Romney," said Ruth.

Romney drew himself up. "I'm only the butler," he said. "I ain't supposed to think." At the door he paused, winked gravely at me and went out.

"I don't know where you got that priceless treasure," I said, "but whatever you do, hang on to him."

Ruth laughed. "It would take nothing less than an atom bomb to shift Romney. Now what's all this about Joe and Tyler Morgan?"

She was pale to the lips when I told her but she soon rallied. She had courage and steadfastness of a high order and I knew that whatever was in store for us, she would see it through.

She rose from the piano stool, slowly and gracefully, and stood in the middle of the room, looking at me. Her eyes were smoke-blue and unfathomable. They drew me like the eyes of a sorceress and I was not aware that I had left my chair until I felt her shoulders shrink under the grip of my hands. I pulled her close against me and kissed her savagely on the mouth. For a moment she yielded then she came suddenly to life and strained away from me. I let her go and she sat down again, rather abruptly, on the piano stool.

Her eyes held mine, her lips were slightly parted and she was breathing heavily. Colour mantled her cheeks and she said in a strained voice, "Why did you do that?"

"Impulse. Why didn't you slap my face?"

"Because I don't yield to impulse. Would it have stopped you?"

"Nothing would have stopped me."

"You'd better go now."

"Yes, I'd better go now." She sat still and very straight watching me to the door, her colour still high. At the door I turned. "I kissed you," I said, "because just at that moment I thought you were the most beautiful and perfect thing I had ever seen. Good night."

Romney, with his usual uncanny anticipation, was waiting to show me the door. "Better wipe the lipstick off your dial, cock," he advised as he helped me into my coat.

"I'll wipe the grin off yours," I growled, and went out into the night.

I walked quickly through the fog, obsessed by my thoughts. The police might not make much of the incident of Joe's gun but when Johnny was found they were going to remember it and they were going to remember also the incident of Ruth's fur coat. It would not take them long to learn that Johnny had been Ruth's fiancé and then they would be after us horse, foot, and guns.

It was deathly quiet in the back streets of Shellbridge and the fog was like thick, yellow smoke. My footsteps had a loud, hollow ring, echoing back to me from every side and, for a moment, I fancied I heard a deeper echo farther down the street. I stopped and the echo stopped also. Then I walked on a few yards and stopped again, abruptly. This time the echo went on too long and I knew that I was being followed.

I crossed the street and the footsteps crossed with me. I quickened my steps and the footsteps kept pace a few yards behind. Then I turned back and the footsteps retreated before me and died away. "Who's there?" I called, and the echo of my voice mocked me in the silence.

I turned again and the footsteps began with mine, furtive, sinister, relentless. If it were Joe, at least I had drawn him away from the vicinity of Ruth's gate which was all to the good. I touched the gun in my pocket, remembered that Joe's gun was in the hands of the police, grinned to myself and embarked in deadly earnest on a game of hide-and-seek.

Several times I doubled back, becoming thoroughly lost in the process but each time my shadow found me out. Once I caught a glimpse of him under the diffused radiance of a street lamp. It was Joe all right. There was no mistaking that long, gangling form. And he wasn't following me for practice. He was a killer and I was the quarry.

Up and down through the wide avenues of the residential quarter, through the narrow, twisting alleys of the slums, across evil-smelling courtyards, I led Joe on a blind tour of Shellbridge until at last I felt the dank breath of the sea on my face and came out on the promenade.

It was a promenade of the dead, choked with impenetrable fog, stretching away into endless silence. I paused to listen, heard the clop clop of Joe's footsteps falter and die away a few yards behind, crossed the promenade to the seaward side and found myself opposite the pier.

At this time of night and in this smother the pier should be deserted. It would be a long, empty arm thrusting out to sea, cut off by the fog from Shellbridge and civilization and there Joe and I could bring our duel of wits to a close. The turnstiles clicked as I passed through and I had gone scarcely ten yards before I heard them click again. Joe was still with me.

I walked on towards the far end and the smell of creosote and seaweed reminded me forcibly of my first acquaintance with the pier when I had saved Ruth from drowning. But the fog was twice as thick tonight, the pier twice as dangerous. On either side amusement buildings would keep me from falling over but at the far end there was nothing and with Joe close behind me there was no going back.

I went on, picking my way slowly across the echoing timbers. The hollow boom of the fog-horn sounded louder than ever but it was not loud enough to drown the echo of Joe's following footsteps. I could not see my hand in front of my face and I had no idea how far the pier stretched. From previous experience I guessed it to be about three hundred yards long but it might be considerably less.

I moved across to the left, tripped over the steps of the silent theatre and a few seconds later heard Joe trip also. I was impressed by the grim determination with which he had stuck to me and, at that moment, the thought flashed into my mind. What if he had another gun?

While I had been in Ruth's house Joe could have been reporting to Tyler Morgan and I had made Tyler my mortal enemy. Tyler could have given Joe his own gun and told him what to do with it, for Tyler didn't do his own killings. He employed Joe. I was convinced in my mind that it was Joe who had run down Spike Murphy and now he was out to finish me.

I felt my way along past the shuttered barricade of the

shooting gallery to the semi-circular tea-troom at the far end of the pier. Behind this tea-room, close to the edge, Ruth's assailant had lain in wait and here I would lie in wait for Joe. The tea-room was dark, its doors barred, its windows shuttered. I felt as if I were at the end of the world and knew that two steps more would take me over the edge.

Had Joe a gun or hadn't he? Did he know that I had a gun too? Would he risk coming any farther in the treacherous fog? I listened but could hear only the water lapping at the slimy timbers of the pier, sucking greedily round the uprights.

I didn't want to use my gun unless I had to, for shooting Joe wouldn't solve anything. It would only drive me farther along the one-way road that lay outside the law. I could hear Joe no longer but I knew that he was there, listening and waiting not more than a few feet away. The slightest error of judgment now would mean my life.

An age of silence dragged past, then, from somewhere in front, I heard the warning creak of a plank. Joe was moving in for the kill but I had the feeling that he did not know how near the edge he was. Again silence. I could hear my heart beating and wondered if Joe could hear it too. He must be very close now.

"Mr. Latimer!" The voice was low and hoarse and not three feet away. I tensed but did not speak. "I don't aim to do you no harm, Mr. Latimer, but I gotta talk to you."

Still I kept silent and the voice began again, coaxing, wheedling, false as a cracked bell. "Just a few words, that's all I want."

"I can hear you, Joe," I said. "Talk." Quickly, I crouched low on one knee and as I did so the blast of gun-fire shook the night, the flash ripped the fog aside for an instant and I heard the whine of the bullet going out and away. Then I gathered myself for the effort and sprang.

Joe swerved instinctively, I missed him completely and the next second I heard the splash as he went in. I had been right. He had not known how near the edge he was.

I backed away a few steps and stood listening. The fog-horn dinned in my ears, a seagull wailed and whirred invisibly by. There was no other sound and after a few more seconds I retraced my steps along the pier. Emptiness surrounded me, silence went with me, there was no one to challenge me. I lit a cigarette, shielding the glowing end with my hand. It may have been a dangerous thing to do but all my nerves were on edge and I craved for a smoke as a parched man craves for water.

In the foyer of the hotel the brightly-lit bar beckoned me. Within I could hear the clatter of many tongues and for a long moment I hesitated on the threshold. Then I went on up the stairs to my room. I wanted a drink badly but I like to prove to myself occasionally that I am a strong character, that I can resist temptation.

In spite of the closed window, my bedroom was thick with fog through which the single light shone dimly. I plumped down wearily on the bed, unlaced my shoes, kicked them off and sat for a long time staring at the wall. Then I put my shoes on again and went down and had that drink. For the second time in my life I drank to Shellbridge Pier.

Someone slapped me on the back, almost causing me to spill my drink and I turned to see Leslie Turner leering at me from behind a large tankard. His face was flushed and he seemed to be in a fairly advanced state of intoxication. "Slowly, old chap," he said. "Don't gulp it down like that or you'll die of arterio-sclerosis before you're fifty."

He slid on to the stool next to mine, drained his tankard to show that he did not practise what he preached, thumped it down on the counter and said, "Fill it up, Molly. Mr. Latimer will pay."

Molly cocked a quizzical eyebrow at me and I nodded. "Put some hemlock in it," I said.

"We don't stock it."

"Pity."

"Why so pale and wan, fond lover?" asked Turner. "Something got you down?"

"Something," I said. "Maybe it's the fog and maybe it's the company."

He gave an exaggerated, theatrical sigh. "I thought we were going to be such chums," he said, "but the atmosphere is much cooler since this afternoon. What have I done to you?"

"Given me an insight into your teaching methods that I'll remember till the day I die. If I were that girl's father, I'd horsewhip you."

"Which girl?"

"Mary Gordon."

"Oh, that one! Thought you meant——" His voice died away into an uneasy silence. Evidently over-indulgence in alcohol had not yet robbed him of discretion.

"You thought I meant your red-haired charmer, Elizabeth Pollock. Yes, if I were her father, I'd horsewhip you, too."

"Who have you been talking to?"

I didn't answer and he thumped his tankard angrily on the counter. "I want to know who you've been bloody well talking to." The red flush at his cheek-bones was more pronounced now and he had raised his voice belligerently. Molly rose from her chair at the other end of the bar counter and came over to us. "Language," she reproved. "This is the cocktail bar of a respectable hotel, not one of your common pubs. If you want to swear, Mr. Turner, swear to yourself or take your custom elsewhere."

"Sorry," growled Turner. "Got a lot to put up with these days. Bloody spies everywhere."

"You heard what I just told you?"

"It slipped out, though what's it matter if it did? Why is it that word could make a fortune for Bernard Shaw, yet when I use it all I get's abuse?"

Molly tossed her head. "Mr. Shaw was a gentleman and a genius. There's no comparison, either way."

She went back to her seat and Turner sat hunched over his tankard, brooding. "Women!" he muttered. "Never marry a woman. They're Hell. Unless they've got money, of course. It's different if they've got money. Here, who's been telling you about Elizabeth Pollock?"

"I saw that smile she gave you this afternoon. It told me all I needed to know."

"Just a little innocent fun, old man. It's damned dull in Shellbridge while the winter lasts and a chap's got to divert himself somehow."

"You've got a full-grown and willing fiancée, so you've no excuse for robbing the cradle."

"Cradle, eh! That kid's hot stuff. She could teach you, I bet."

"And who taught her in the first place? You or some swine like you. Away and drink by yourself. You make me sick."

Molly came forward again. "What are you two quarrelling about?" she demanded. "Break it up, will you. How's the new Planning Scheme going, Mr. Latimer?"

"It hasn't begun yet. The first thing I have to do is to make an exhaustive survey of the town and who could survey anything in this smother?"

She leaned her elbows on the counter, determined to keep the peace between Turner and me. She was looking very attractive tonight, her colour high and not a hair out of place. "We hear a lot about Planning these days," she said, "but it isn't a new thing, is it? I mean, they had it in ancient Egypt. I once read there was a workman's village built thousands of years ago in Egypt that was an example of a perfectly planned little community. It was for workmen building one of the pyramids."

I looked at Molly with a new interest. Turner had told me she was intelligent and could talk on any subject, but I hadn't expected to be regaled with a history of Town Planning down the ages. Characteristically, however, Turner wasted no time in disillusioning me.

"Once read," he sneered. "You read it this afternoon on purpose to impress. I met her coming out of the public library, Latimer, with a book on Town Planning by Sir Patrick Abercrombie tucked under her arm. You can't beat women for pure cunning. If she fails with Peter Randall, there's always you as a second string. Get it?"

Molly's face was scarlet and her green eyes blazed at Turner. If there had been a bottle handy on the counter, I believe she would have broken it over his skull, but fortunately for him there was nothing within reach that she could have used as a weapon. She was struggling to speak when there was a hacking cough from behind and Peter Randall joined us.

Molly was all smiles now, hastening to pour him a double whisky and looking apologetic when she whisked away the money.

" 'How happy could I be with either were the other dear charmer away,' " murmured Turner wickedly, but Molly turned her shoulder to him and affected not to hear.

"How's the cold, Peter?" she asked.

Randall coughed again to let us hear how it was and Molly said, "You shouldn't be out on a foggy night like this."

"He couldn't keep away," said Turner, "As the moth returns to the candle-flame so Randall returns to the barmaid."

Randall gave him an evil look, saw that he was three parts

drunk and decided to humour him. "How's the Play?" he asked. "Got a West End Producer hooked yet?"

Turner shook his head and, just for a second, he looked almost sober. His shoulders drooped and the hard, blue eyes dulled momentarily with the terrible awareness of failure. Then the shadow passed. "Not yet," he admitted, "but I've hopes. Your sister's working like blazes on Ruth Mannering."

"Ruth knows the big shots in the musical world," said Randall, "but I don't know about the drama. However, money talks."

"Her money only says the one thing: 'Don't give me away.' I bet you've tried to bite her ear for plenty."

Randall looked down at his drink, his face inscrutable. "She isn't an easy touch. It seems she's got principles."

"With all that jack she doesn't need principles."

"She has them all the same. She'd give you a hundred thousand quid for a new Town Hall for Shellbridge quicker than she'd give you a fiver for a night out with a blonde."

"Don't it make you mad?" said Molly, forgetting her painfully acquired English at the thought of gold.

I withdrew a little from the counter and stood watching them unobtrusively. Three possible murderers, I thought, and just at that moment they looked it. Greed had them in thrall and all three of them stood to gain immeasurably from Ruth's death. Diana would back Turner's plays all right, once she got her share of Ruth's fortune, and Peter would lift Molly out of her present environment into the life of luxury she evidently craved. A girl who would swot up Abercrombie on the Town Planning of Ancient Egypt, just to gain an alternative string to her bow, was capable of anything.

In bed that night I lay thinking until I felt all churned up inside. I thought about Joe in his watery grave, about Tyler, about the Randalls, Henry Crane, Leslie Turner, and Molly Piggott, but most of all I thought about Ruth. I tried to analyse my feelings for Ruth. What was it that had turned me in the space of a night from an ordinary, level-headed, law-abiding citizen into an accessory to murder? Was it love in Arcady or desire under the elms? Did I want her to love and to cherish, forsaking all others or did I just want her? I kept seeing her in my mind's eye as the girl in the Velasquez picture and I tossed and turned, sweated and grew cold, rumpled the bed-clothes and ruffled the pillows until at last I fell into a tormented, nightmare-haunted sleep.

Next morning, just as I finished breakfast, I was called to the telephone. It was Mary Gordon.

"Mr. Latimer? About Elizabeth Pollock. She *was* out in Mr. Turner's car the night before last. She went to a dance with some of her crowd at Man o' War Bay—that's a village three miles down the coast—and he turned up at eleven o'clock and took her home in his car. He kept her out ever so late and she had to get in by the window and he tried to kiss her."

"That was frightfully enterprising of him," I said. "Thanks, Mary. I'm most grateful." As I replaced the receiver I was thinking that if Mary's evidence let Turner out of Tuesday night's London adventure, it put Henry Crane very much on the spot. I had a feeling he wouldn't be able to explain away the use of his car so easily and, at that moment, he went up in my mind to Suspect Number One.

CHAPTER NINE

A VISITOR FROM MARTINIQUE

THE cocktail party began at eight o'clock in an atmosphere of sweetness and light, in which, however, it was not to be allowed to continue. Ruth was wearing a short dress of steel grey satin with touches of dark red. She looked wonderful in it but tonight the colour was *on* her cheeks not *in* her cheeks and there were signs of strain behind her eyes, particularly when they met mine. The neckline of her frock left part of her shoulders bare, revealing an angry bruise on the ivory flesh and, when she saw me looking at it, she said with a half smile, "Your handiwork, Philip."

"Last night?"

"Yes."

"I'm sorry." There was a buzzing in my ears tonight and I felt strangely lethargic. Lack of sleep combined with semi-concussion were not the best aids to sparkling conversation.

"You should be." Her smile robbed the words of their sting and I knew that she harboured no resentment.

"I'm not sorry I kissed you. That was something that had to be done and it was done. But I would not have hurt you for anything in the world."

"You just don't know your own strength, do you?" She turned to greet the Randalls and Molly Piggott who had followed me into the room.

Diana the Huntress looked more striking than ever in a black velvet frock with a bustle. She wore black lace gloves with a gold bracelet at each wrist and the ebony cigarette holder was soon in evidence. A treble string of pearls set off her long, creamy neck and you could almost have tripped over her earrings. She arched an eyebrow at me, blew smoke in my face and began to gush to Ruth.

Peter, who seemed ill at ease, engaged me in a dull conversation about Town Planning, and Molly Piggott, who had ruined the effect of a nice red frock with too much cheap jewellery, stood shyly in the background. Then Leslie Turner entered with

Henry Crane; Romney, the long suffering, came round with a tray of drinks and the conversation became general.

Turner was untidy as ever and the brightness of his sharp blue eyes seemed to emphasize the shabbiness of his suit. His tie was badly knotted but he had remembered to put on a clean shirt. He seized avidly on a drink from Romney's tray, drained it at a gulp and picked up another. Then, with an adroitness that commanded my admiration, he cut out Diana from the others and manœuvred her over to the far side of the room where they began to whisper fiercely together.

Henry Crane, in a double-breasted dinner-suit, was the only man in evening dress and his personality dominated the room. The suit was as well cut as his features and his poise was that of an important business man who slightly despised the company in which he found himself. His eyes flickered when they lighted on me and his strong white teeth almost bit through his cigar. Then he turned his shoulder to me and began to talk quietly to Peter Randall.

Molly Piggott still stood forlorn, so I found her a chair and a drink and stayed by her until I saw that she was more at ease. I saw Ruth watching me with an approving eye, then she came over and spoke to Molly, too.

The last to arrive was Patrick Conway, gravely formal in a dark grey suit and a stiff white collar. His tight mouth was relaxed in a confident, self-satisfied smile and he made no apology for being late. He nodded to me, brushed up his smile for Ruth and quickly took Henry Crane away into a corner. They seemed to have much to say to each other.

I had a moment alone with Ruth again and said quickly, "Anyone else coming?"

"Just John Wilmot, the Town Clerk. I don't know what can be keeping him, for he always makes such a point of punctuality."

Tongues, loosened by Martinis, were now wagging freely and about ten minutes later I missed Crane. One moment he was whispering with Conway, the next he was gone. I wandered out of the room behind Romney and saw that the light was on in the dining-room.

"Who's in there?" I asked.

"His Highness the Alderman, I expects."

"He seems to make himself pretty free of the place."

"This is Liberty Hall so far as Miss Ruth's friends is concerned and, blimey, don't they love it! Ruth Mannering is sich a dear friend of mine," Romney broke into a high falsetto, "and I often visits her in her lovely home. She has a *salon,* y'know, an' doesn't mind her friends dropping in any old time to hear her play."

"Henry Irving's dead," I said. "Let him stay in his grave." Romney stalked off to the kitchen, looking wounded and I popped my head round the dining-room door. Crane was there all right, staring, as if hypnotized, at the Velasquez picture.

I went in and stood behind him and when, at last he turned away from the picture, the look of rapacity on his face was positively primeval. Here was a man who would go to any lengths to get what he coveted whether it was a woman or just an *objet d'art* and anyone looking at him now would have been justified in doubting his sanity.

When he saw me he went very still as if suffering from arrested motion as well as arrested development. "Are you by any chance following me?" he asked, and his voice was dangerously smooth.

I nodded towards the picture. "I wanted another look at it, too."

His lip curled. "If it was going for twenty quid, you couldn't buy it."

"The point doesn't arise," I pointed out. "It's not for sale."

"Am I to interpret that as a gibe?"

"Interpret it any dam' way you please," I said. "Why do you want the picture, anyway? Because Velasquez painted it? Because it resembles Ruth? Or because you just like looking at pictures of naked women?"

"Because it's unique, because it's one of the great art treasures of the world, and because it appeals to me personally." There was a vein throbbing in his forehead and he was holding himself in with an effort. It was no time to tackle him on the subject of his car and I turned away with a shrug. "It's nice to know there are some things money can't buy," I said, "but I'm sure Ruth will let you look at it as often as you want."

"Who said you could call her Ruth?"

"She did," I said, grinning in his face. "Another of the

I

pleasures money can't buy." I left him there, on the point of exploding, and went back to the drawing-room.

The party had taken on further momentum and Leslie Turner and Diana Randall were sitting on the couch looking into each other's eyes. His arm was round her shoulders and the world appeared to be well lost for love. Ruth was talking to Molly Piggott and Peter Randall was wandering about the room picking up ornaments, appraising them with his eyes and putting them down again. I watched him carefully but he did not go near the escritoire where the paper-knife lay. He seemed, in fact, consciously to avoid it.

"Have you seen Henry?" asked Ruth as I came in.

"He's having a session with the Spanish Nude," I told her, "and his emotions are disturbed."

Turner sniggered, Henry came in just in time to hear my remark and his scowl was so eloquent that I stepped hastily out of range. He went over to join Ruth and Molly and then Romney came in with a tray of savouries, lovingly prepared by Mrs. Romney with the object of stimulating thirst. I took one and another drink, felt slightly faint and sat down on the nearest available chair.

About ten minutes later Wilmot arrived looking flustered, his white hair unbrushed, his red face noticeably pale. "I'm terribly sorry to be late," he said, "but there's been a spot of bother over that snake."

I saw Crane stiffen. "The fer-de-lance for the Zoo?" he asked. "What's happened to it?"

"I'm afraid it's escaped."

"Escaped! How the blazes could it have escaped?"

"That fool of a carter," said Wilmot. "He must have taken the bend at the foot of the hill into the town too fast and shaken the crate off his lorry. When he reached the Zoo the crate was gone and the Superintendent phoned me at once. I got the police cracking and they found the crate at the foot of the hill. It had been smashed in falling from the lorry and the snake was gone."

"Is it dangerous?" asked Ruth.

"Exceedingly dangerous; just about the deadliest type of snake in existence. There was a time when there were more deaths in Martinique from the bite of the fer-de-lance than from any other cause. The police are carrying out a search of the area now but goodness knows where it may have got to in this fog."

I was aware of a feeling of uneasiness. It might have happened as Wilmot said but somehow I could not bring myself to believe it. Crane knew that the snake was to have been delivered at the Zoo tonight, Peter Randall as a Councillor would know also. He could have told Molly Piggott and his sister, and his sister could have told Leslie Turner. Crane could have told Conway and indeed it was possible that half Shellbridge knew. Suppose——?

I turned to Wilmot. "Do you know if the carter stopped anywhere between the Borough boundary and the Zoo?"

"Judging from the smell of him, he stopped at the first pub in the town but then he always does. His habits are well known."

Wilmot's reply intensified my fears. Someone could have been waiting for the lorry in the fog close to the pub, transferred the crate to a car, smashed it at the foot of the hill to make it seem like an accident and stolen the snake. There is a way of handling snakes if you know how—I had done it myself in Africa. You catch them just behind the head and if you are quick enough there is nothing they can do about it.

"How big was it?" I asked.

"About three feet long, I believe. It wasn't fully grown."

Ruth sat down at the piano and I looked at her guests. Her death would benefit them all. Crane could have his picture and unchallenged authority in Shellbridge. Peter Randall would have unlimited money and Molly Piggott would have Peter. Diana Randall would be able to back Turner's plays. Conway would gain a small fortune out of her estate, and retain Crane's patronage. Yes, Ruth's death would solve all their problems and one of them had already tried to bring her death about. Which?

Ruth began to play and, as the others gathered round the piano, I slipped out to the hall. I was feeling slightly sick and my head seemed to ache more and more from my ordeal at the Mermaid Club. I hadn't noticed it much until the evening but I was acutely conscious of it now.

There was a brief-case in the hall bearing the initials H. C. It was locked and I picked it up, shook it and felt all over it. It could easily have held a three-foot snake but there was

obviously no snake there now. I turned to see Romney watching
me from the kitchen door and beckoned him over. "I want you
to show me Miss Ruth's bedroom," I said. His face was eloquent
and I added, "And none of your coarse remarks, please."

He shrugged massive shoulders, led me upstairs and into a
room that took my breath away. A four-poster bed in carved
light oak, honey-coloured panelling, a honey-coloured carpet
with tiger skin rugs on each side of the bed and in front of the
dressing-table. Curtains and bedspread of almond green quilted
satin. One picture, a ballet scene by Degas, and one lug arm-
chair upholstered to match the dressing-stool and the curtains.

"I suppose Queen Elizabeth slept here," I commented.

"Miracle if she did," said Romney, "seeing the house wasn't
built till just before Queen Victoria's time."

I pulled back the bed-clothes and lifted the pillows but there
was nothing there. I looked in the wardrobe and opened every
drawer while Romney watched me with a cold eye. I searched the
adjacent dressing-room and bathroom without result and then
Romney said, "Would it be too much to arsk what you was
looking for?"

"A snake, Romney."

"I must have made them Martinis pretty strong." I told
him about the fer-de-lance and his face changed. "Leave it to
me, cock," he said. "If it's in this house, I'll find it, and if you
got any sense you'll go home. You look sick."

I shook my head. "I've got to know, Romney," I said. "I
couldn't sleep without knowing. Let me help you search."

We searched the house from end to end, thoroughly. It was
the first time I had been through it all and it was quite a house.
The furnishings would have fetched a fortune in any sale-room
and the pictures would have filled a fair-sized art gallery. We
searched in the most unlikely places as well as all the places
where Ruth might possibly go before morning, but we found
nothing.

I was constantly on edge. From time to time the old timbers
creaked and each creak made me start and caused perspiration
to break out on my forehead. A fer-de-lance can strike with
bewildering speed and to come upon one unaware would mean
certain and painful death.

In one room we disturbed a mouse and my heart almost

failed me as the 'timorous beastie' scuttled across the floor and vanished into a crack in the wainscot. As for Romney, he went chalky white and leaned against the door for a moment, unable to speak.

"Have to get a cat," he said at last. "I hates cats but I gotta admit they has their uses. You an' your ruddy snakes'll be the death o' me."

We came at length to the downstairs cloak-room where a camel coat belonging to Ruth had been thrown carelessly over a chair. As we switched on the light we saw one of the sleeves move and we both stuck in the doorway trying to get out fast. "Steady," I said, "don't panic."

"Look 'oo's talking," said Romney. He had armed himself with a poker and in a sudden access of bravado he poked the coat on to the floor. Nothing wriggled out from underneath it and there was nothing on the chair.

"Try the pockets," I suggested.

"You try the pockets, cock," urged Romney. "This snake hunt was your idea."

"Pat them with the poker, you clown."

Romney obeyed without result and, not to be outdone in courage, I picked up the coat and shook it. Romney retreated a couple of steps but nothing happened. "The vibration of our footsteps must have shaken the sleeve," I said.

"Methought I saw an aspic's trail," declaimed Romney. He giggled, paused for effect and added, "Romney the well-read butler."

"Romney the drunken butler," I said. "If you take my advice you'll lay off your mistress's liquor."

"I ain't touched her perishing liquor."

I looked at him again. The thought had crossed my mind that he was gloriously tight but it wasn't alcohol that was making him act the clown more than usual. It was fear. The movement of the coat-sleeve had shaken Romney even more than it had shaken me and I was in a cold lather of sweat from head to foot.

"This is the end of the line, cock," he said. "There's no snakes in the house except the pink ones some of 'em'll be seeing in the droring-room before long."

"We'd better try the garden."

He gave me a withering look. "The garden! 'Oo the 'ell could find a snake in the garden on a night like this before it finds us? Besides, what would he put it in the garden for if it's only Miss Ruth he's after. Might bite anyone in the garden."

"He may have hidden it in the garden in a brief-case or attaché-case or something, intending to introduce it into the house later. It's the case we've got to look for."

"O.K. I'll get a couple of torches."

The garden was a vast wilderness in the fog-laden night but we quartered it methodically, poking behind bushes and peering into outhouses. The ripple of Ruth's piano music accompanied our search, ending abruptly in a burst of hand-clapping. Then the piano began again but Ruth was not playing her own music this time. She was playing popular airs and the guests entered zestfully into a bout of community singing, making more noise than harmony.

"Wine is a mocker," said Romney. "Strong drink is raging," and on the last word he put his foot through a glass frame with a terrifying crash.

The crash occurred just as there was a lull in the singing and inside the drawing-room the music stopped. There was an eloquent pause then the french windows were wrenched open and a band of light was thrown across the drive. "Can you make a noise like an amorous pussy?" whispered Romney.

I saw Peter Randall framed in the open window. "What the hell's going on out there?" he demanded.

"It's all right," I called. "Romney's mislaid something and I'm helping him look for it."

Randall grunted, turned away and closed the window. The music started up again and then the chorus of voices. "It's no go," said Romney, "there ain't nothing here."

"Doesn't seem like it," I admitted, "but I'm certain that snake didn't escape by accident. Someone pinched it and he didn't pinch it for a household pet. Keep your eyes skinned when the party's over, Romney, and have another look in Miss Ruth's bedroom before she retires for the night."

We went back to the house and I stood looking again at Henry Crane's brief-case in the hall. "What does he want with a brief-case, anyway?" I said. "It doesn't go with evening dress."

"He always carries a brief-case," said Romney; "adds to his importance."

The telephone rang and Romney, lifting the receiver, said in dignified tones, "Miss Mannering's residence." It was the Chief Constable for Wilmot. The snake had not yet been found and the Chief Constable proposed to ask the B.B.C. to broadcast a warning after the midnight news. Wilmot agreed and as he turned away from the phone he looked ten years older.

"Don't take it to heart, Mr. Wilmot," I comforted. "It isn't your fault."

"That won't stop me being blamed for it. I get the blame for everything that happens in this bloody town. Last year the local paper announced summer time a week too soon and half the population turned up at church next day an hour early. I even got the blame for that. Coming in?"

We re-entered the drawing-room together to be greeted with 'Old Man River', sung at full blast by the assembled company. Ruth gave me a half-smile, switched to 'Go Down Moses', and Wilmot and I joined in.

Perhaps it was my contribution that ended the community singing, for after we had given 'Go Down Moses' the limit, Ruth paused, her slim, white fingers resting on the piano keys. Then Molly said, "Do please play one more piece for us, Miss Mannering. Do you know the *Ritual Fire Dance*, by de Falla?" Her voice shook with excitement at her own daring.

"Well," said Ruth, and we stood back as she began to play. She made a magnificent job of it and it was impossible to listen to the wild music unmoved. It set the blood drumming in my veins and I was hard put to it to keep from sweeping her up from the piano stool and carrying her out of the room. If only I could be alone with her, now, even for a few minutes. There was magic in her hands. They could stroke away my headache as easily as they stroked the piano keys.

Molly listened with a face of rapture. It was obvious to me that she had not had the slightest idea what she would be hearing and was delighted with the success of her choice. The Shellbridge public library must be a wonderful help to her in her social ambitions.

Turner was standing next to me and his sneering voice grated in my ear, "It might be Mozart's *Fantasia in C Minor* for all Molly knows."

"Shut up," I snapped, and moved away from him.

The intoxicating music stormed to its majestic conclusion and the applause was spontaneous and prolonged. Then Diana, who was now sitting on the arm of Turner's chair, colour heightening her cheeks, called out, "Let everybody do something. Let's have a real Victorian evening. Mr. Latimer looks like a singer."

I shook my head, well aware that singing was not my forte. Shortly after my boxing days I had played the clarinet in a dance band, but there was no clarinet available and in any case that stage of my life was behind me for ever. "Sorry," I apologized, "I'm a good listener but a poor performer."

Turner pulled Diana off the chair-arm on to his knee and she sat with one arm round his neck, a martini glass held high in her other hand. It was easy to see that their attraction for each other was purely physical. It showed in Diana's long, sensual underlip, in the violet shadows under her eyes and I thought sourly that Turner had the dazed look of a mongrel street cur after a bitch. When they were done with passion they would have nothing left. They just about deserved each other.

"What about you two doing something?" I said. "A duet, perhaps?"

"Diana doesn't sing," explained Turner, "but she can recite a bit."

"Splendid," I said. "You can coach her up in the Letter Scene from *Macbeth*."

Turner leered. "She's got the right figure for it, anyway, hasn't she?"

Diana tittered and in a moment of revulsion that I could not control, I blurted out, "It would be a better way of employing your time than taking schoolgirls out in your car."

All in a moment Diana was still. Then she said in a tight voice, "So he takes schoolgirls out in his car, does he?"

"Correction," I amended. "One schoolgirl. A red-headed, precocious hussy called Elizabeth Pollock."

"My poppet," said Diana, regarding him with a smile that was wholly evil. Her voice was silky and caressing. She raised the Martini glass, held it poised for a second above Turner's head and slowly tilted it. The contents of the glass spilled over his hair and flowed stickily down his cheeks. He uttered a hoarse roar and raised himself with a convulsive heave, causing Diana to tumble on to the floor. "Bitch!" he spat, his eyes wildly staring. Then they focused on me. "As for you!" He paused, his face working, then he strode to the door and out of the room.

Diana picked herself up, the unholy smile still lighting her face and Ruth, stepping forward, twitched the empty glass dexterously out of her hand. "No more Martinis for you," she said. "You've had more than enough. We've all had more than enough, including Philip. Philip, since you caused the disturbance, I sentence you to sing and I'm taking no refusal."

Her eyes were stormy, warning me that I had gone too far, that further misbehaviour would not be countenanced.

"Sorry," I apologized. "Drink brings out the worst in me, but don't condemn me to sing all by myself. I'll sing a duet with somebody. What about you, Molly?"

Molly bridled, pleased at being asked, and after a small show of hesitation, agreed to join me in the 'Keys of Heaven', the music for which Ruth found in her cabinet. I had no voice and knew it and after the first few bars the audience knew it too but nobody threw anything. Molly had a shrill, wavering soprano that was quite pleasing to the ear, but we mimed the song much better than we sang it.

When the applause had died down, which did not take long, Molly squeezed my hand. "I think you're awfully nice," she whispered, "and I'm sorry for that routine I gave you last night about ancient Egypt." I grinned at her, then Peter Randall took her by the hand and led her back to the couch.

"That was very nice," commended Ruth, "and now it's Henry's turn."

Henry gave a sickly smile, left the room and returned in a few seconds bearing his brief-case. I watched him warily as he opened it and then the mystery of the brief-case was revealed. Henry had brought his music. He went over to the piano, stood with a self-conscious smile on his face and announced, "I'd like to sing you the Aria from Turandot, 'None Shall Sleep Tonight'."

I started and saw that Ruth's face was as startled as my own. It could only be coincidence, of course, but it was a grim reminder of the night we had buried Johnny, searched his London flat and suffered at the Mermaid Club. 'None Shall Sleep Tonight.' If only Shellbridge had been ancient Pekin and Ruth the Princess Turandot, she, too, could have decreed that none must sleep till

Johnny's murderer was brought to light. It would have given me a certain grim satisfaction to keep the whole town awake while the hunt for the murderer went on. A pity it wasn't practicable.

Henry's voice was powerful but it had a hard note with no music in it. The ornaments in the room rattled and if Ruth had opened the french windows they could have heard him at the other end of Shellbridge. Since he was Alderman Crane and a dominating influence in the town, he was given an encore which he accepted as his lawful due. He sang one of the songs from *Merrie England* and when the last booming note died away, I was surprised I could still hear. He did my headache no good at all.

Then Leslie Turner came back, walking very cockily and trying to look as if he had stayed outside on purpose till Crane's turn was over. He went straight across to Diana, who turned her back on him, but he put a hand on her shoulder, spun her round in an odiously masterful manner and began to talk to her very rapidly and fiercely in an undertone. He had both hands on her shoulders now and looked as if he were gripping them very tightly. She wriggled a little but he only held her the tighter and then I saw her hand go up.

I thought at first that she intended to slap his face but instead she stroked his cheek and her face broke into a smile that left the Mona Lisa nowhere. There were red marks on her bare shoulders when he released her but it seemed that, like most over-sexed women, she responded to rough treatment like a flower opening to the sun.

"What about a song from you, Mr. Turner?" asked Ruth.

He swaggered over to the piano and sat down. "Leslie Turner in Songs at the Piano," he said. "The rage of European capitals and I mean rage. Never saw people in such a rage." He paused for a laugh which was not forthcoming, rippled his fingers over the keys and looked round the room. "Now what shall I give you first?" he asked. No one spoke. "I know," he went on. "I'll sing that well-known song of frustrated love, 'The Lute Player', and I'll dedicate it for obvious reasons, to our friend Latimer here, the double-dealing Planner."

In an exaggeratedly deep baritone he began to sing, " 'She was a lady great and splendid, I was a minstrel in her hall' ";

which was as far as he got because, at that point, I slammed the lid of the piano down on his hands.

He jumped up with a scream of pain, folded his arms and bent over, squeezing his hands against his arm-pits like a school-boy who had just been strapped. Ruth pressed the bell-push and Romney entered, eyebrows raised in his best, well-bred butler manner.

Ruth's voice was as cold and impersonal as a dentist's receptionist's. "Mr. Latimer's hat and coat, Romney. He's leaving us."

I stood looking at her but her eyes were fixed on a point somewhere beyond my right shoulder. Her face was like a death-mask. I gave her a slight bow which she ignored, then, "Thank you for a very jolly evening," I said, and followed Romney out. I thought my head would burst at any moment and sickness was rising in my throat so that I almost choked.

"Been an' blotted yer copy-book, have yer?" asked Romney.

"Looks like it," I admitted, "but that bunch would try the temper of a saint."

"Don't I know it! If I hadn't been a saint meself I'd have poisoned them years ago."

I felt near to collapse and as I nosed the Bentley through the fog, dizzy spell after dizzy spell assailed me. I had had great hopes of the cocktail party but I had accomplished precisely nothing. All I had done was to stir Ruth to anger and I was no farther forward in locating which of her friends had killed her fiancé and tried to kill her. It would have been difficult (I saw that now) to get anything out of them while they were in each other's company, but at least I had been able to confirm my previous impressions of their characters. There was not one of them, except perhaps John Wilmot, who would not be capable of murder, and the problem of selection was as formidable as ever.

If only I had gone to the police in the beginning, but it was too late now. The murderer must be laughing his head off in secret, but perhaps the last laugh was yet to come.

I was glad to reach the hotel garage and it took me all my time to drag myself upstairs to my bedroom. I undressed in a dream, struggled wearily into my pyjamas, pulled back the bed-clothes—and leaped away with a split second to spare as the fer-de-lance struck.

CHAPTER TEN

MURDER WILL OUT

FOR a moment I could only stand and stare as if hypnotized. The fer-de-lance was a dark, writhing shape on the white sheet. It had thrown its body into a coil and its tail was beating a rapid tattoo on the bed while its slender neck, raised in the posture of defence, swayed from side to side. The narrow, triangular head was alert, the cat's eyes dilated and glittering like drops of dew in moonlight.

The shock had driven away my sickness and when my heartbeats had slowed down a bit, my first thought was, 'Why me?' It was Ruth whose life was threatened, Ruth who should have been the destined victim, yet the snake had been placed in my bed, not hers. To someone in Shellbridge I had become the enemy, but why?

Was it because I knew that an attempt had been made on Ruth's life? Or because I knew that Henry Crane's car had been out of Shellbridge the night Ruth and I had invaded Johnny's flat? Or could this have been the handiwork of Tyler Morgan? Somehow I couldn't see Tyler monkeying with snakes, and I wondered if he had missed his henchman, Joe, yet.

The snake's black, forked tongue flickered and I caught a glimpse of its hooked, swallowing teeth. "I'll get around to you in a minute," I said, looking round for a weapon. I could have shot the brute easily enough but I wanted to take it alive.

I approached it warily, snatched a pillow from the bed and got away again, just in time, while it lashed itself into a frenzy. Its skin was olive grey banded with yellow and it had a nasty black streak from the right eye to the angle of the mouth that added to its wicked appearance. It raised its head, quivering with menace, and I lammed it good and hard with the pillow.

The coils began a wild, sinuous dance and I realized with a sinking heart that the pillow was not enough. I thought of using the butt of my gun as a club but in order to do that I would have to advance my hand pretty close to the snake and I had no stomach for that. Then I remembered seeing a window-pole leaning against the corridor wall and it took very few seconds to possess myself of it and return to the fray.

The snake, slightly dazed, was still threshing about on the bed and the problem now was to find the happy medium, to hit it hard enough to stun yet not hard enough to kill. Wilmot would never forgive me if I killed it.

The window-pole was an unhandy weapon and the first blow did little harm except to the snake's temper. With the second I was more fortunate, however, and saw, to my relief, that the writhing coils were slowly going limp. I tumbled some ordnance survey sheets out of my brief-case, gripped the dazed reptile just below its evil, pointed head, stuffed it into the brief-case and closed the zip fastener. After that, I felt sick again and had to make a hurried dash to the bathroom.

I dressed hurriedly and went down to the bar for a brandy, getting in just before it closed. The girl who had taken Molly Piggott's place for the evening was a stranger to me and as I sipped the brandy I said casually, "Mr. Randall been in tonight?"

"He was in about half-past seven and took Molly off to a party."

"Did you notice if he was carrying a brief-case?"

"I couldn't really say."

The ancient hall porter was in evidence for once but he hadn't been about when Randall had arrived. He was seldom available when he was wanted and I wondered what dark secret life he led below stairs. The key of my room had been hanging on a hook in his office and Peter could easily have borrowed it.

By the time I had the Bentley out of the garage the snake had partly revived and I could hear it thrashing about inside my brief-case. Fortunately, the case was the latest type of 'business man's overnight' and the zip fastener left no room for the snake to crawl out at the ends. I drove to Ruth's house, Romney admitted me with a grunt of resignation and, selecting a walking-stick from the hall in case of need, I burst into the drawing-room. Ruth was at the piano again, the others clustered round her, but she stopped playing in surprise at my abrupt entry.

I opened the brief-case and let the fer-de-lance fall to the carpet where it lay collecting its wits. "Surprise!" I said brightly.

Diana Randall screamed, Henry Crane went white as a sheet,

Peter Randall swore and backed away. The others exhibited varying degrees of terror and confusion and the fer-de-lance began to writhe towards them across the carpet. It was still pretty somnolent but recovering fast.

"Get that thing out of here!" Crane's voice cracked with hysteria and Molly Piggott said quietly, "Why, it's half stupid!" She bent quickly, caught the snake neatly behind the head and held it out to me. "Put it back in your brief-case," she ordered. "You ought to have had more sense."

I let her drop it into the case, zipped the case up and handed it to John Wilmot who took it with a certain reluctance. "Where did you find it?" he asked.

"On the floor of the garage at the Ocean Hotel," I said. "I didn't know you had such a way with snakes, Molly."

Molly tossed her blonde curls. "I'm not afraid of snakes," she said, "for I've handled them often enough. My brother's the keeper of the reptile house at the Zoo."

Wilmot turned to Ruth, asked permission to use her telephone and went out, carrying the brief-case at arm's length. Henry Crane, whose colour was slowly returning, rounded on me. "You ought to be horsewhipped for that," he said, "frightening ladies."

"Not only ladies," I said, grinning at him.

Diana Randall gave a high-pitched laugh. "He has you there, Henry," she said. "You were scared right down to your shoes."

The party broke up after that and I was left alone with Ruth. "Now what was all that about?" she demanded. "I thought I'd seen the last of you for tonight. Indeed, after your behaviour, I hoped I'd seen the last of you for good."

"The snake wasn't on the garage floor," I said. "It was in my bed and I'm sorry about my behaviour. I was feeling sick and Turner's impudence finished it."

"You looked sick. What do you mean, the snake was in your bed? Oh! You mean someone put it there!"

"Someone must have put it there. It could never have got there on its own."

"Why did you say you found it on the garage floor?"

"Because it could have crawled there by itself. If I had said it was in my bed, I would have had to have called in the police and we can't afford to attract any more police attention."

"No, we certainly can't."

"I dumped the snake on your carpet because I wanted to see who was afraid of it and who wasn't. I must say Molly surprised me."

"If she had put the snake in your bed, do you think she'd have given away the fact that she could handle it?"

"You've a point there but she was well placed to have put the snake in my bed or to have given Peter the key of my room. They might well be in it together."

"Could Peter have got the key of your room for himself?"

"Quite easily, as it happens. It was hanging quite near the register and the hall porter wasn't around. He never is when he's needed."

"Then anybody might have done it?"

"Anybody who could handle snakes. Whoever it was must have half doped the brute to keep it from crawling out of the bed again."

"The warmth of the blankets would induce it to stay."

"Perhaps, but I think it was doped, too. It wasn't quite quick enough or it would have got me when I made to climb into bed. Whoever did it wouldn't be expecting me to go to bed so soon and the effect of the dope hadn't quite worn off."

"It was a dreadful thing to do."

"We're up against a rather dreadful person. I thought it was Henry until he panicked."

"Do you think the panic was genuine?"

"It looked genuine. He changed colour. Do you know if Conway's had any experience of snakes?"

"He might have; he was in India during the war. So was Peter, and Peter's the Convenor of the Zoo Committee."

"Then there's the fair Diana," I said. "I wouldn't be surprised if she had an affinity with snakes. She's a bit of a snake herself."

"What about Leslie Turner?"

"I've reason to know that he's a nasty bit of work," I said, "but he looked scared too."

"I can't understand why anyone should want to put a snake in your bed."

"Because I know you're marked for death," I said. "That's one reason, anyway."

There was a tapping at the french window behind us. Ruth jumped nervously and clutched my arm. "Steady," I exhorted. "I'm glad you've had the sense to keep that window locked at last."

I went over to the window, jerked it open and Diana Randall, cool as an April breeze, swept into the room. "Terribly sorry to disturb you both," she said nastily, "but I left my bag."

"On purpose?" I asked.

"Don't be silly. You scared me into forgetting it with your beastly snake." She bent over an arm-chair, lifted the cushion and there, sure enough, was the bag. She put it under her arm, looked quizzically at us both, then turned to Ruth. "I rather hoped I'd find you alone. I wanted a word with you."

"I suppose that's my cue to say I was just going," I said.

"Oh, don't let me chase you away. You seem to have so much to say to each other. Ruth and I can talk in the library." She gave Ruth a dazzling smile. "I won't keep you long, dear."

She laid her bag down on the chair again and accompanied Ruth to the library which was across the hall next to the dining-room. I had a quick look through the bag but it contained nothing incriminating, then I tiptoed across the hall and stood just outside the library door. "So you won't do it?" I heard Diana say.

"I'm sorry." Ruth's voice was quite gentle, even compassionate. "If I liked the play and thought it had a chance I'd put up the money with pleasure, but I don't think Leslie will get any farther with that kind of stuff. It's nasty."

"Nastiness pays in the West End."

"Not nastiness just for the sake of nastiness."

"Well, I believe in Leslie, that's why I'm going to marry him. I believe he's got a great future."

"Not with that kind of play."

"You'd never miss the money and you'd get it back with interest."

"It's not a good play, Diana, even if he toned down some of his dialogue."

"What do you know about plays, anyway? This may sound beastly, but I can't help saying it for it's true. There are times when I wish you were dead. You've all the money in the world and you won't spend a penny of it to help your friends."

"My friends are only my friends because of the money."

I slipped back to the drawing-room, lit a cigarette and stood in front of the fire, leaning against the mantelpiece. Ruth was in the toils all right, beset by rapacious vultures. I hadn't relocked the french window and as I stood looking at it, Henry Crane pushed it open and stepped into the room. "You still here?" he snapped.

"As you see."

"Where's Ruth?"

"In the library with Diana Randall."

"That shock-headed Jezebel! Blast it, I wanted a word with Ruth alone."

"About that picture?"

"Mind your own business."

"Bet you a quid she won't sell."

The veins on Crane's forehead stood out. "Look here, Latimer," he burst out, "kindly remember that you're an employee of Shellbridge Corporation and that you're speaking to one of its senior members."

"Hardly an employee," I said. "I have a contract to provide your Corporation with an Advisory Plan for the future development and proper lay-out of the town. When I've done that, I take my fee and go on my way rejoicing."

"Contracts can be broken."

"At the cost of heavy damages."

"I'd pay the damages myself just to be rid of you."

"Then everyone would know that you'd put your personal concerns above the interests of the ratepayers."

He glared at me and I fanned his anger with a seraphic smile. "Why have you honoured me with your enmity?" I asked. "Is it because I know your car was out of Shellbridge the night before last when you tried to make out it had never left the garage?"

"So you were the man prowling round my garage!"

"I deny that."

"Then how did you know my car had been out?"

"Ruth saw it in London that night and recognized it." I had drawn a bow at a venture but from the momentary dismay on Crane's face I knew that the arrow had found a target and then, before my eyes, came a sudden vision of the street outside the

J

Mermaid Club. I remembered parking the Bentley between a Rolls-Royce and a Daimler and I had a vague recollection of noticing, beyond the Daimler, a large black American car that might well have been Crane's Buick. "Outside the Mermaid Club," I said, and knew I had scored a bull. Just for a second Crane's guard was down then he recovered himself.

"What were you doing at the Mermaid Club?" he asked. "It was no place to take Ruth."

"I've been a member for some time."

"Then you're a member no longer. It was my money that financed the Mermaid Club and I can ensure that its doors are closed to you."

His money! That tied him up with Tyler Morgan and perhaps with Johnny. Someone from Shellbridge had met Johnny at the Mermaid Club and had contrived that Johnny should meet Ruth. And someone from Shellbridge had murdered Johnny. For a minute I was lost in thought and when I was aware of Crane's presence again it was to see him watching me with cold intensity.

"How dare you take Ruth to the Mermaid Club! Come to that, how dare you take her anywhere. She's not for you."

"Nor for you. She's engaged to some American called Kingdom, also a member of the Mermaid Club. Ever meet him there?"

"No. I didn't know he was a member. Can't stand the fellow and Ruth isn't going to marry him, I'll see to that. If she marries anyone it will be me."

"Sure of yourself, aren't you?" I said. "Why were you so keen to keep it dark that you'd been out in your car that night?"

"Because the less Shellbridge knows of my private life the better. I was having a bit of fun at the Mermaid Club, if you must know."

"With a girl?"

"How else does one have fun at night clubs?"

I was silent. If he had been in the dance *salon* of the club with a girl, Ruth and I would have seen him. He could easily have been the intruder in Johnny's flat and have gone on to the Mermaid Club after Ruth and I had interrupted him.

"Is anyone else from Shellbridge a member of the Mermaid Club?"

"Not as far as I know, but I don't go there very often."

"Afraid someone from Shellbridge might see you in the halls of vice?"

At that moment Ruth came in with Diana. Her colour was high and Diana's expression was venomous. "Ah, Henry," she sneered, "the moth returns to the flame."

Henry gave her a look of intense dislike. "There are times when I find your impudence insufferable, Diana."

"You needn't suffer it then. You can go out the way you came in."

"I want a few words with Ruth."

"You won't find her in a yielding mood." Diana snatched up her bag and cocked a plucked eyebrow at me. "Care to do your Galahad act again? Unless you're afraid to leave Henry alone with Ruth."

"I'm more afraid of being alone with you," I said, "but I'll take a chance."

We went out by the french window into the fog and Diana tucked her arm in mine. I felt her shudder with the cold and then she said hopefully, "Isn't it dark tonight?"

"It is," I agreed, "and of course you have no oil for your lamp."

"I'm afraid I don't get it."

"I didn't think you would. It's a biblical allusion."

"Oh, that puts me on the track. So you think I'm a foolish virgin?"

"No, just foolish."

"You don't have to go out of your way to be insulting just because I asked you to see me across the garden. You've a very bitter tongue tonight. Something's made you hopping mad, I can see that. What is it?"

"I must have caught some venom from that fer-de-lance."

"You're a very strange man and you seem to have a good deal of influence with Ruth. How do you manage it?"

"By not sponging on her."

"Do you know anything about Plays?"

"I've seen quite a number."

"Leslie's written a perfectly wonderful play but the West End managers just won't take the risk of putting it on. I've been trying to get Ruth to back it but she won't listen to me. You wouldn't like to have a shot at persuading her?"

"What's in it for me?"

"I might persuade Leslie to cut you in on the profits."

"And if there are no profits?"

"So you won't take a risk either?"

"I'm taking one now," I said; "alone with Diana the huntress."

"Don't forget I'm engaged to Leslie."

"Don't you forget it."

I heard her chuckle as we passed through the gap in the hedge into the garden of her cottage. The cottage was dark and I said, "Is everyone in bed?"

"Our housekeeper is, but Peter's still out. He went home with Molly. Coming in?"

"Ruth will be expecting me back."

"Cautious, aren't you? Come to tea tomorrow afternoon. About four."

"Thank you. I'll look forward to that."

She halted at the cottage door and brushed against me. Her hand tightened on my arm. "If you could get Ruth to back Leslie's play, you'd find me not ungrateful." Her voice was soft, her face provokingly uplifted, close to mine.

"I'd have to read the play first," I said, chucked her under the chin and left her. Henry had called her a shock-headed Jezebel. He knew her all right.

When I reached Ruth's drawing-room, I heard the sound of high words within and paused to listen. "For the last time," Ruth was saying, "I won't sell that picture."

"Not even for forty thousand?"

"Not even for every penny you've got."

"But you could buy twenty pictures, all masterpieces, for what I'd give you for the Velasquez."

"I don't want twenty pictures. I like the Velasquez. I think it's one of the most wonderful pictures ever painted."

"You just want to keep it out of vanity because the model happens to resemble you."

"That may be so, Henry, I don't deny it, but the fact remains I'm not selling."

"And you won't marry me either?"

"No."

"Am I so repulsive to you?"

"Of course not. You know very well I'm engaged to Johnny Kingdom."

"He's only after your money."

"How do you know that, Henry?"

"Instinct. I can smell a fortune-hunter miles away. That fellow Latimer's another of them. Show him the door, Ruth."

I stepped into the room and Ruth said, "I think you'd better leave now, Henry."

Henry jerked his head at me. "I'll leave when he does, not before."

Ruth pressed the bell beside the fire-place and Romney came in like a fat robot. "Show Mr. Crane out, Romney."

For a moment Crane hesitated, his face red with anger and mortification, Then, shrugging his shoulders, he followed Romney to the door.

When he had gone Ruth said, a trifle listlessly, "Are you feeling better now?"

"Yes," I said, "my head's still buzzing a little but I don't feel sick any more."

"Then you can go too, if you like. I've had just about as much as I can stand for one night."

"Don't visit your anger on me," I said. "I've done nothing to deserve it."

She looked at me uncertainly for a moment then she said. "No, you haven't, have you? Poor Philip! Sit down and have a drink or would you rather have coffee?"

"Coffee would be very nice, thanks."

She rang for Romney again, ordered the coffee and sank wearily into the chair opposite mine. She put up a hand to brush back her hair and I saw Johnny's engagement ring glittering on her finger. It was quite a shock.

"When did you restore that to the place of honour?" I asked.

"I put it on for the party," she said. "No one noticed before that I wasn't wearing it and I thought that—when they find Johnny—it would be better if I were still engaged to him."

"A wise precaution," I commended. I was thinking that she had worn the ring all evening and I had never noticed. I had been watching her hands on the piano keys, too, and yet the fact that she was wearing the ring had not registered. It showed the state I had been in. I must have been little better than a Zombie.

"Philip, what are we going to do?"

Before I could answer, Romney arrived with the coffee and biscuits and at the same moment Peter Randall pushed open the french window and popped his head round it. "Lucky me," he said, "just in time for supper."

I saw the light of anger blaze up in Ruth's eyes and she said with ice in her voice, "How much is it this time and what's it for?"

Peter leaned against the window, smiling down at her, but the smile was mechanical. "My dear cousin," he said, "my dear, sweet cousin, that was most unkind but I would like a word in your ear if it's not too inconvenient."

"It's most inconvenient."

"It'll only take a minute."

Ruth sighed. "Very well, Peter," she condescended, "I'll give you five minutes in the library if Mr. Latimer will excuse me."

"Go right ahead," I encouraged, "I'll be quite comfortable here."

I gave them a minute to get settled then tiptoed to the library door. "It's a pretty good wheeze," Peter was saying, "and it's sure to bring us in stacks of coin. This pal I was at school with has a farm in Cornwall and there's a well in his grounds that's supposed to have been blessed by the piskies— that's some kind of Cornish fairy. They put a lucky spell on it, or something, and people come from miles around to throw pennies in and wish. Of course, when it's dark, this pal of mine rakes in the pennies and now he's got the brilliant idea of trying to sell the water, putting it up in bottles, advertising its lucky properties and flogging it at a bob a nob. He's offered to take me into partnership but will need some capital to buy the bottles and start an advertising campaign."

"I must say it sounds pretty dubious to me," said Ruth.

"Look at it this way," persuaded Peter. "Suppose we sell five hundred bottles at the first go, which we think a pretty conservative estimate, some of those five hundred people would be due for a stroke of luck, anyway, bottle or no bottle, I mean the law of averages and all that. Suppose five of them were lucky, won a football pool, say, or got a legacy and wrote to tell us about it—we'd ask them to do that in the advertisement— we'd publish the letters and then the orders would simply roll in."

"Suppose you don't get any letters?"

"We'd be sure to get some. After all, the world's full of mugs."

"Well, I think it's downright dishonest."

"We'd give you fifty per cent of the profits for putting up the money."

"I've no intention of putting up the money."

"But, Ruth, you've got such stacks of the stuff. You've always given it to me before."

"And you've always lost it."

"I won't lose it this time."

"No, Peter. I'd help you with pleasure if it was something worth while, but a thing like this——"

I returned to the drawing-room, selected a biscuit and poured myself out some coffee. Then, a few minutes later, I heard the front door slam. Evidently Peter had gone off in dudgeon without waiting for his supper.

Ruth came in looking dispirited and I said, "Your coffee will be as cold as the water in the piskies' well."

"What does it matter?" She sipped the coffee thoughtfully, then she stiffened. "So you were listening?"

"Yes. I also listened in to Diana and Henry. Do you know what I think? If you want to live to be an old, old lady, you'd better give the whole of that two million to a deserving charity, quick, and make it public that you've done so."

"I'm in no mood for witticisms."

"There's many a true word spoken in jest."

"Let's forget our troubles while we have our supper and talk about Town Planning. Have you made any progress?"

"Not yet. The first step will be to have a survey made of the town and that's not very practicable while the fog lasts. I had hoped to arrange for some aerial photographs to be taken."

"There's a cliff above the town called Woodman's Point where you can get a marvellous bird's-eye view of the whole of Shellbridge. It's a favourite spot of mine and if the fog clears tomorrow, I'll take you to it. If you think it would be suitable, you could have photographs taken from there."

"I'm having tea with Diana tomorrow at four. She wants me to persuade you to back Turner's play."

"You'll have a job. Suppose you call for me at two, then, and we'll go to Woodman's Point first."

"If it's clear enough."

"Naturally." She poured me a second cup of coffee and one for herself. The fire glinted between us, its warmth inducing drowsiness and I felt as if I were sinking deeper and deeper into the depths of my capacious arm-chair. It was all very cosy and companionable and if only I could have rung for Romney to bring my slippers, it would have been perfect.

I blew smoke rings at the ceiling and Ruth said, "You're awfully good at that, I've noticed you do it before. I wish I could do it."

"Some day I'll teach you. Do you know, I can't get over sitting here like this. A few days ago we had never met and now here we are, having gone through so much together that I feel there never was a time when I did not know you."

"I feel that, too."

"And yet I know almost nothing about you, your childhood, the books you like to read, the food you like to eat, the films you like to see—do you go to see films?"

"Often. I loved *The African Queen*."

"I liked that one, too."

"I met Katharine Hepburn once," she said and went on to talk of celebrities she had known. She had dined more than once with the Oliviers had had the good taste not to refer to them as Larry and Vivien as most of the people who have shaken hands with them once seem to do. She had met a great many famous people and had once played the piano before Royalty.

I told her about the time I had met Field-Marshal Smuts in Africa but that was as far as I could go in celebrity matching so I changed the subject to my early struggles. She listened very attentively, her face grave, her eyes alight with interest and I knew she felt more sympathetic and yielding towards me at that moment than she had ever done before. I believe that if I had tried to take her in my arms then anything might have happened, but I didn't take advantage of her lowered guard. I wanted her the hard way or not at all.

We were silent for a little, then she began to tell me about her father and mother, about how she had been brought up in this big, old house and never really felt at home anywhere out of it. She told me how she had driven an ambulance in London during the flying-bomb period and how, after she had answered an emergency call to an hotel that had received a direct hit, the first body they carried to her ambulance had been her mother's. They had never found her father. She hadn't even known they were in London. It seemed they had come up to see her as a surprise and had not got in touch with her before the bomb fell.

That put paid to the ambulance driving—she had been just eighteen—and she had joined the Wrens for a spell. She had been composing music for a year or two before that time without much success but she said that something seemed to change in her after the shock of her parents' death. "I seemed to feel everything so much more deeply after that," she said, "and it made a tremendous difference to my music. I wrote a sonata that was used in a film and played it myself for the sound-track. It caught on and after that I was made."

"I remember the film," I told her. "It was *The Song of the Lotos*, wasn't it?"

She nodded. "It wasn't a very good film, really, but they seemed to like my music."

"You have a wonderful gift," I said. "You're a wonderful person altogether, I'd be quite in awe of you if it wasn't that you had one or two endearing human weaknesses."

She sat up straight at that. "What weaknesses?"

"Well, vanity, for one. You have a lot of mirrors in the house set in strategic positions, and you're mad about that Spanish picture because you think the girl's like you. She is too, I noticed it right away. Then it pleases you to have that bunch of parasites hanging about you, praising your music and battening off you. You like running your *salon* and being the rich and beautiful and talented Ruth Mannering."

"You're pretty vain yourself over your old Town Planning schemes. It shows in the rather *outré* shirts and ties you wear, the streamlined suits and that knife-edge crease in your trousers. And you're so touchy if you think anyone's criticizing you or patronizing you."

"You're pretty touchy yourself. We're a well matched pair, in fact."

"We do seem to have a lot in common. We're both artistic, we like the same things and now we seem to have the same weaknesses."

"And somebody wants to murder both of us," I said. "How are we going to stop him?"

She yawned daintily behind her hand. "I don't know and just at the moment I'm too sleepy to care."

I took the hint, laid down my empty coffee cup and rose. She rose also and walked with me to the drawing-room door where we stood talking some more. I was aware that, after our pleasant, relaxed half hour over the coffee, constraint had risen again between us. Our conversation had become formal, almost stilted and I could see she was wondering if I would try to kiss her again and if so, what she would do about it.

We looked at each other for a moment in silence then I grinned at her. "You could always solve your problem by ringing for Romney to show me out again," I suggested.

"I'm sure that won't be necessary." There was no answering smile and as she opened the front door for me the telephone rang in the hall. She bit her lip in vexation. "What now?" she snapped.

"I'll leave you to it," I said. "Good night, Ruth."

"Good night, Philip."

As I made to step into the Bentley the door of the house opened behind me and Ruth called urgently, "Philip!"

I turned and she led me back to the drawing-room. Her lipstick seemed unusually vivid and then I saw that her face had gone dead white. "Ruth, what is it?"

She was silent so long I thought she had lost the power of speech, then she blurted, "Johnny's been found."

CHAPTER ELEVEN

FEAR IN THE NIGHT

"Found!" I echoed. "Who found him?" I plumped down in the chair and put my head in my hands. I felt dead inside and at that moment I wouldn't have cared if the roof had fallen in.

"Some children playing on the sands," said Ruth in a flat voice. She was looking away from me towards the french window, where a gap in the curtains revealed the yellow fog pressing against the pane. The room was full of it.

"Children!" I exclaimed, horror flooding my mind. "What a ghastly thing for children to find! I didn't think anybody would go near those sands till next summer."

"Children will go anywhere, any time. Philip, we must face it now. What are we going to do?"

"There comes a time in a mess like this when nothing seems to matter any more," I said, "and so far as I'm concerned, this is it. I just couldn't care less."

"If you've reached the point where nothing matters any more," said Ruth, "it means that you're defeated. Somehow I didn't think you'd be so easily defeated." I was silent and she went on quickly, "Isn't there a point in an aeroplane flight called the point of no return, where it's just as easy to go on as to go back?"

"Or just as difficult. We reached the point of no return when we buried Johnny."

"So it is defeat then?"

I sat with bowed head, gazing at the pattern on the carpet but not seeing it, seeing only the lonely sand dunes, hearing only the voices of children happily playing until——

Suppose the worst should happen and I were put on trial and the parents of the children were sitting in the court hating me, willing the jury to condemn me. "Billy was never afraid of the dark till he found the body of that man." I could hear the voice of the outraged mother bearing witness against me, if not in court then at the Judgment Seat. What had I done to those children?

"I wonder if the extradition laws operate in Mexico," I said.

"You mean to run away?"

"Not alone."

Ruth was silent and my thoughts ran on. They watched the ports, didn't they? And the airports too. It must keep them quite busy barring all the exits to fugitives from justice. We'd need money and the right connections. Well, Ruth had money and money could buy the connections. Her voice broke in on my mental wanderings like a cold douche.

"If you go at all it will definitely be alone."

"I'm not going anywhere without you."

"What sort of existence do you think we'd have in Mexico?"

"An idyllic one; dreaming in the hot sunlight, waited on hand and foot by smiling peons——"

"And listening all the time for the sharp rap on the door that would mean they had caught up with us. No, Philip, we've done nothing to be ashamed of, nothing that could give us any cause to flee the country. I'm disappointed in you, Philip. I thought you were made of sterner stuff, that it would take much more than this to make you acknowledge defeat."

The import of her words broke over me suddenly like an invigorating wave and I jumped to my feet. "I must be crazy," I exclaimed. "Of course it isn't defeat. It was the thought of those children that rather broke me down for a minute. Was that the police on the phone?"

"Yes, the local inspector's on his way here now."

"Can you handle him?"

"I think so. I'll plead complete ignorance of the whole thing."

"I'd better clear off then, good luck."

I had the Bentley moving in ten seconds flat and, as I turned out of the avenue where Ruth's house stood, I narrowly missed another car coming towards me. The police car, without a doubt. Its yellow fog-lamp chilled me and passed on.

Back at the Ocean Hotel, I went straight to bed but even as my head touched the pillow I knew I wasn't going to sleep. None shall sleep tonight! None shall sleep tonight! The words pounded in my head. I was desperately tired, my head ached persistently but the turmoil in my mind would not let me rest. It was the same problem—the only problem. Over and over again I wondered how Ruth had got on with the police and whether it was Henry or Peter or Diana or Turner or Molly Piggott or Conway who had tried to murder her.

Then all at once I sat straight up in bed. The french window! Peter Randall had been the last to come in by the window and he had gone out by the front door. After his departure I had pushed the window to and I was certain that in the general excitement I had forgotten to lock it. Suppose Ruth had thought I had locked it and not made sure for herself! After her interview with the police she would probably be too upset to think of the window and Romney might not have thought of it either. He might have gone to bed before Ruth, believing that she would attend to the window and I had a ghastly vision of a dark, furtive figure, pushing the window open and gliding into the room, crossing the hall and climbing slowly and quietly, a step at a time, up the long staircase to Ruth's bedroom.

I tried to push the thought out of my mind but once I had given birth to it, it would not leave me. It was growing in stature and in terror till it dominated me like Frankenstein's monster. I knew it was silly yet I had the feeling that there was something wrong, that Ruth was in imminent danger. There was no accounting for the feeling save the fears of a disordered mind, but it persisted. I couldn't even try to sleep, feeling like that.

I dressed hurriedly and uncertainly in the dark, conscious all the time of my aching head. I could not even wait to put on the light although I lost precious seconds feeling feverishly for my shoes. In the hall the night porter gave me a peculiar look and I said over my shoulder, "Can't sleep. Just going out for a breath of fresh air." The swing doors vibrated behind me and the fog hit me like a wall. Fresh air! No wonder the porter thought me queer.

I didn't risk the Bentley again for the fog seemed thicker than ever but walked with ever quickening steps along that now familiar route. It was a long walk and a lonely one but it helped to clear my head. It was almost two o'clock in the morning and I had Shellbridge to myself. All of it.

Ruth's front gate stood open and although that was probably not unusual it intensified my fears. I went in and round to the back, straight to the drawing-room windows. They were locked after all and the curtains were drawn. Relief made me dizzy but I could not get rid of the feeling that all was not well.

I glanced up at the dark first-floor windows. Which was the window of Ruth's bedroom? Where did Romney sleep? Then something drew my gaze down to the tall windows of the dining-room and with a shock that set the blood pounding in my veins I saw a thin ray of light moving slowly and purposefully across the inner wall. There was someone in Ruth's dining-room with a torch.

I slid the gun out of my pocket, flicked the safety catch off and moved up close. The middle window of the dining-room was wide open and I saw that a small circle of glass had been cut out of the upper pane, close to the catch.

The torch beam steadied on the Velasquez picture and I saw the hands of a man reach up to take the picture down. The torch was in his left hand and for a moment, as he struggled with the picture, the beam shone sideways on his face. It was the face of a stranger.

I stepped in through the open window, rammed the muzzle of my gun into the stranger's back and said, "Keep your hands as they are and don't move. This is a gun."

He squealed like a frightened animal, let go the picture which fell with a crash to the floor and stood shaking with fear. He still held the torch, the beam of which now pointed at the ceiling and I took it quickly from his unresisting fingers. "Back against the wall," I ordered. "Keep your hands up."

As he obeyed, I backed away from him, found the switch near the door and switched the light on. Upstairs a door closed, sounding startlingly loud in the silence of the house. "Keep still," I said, "I think we're going to have company."

"Look," said the burglar in a hoarse, shaking voice, "why don't you point that gun somewhere else? Scared stiff of guns I am."

The door opened and Romney came in. He was carrying a heavy brass poker and looked unbelievably fierce. Ruth was close behind him, peeping over his shoulder. She was wearing her crimson velvet house-coat and looked infinitely lovelier than the girl in the Velasquez picture.

When she saw me, the surprise on her face was comical to see but I smiled at her reassuringly and said, "Don't worry, the marines have landed and have the situation well in hand. I caught this beauty trying to steal the Velasquez. Ever seen him before?"

Ruth looked at my shrinking captive. "Yes," she said. "That

night at the Mermaid Club. You remember I was put in another room with a man to watch me? This was the man."

I remembered Ruth saying that he had horrible eyes and that he had kept looking at her and licking his lips. He was still looking at her and licking his lips but for a different reason. They were dry with fear. He did have horrible eyes, too, red-rimmed, colourless, and constantly blinking. Altogether, he was an unpleasant piece of work.

"So you're one of Tyler's boys," I said. "What's your name?"

"Sam Gunter." The first shock of fright was wearing off and he was sullen now.

"See if he has a gun, Romney."

Romney searched him roughly, producing a gun and a knife. The knife had a curved point like a linoleum knife and had evidently been intended for cutting the picture out of its frame.

"At last we really got a use for bluebottles," said Romney. "Shall I phone them now, Miss Ruth?"

"Don't let's be hasty," I intervened. "First, I'd like to have a little talk with Sam. Who put you up to this, Sam?"

Sam shrugged his shoulders. "You might as well get the cops, mister. I ain't talking."

"Perhaps I might be able to persuade you," I said. "Ruth, will you and Romney leave us for a few minutes."

Ruth hesitated. "Will you be all right?"

"Of course. Please do as I ask."

"Very well. We'll be at hand if you want us."

When they had gone I pocketed the gun and grinned menacingly at Sam. "Now, Sam, who instructed you to steal this picture?"

"Tyler, if you got to know."

"And who instructed Tyler?"

"That would be telling."

"If you tell me the truth, I might persuade Miss Mannering to let you go."

"I ain't talking."

I moved purposefully towards him, clenching my fists and he backed away from me. Every vestige of colour had drained out of his face and not for a second did his frightened eyes leave mine. Then I shot out a foot and tripped him up so that he fell backwards into a chair. I stood over him and he sat glaring up at me.

"Don't you dare touch me," he quavered. "The cops won't stand for it."

"The cops will probably add to it when they get you alone in a cell. You broke in here and were caught and any bruises on you will be put down to the fact that you resisted capture and had to be forcibly restrained."

He lashed out at me with his right foot but I stepped back in good time and kicked him on his outstretched ankle. He uttered a rather pathetic howl of pain, heaved himself to his feet and came at me with flailing fists. I stopped him with a straight right that caught him flush on the mouth and sent him reeling back against the wall. He stood there staring at me wildly, hands hanging at his sides, shoulders slumped. A dark thread of blood showed up on his lower lip and dribbled slowly down to his chin.

I stood regarding him with what I hoped was a sinister smile. "Don't delude yourself that this hurts me more than it hurts you, Sam," I said. "I'm enjoying myself. Your boss, Tyler, and I have something in common in that we both used to be professional boxers. I'm a bit out of practise, but it's wonderful how it comes back to one."

He licked the blood from his lip. "I ain't talkin'," he repeated.

"That night at the Mermaid Club, you frightened Miss Mannering and I'm afraid you're going to have to pay for that. You see, I'm by way of being rather fond of Miss Mannering and I hate the thought of her having been frightened. She was particularly frightened of your eyes so I think I'll blacken them both for a start."

"I tell you I ain't talkin'." All at once he grabbed an armchair, pushed it in front of me and made a dash for the window. I got round the chair just in time and tripped him up again. He fell with a crash that shook the room, bounded immediately to his feet and made a blind rush at me. It was like shooting a sitting bird but I had no compunction whatever. I stepped back and let him have it, good and hard with my right fist again, but this time I aimed for the point of his jaw. Once more he reeled back against the wall, slid slowly down to a sitting posture and rolled over flat on his back.

I stood rubbing my knuckles for a few seconds till his eyes blinked open, then I sat on his chest, took hold of his tie and began to pull it tight. After a moment he gagged, rolled his eyes and his tongue came out. "Talk, Sam," I said, "talk while you can because in ten seconds you won't be able to talk. Not ever."

I tightened the tie some more and Sam gurgled, choked, rolled his eyes frantically and gave in. "Gimme a chance, mister," he croaked, "and I'll talk."

I nodded, loosened the tie but continued to sit on his chest just to be handy. Sam drew several deep breaths. "It was a bloke called Crane," he said, "Henry Crane. He saw Tyler about it at the Club two nights ago and fixed up for us to swipe the picture when he gave the say so. He wanted to try and get it legal first and we was only to act if that didn't come off. Tonight he phones and gives us the office to carry on. Tyler and Joe wasn't there but I was to do the job, anyhow. There was a couple of thousand quid in it. Good pay."

"The picture's worth about twenty times that," I said. "So Tyler and Joe weren't around tonight?"

"No. They've gone off somewheres on some lay of their own an' we've had no word. Hope they ain't got in bad with the cops."

"And nobody at the Mermaid Club knows where they went or what they were after?"

"Not a soul."

I got off Sam's chest. He stood up shakily and I made him sit down at the table, tore a couple of sheets out of my note-book and handed him my fountain-pen. "Write what I dictate," I said, "and so far as I'm concerned you can go free."

"Okeydoke, mister. Shoot."

I dictated slowly, "I, Sam Gunter, of the Mermaid Club, London, hereby certify that I was offered two thousand pounds by Alderman Henry Crane of Shellbridge, to steal a valuable picture by Velasquez from Miss Ruth Mannering, also of Shellbridge."

I made him write out a second copy and sign them both, then I jerked my head towards the window. "Beat it," I ordered, "and from now on, keep out of Shellbridge."

"Thanks, mister," he said. "I'll remember you in my prayers." He was out of the window and away like a streak of lightning and, having closed and secured the window, I crossed the hall to the drawing-room where Ruth and Romney awaited me.

K

"Sam talked," I said. "So I let him go as a reward."

Romney shook a sorrowful head. "Crazy," he said, as if to himself. "Everybody round here's crazy except me."

"Go to bed, Romney," said Ruth.

"And keep your mouth shut," I added. Romney looked at me reproachfully over his shoulder as he left the room.

Ruth had her chin tucked into the high collar of her close-fitting house-coat as if she wanted me to see as little of her as possible and when I handed her a copy of Sam's confession, she read it without a word.

"So there goes one of my chief suspects," I said.

"Henry?"

"Yes. Up till a few minutes ago I had every reason to believe that he had tried to drown you and that he had killed Johnny. His reaction to the snake shook me a little but it was just possible he had put that on. He knew the snake was due to arrive tonight and could have pinched it from the lorry and put it in my bed. His car was out of Shellbridge the night we searched Johnny's flat, but if he was trying to kill you, he wouldn't have needed to steal the picture."

"No," said Ruth, a trifle bitterly. "Peter and Diana would have let him have it cheap. All they can think of is money."

"So Henry's out," I said. "His car was at the Mermaid Club, not because he'd just come from Johnny's flat but because he was arranging with Tyler to steal the picture so, naturally, he would lie about the car being out that night. I must say, though, I'm surprised at his trying to get the picture that way. He could scarcely hang it on his wall."

"No," agreed Ruth, "but he could gloat over it in secret. Henry's like that. He has to get what he wants by fair means or foul. Sometimes I think he's not quite right in the head."

"I suppose the fact that you no longer had the picture would be enough."

"Yes, my loss would have been his triumph but he's megalo-maniac enough to believe that possession is nine points of the law and that in the end I'd have taken his money and let him keep the picture."

"I couldn't sleep for worrying," I explained. "I thought you might have forgotten to lock the french window. That's why I came."

"I locked it after you'd gone. Why are you so concerned about me?"

"If you don't know that," I said, "you must be as guileless as a new-born babe."

She blushed as crimson as her house-coat and stood gazing at me, her lips slightly parted, her deep blue eyes unfathomable. "I can't get you out of my mind," I went on. "I've never had much to do with women—I've been too busy trying to make a career out of nothing—but I've never met anyone like you. I'll remember you till the day I die."

"Are you trying to tell me you're in love with me?"

"You wouldn't believe me if I did. You think every man you meet is after your confounded money. Why don't you give it away?"

Her voice was very soft. "I'll give it away if you want me to."

"Don't you dare," I said. "I'd never forgive myself if you did that because of me."

"You're unhappy because I've got money and you'd be just as unhappy if I didn't have it any longer."

"That's about it."

"You don't want me with money and you don't want me without it?"

"Put that way it sounds pretty crazy."

"It is crazy."

"Perhaps it'll straighten itself out. Meantime we've got enough trouble. What did the police inspector say?"

"Not much, really. He was very polite. Wanted to know when I'd last seen Johnny and what my movements were on the day he was killed. He wanted to know all about Johnny, of course, who he was and so on, but I said I knew nothing about him. They've established the time of death to within an hour or two, they've been through his London flat and they've traced his connection with the Mermaid Club."

"It hasn't taken them long," I commented.

"He was found yesterday but they've been keeping it dark and they're calling in Scotland Yard. It seems the Yard are interested in the Mermaid Club."

"That's nice. It means that before long we're going to have a lot of what Romney calls bluebottles buzzing round our ears. Tell me, though, when Peter was in bed with the cold could he possibly have got out without his sister or the housekeeper knowing?"

"It would be difficult. Besides, it wasn't Peter's car at Johnny's flat. It had a different gear change, remember?"

"All the same, Peter is now suspect number one. Take the murder of Johnny. Suppose Peter, having failed to drown you, had tried to see you next day, to propound his get-rich-quick scheme and had come in by the french window as usual. You weren't there and he hung about waiting for you to come in, fidgeting with impatience, picking up things and laying them down—I saw him do that at your party—perhaps toying with the paper-knife on your desk. Then, suppose Johnny, whom you had sent away the night before, came back to try and effect a reconciliation. He comes round to the french window, sees a new Bentley standing in the drive and goes over to have a look at it. Perhaps he opens the boot and looks in.

"Peter sees him there, goes out to speak to him, perhaps carrying the paper-knife, and Johnny accuses him of having tried to drown you. Peter, on impulse, stabs him in the back, bundles the body into the boot and slips away through the fog without waiting to see you after all."

"It could have happened like that."

"I'm certain it happened just like that. Only it might not have been Peter in the drawing-room. It might have been one of the others."

"Not Molly Piggott," said Ruth. "She wouldn't have come in by the french window. Neither would Leslie Turner."

"No," I agreed. "It narrows it down a bit, doesn't it? Well, I'm off again. See you tomorrow at two if the fog permits."

Next morning, to my pleased surprise, the fog was considerably thinner and I got down to work in the office that Wilmot had made available. At eleven o'clock Wilmot looked in to take me for a coffee and we went to the English Garden Café which was the current fashionable resort. We had not been sitting long when Peter Randall and Conway joined us and a few minutes later Henry Crane arrived. I could just see the back of his Buick through the café door.

He greeted me with an acid remark about busy Planners, then Ruth came in with Diana Randall and before long a good going gossip party was in progress. News of Johnny's murder had not yet been made public and Ruth, of course, did not mention it.

She was very gracious to me this morning and remarked that the fog had cleared in time for our visit to Woodman's Point. Diana pricked up her ears and Ruth had to explain that she was taking me to Woodman's Point at two o'clock so that I could see if it would be a suitable spot from which to take photographs of the town.

Henry Crane looked displeased. "You needn't have bothered Miss Mannering, Latimer," he said. "I could have driven you to Woodman's Point myself."

"Not with a flat tyre," murmured Diana, wickedly.

"What flat tyre?"

"Your nearside rear tyre's flat, Henry. I noticed it as we came in. Didn't you know?"

"Of course I didn't know, blast it!" Henry gulped his coffee and stood up. "I suppose I'll have to change the wheel."

"Ring up a garage to send someone."

"No. I despise people who can't change wheels. I'll do it myself."

"I'll give you a hand," I offered and followed Crane to his car. He paused with his hand on the lid of the boot and gave me a sour look. "You'd better get on with your Town Planning," he snapped. "I don't need your help."

I handed him Sam's confession and stood back to watch his face. It was as good as a play.

He read slowly, his face going red and white in turn, then, savagely, he tore the confession to fragments and scattered the pieces in the gutter. "Temper!" I admonished. "Fortunately, I've got another copy. It's going to my lawyer in a sealed envope with instructions to hand it to the police in the event of my untimely decease. Ruth knows about it, too."

"Ruth knows?" His voice was faint.

"Yes, so you'll behave yourself in future, won't you, Henry? And in view of your attitude to me, you can change that wheel yourself."

I arrived at Ruth's house about a quarter to two. Fog still shrouded the sea and wisps of it clung about the town but it was clear enough for Woodman's Point. I was gleefully describing the discomfiture of Henry when the bell rang and a moment later Romney appeared. "The dam's bust," he announced. "Detective-Inspector McKellar of Scotland Yard."

CHAPTER TWELVE

McKELLAR INVESTIGATES

THE inspector certainly looked like a messenger of doom. He was tall, in the early forties, with curiously high, straight shoulders, an out-thrust head, close-cropped, grizzled hair, a piercing gaze, and the grimmest expression I had ever seen on a human face.

He took a lightning inventory of the contents of the room, of Ruth, noting her strained expression, of me, standing protectively at her side, for we had both risen at his entry. Then he thrust his hat out behind him into Romney's reluctant fingers and with a backward jerk of his head indicated that Romney could go. Romney went, closing the door slowly as if he hated to be shut out, and the inspector waited, head on one side, listening, till he heard the butler's footsteps retreat along the hall and the door to the kitchen close. Then he came forward into the middle of the room.

"Miss Mannering? I'd like a word with ye alone." He spoke with a marked Scots' accent and seemed proud of it.

Ruth turned to me with a half-smile. "This is my good friend, Mr. Latimer, Inspector. I'd like him to stay, please."

"Your solicitor?"

"No, just a friend. I don't think I'll need a solicitor."

"Nobody needs a solicitor yet they seem to thrive." It was clear that the legal profession were his enemies, that they came between him and the swift arrest of his lawful quarry. He looked as if he had never been young, as if he had come fully fledged into the world, a ruthless hunter of men.

"Do sit down, Inspector."

"After you, Miss."

At least he had manners. He waited till we were both seated then he took the chair Ruth indicated, moving it round to get a better view of her. Me he ignored.

"As ye'll have guessed," he said, "I'm investigating the death of your fiancé. It must have been a great shock to ye."

"It was. I can't realize it yet."

"That's natural, Miss. Please accept my sympathy."

"Thank you, Inspector, but must I go over it all again? I've already told Inspector Greer everything I know."

"Aye, just so. I've had the privilege of studying his report but it's important I should hear your side of it at first hand, so ye'll not mind just answering a few questions."

"Of course not if it will help you."

The inspector nodded but his bleak expression did not lighten. He took Ruth rapidly over the same ground covered by the local inspector the night before and she answered his questions firmly and quickly in a voice that did not betray her feelings. I made no attempt to interrupt and, at first, the inspector continued to ignore my presence. Towards the end of his interrogation, however, he glanced at me occasionally, a chill glance that boded ill and I began to feel uncomfortable. Then, all at once, he unmasked his batteries.

"I understand ye're Town Planning Shellbridge, Mr. Latimer?" I nodded. So he had known who I was all the time and that solicitor crack had been intended as a sneer. "And that ye arrived the night before the murder?"

"So it seems." I could feel the tension rising in the room.

"And at once made the acquaintance of Miss Mannering?"

"Yes."

"With whom ye've been spending a good deal of time since?"

"Shellbridge gossip," murmured Ruth. I was conscious of her eyes upon my face, warning me.

"I never listen to gossip, Miss."

"Miss Mannering is a member of the Planning Committee," I said.

"Aye, just so. That would be your Bentley standing in the drive?"

"It would."

"A new car, sir?"

"Very new."

"Then perhaps ye would explain, sir, how the sand got into the boot."

The inspector's words were like a blow over the heart and for a moment I sat just looking at him, striving with everything I had to keep dismay from showing in my face. I had swept and garnished that boot and if the inspector had found sand in it he had very sharp eyes indeed.

With an effort I rallied my forces. "Inspector," I said with dignity, "am I to understand that on seeing my Bentley in the drive, you actually took the keys from the ignition lock, unlocked the boot and looked inside?"

"I did, sir."

"Was that proper procedure?"

"Mr. Latimer, I'm looking for a murderer, the murderer of John King alias Kingdom, who was stabbed to death with a sharp, thin-bladed instrument, conveyed to Shellbridge beach, probably in the luggage boot of a car and there buried. The owner of any car connected with this house is under suspicion and I would like an answer to my question. How did the sand get into the boot of your car?"

"Sand gets into everything in Shellbridge."

"I've also looked in the luggage boots of Miss Mannering's two cars. They've been in Shellbridge much longer than yours and there's no sand there."

"As you seem to have found out, I'm the Town Planning Consultant to Shellbridge Corporation and of course I must get to know the town. I've been driving round it extensively the last few days and have been down at the beach more than once."

"In the fog?"

"I can't let fog hold up my work. The sooner I get this job done the sooner I can take my fee and go on to other work."

"Aye, just so. Miss Mannering, ye told Inspector Greer last night that ye had no knowledge of the deceased's past. When ye met him at first ye accepted his story that he was a rich man in America and later ye agreed to marry him. Is that right?"

"It is."

"Ye knew nothing of his antecedents?"

"Nothing at all."

"Ye knew him only as John Kingdom?"

"Yes."

"Then how was it, Miss Mannering, that when I referred to him a few moments ago as John King alias Kingdom, ye betrayed no surprise?"

I saw Ruth's knuckles whiten and had no doubt that the

inspector saw too, but she faced him unflinchingly. "I'm afraid I couldn't have taken it in, Inspector, but actually I'm not unduly surprised. I was beginning to suspect that Johnny—Mr. Kingdom—wasn't quite what he had pretended to be."

"What made ye suspect that?"

"When I pressed him for particulars of his life in America he was—evasive."

"Ye're still wearing his engagement ring?"

"Yes."

"But no mourning?"

"I don't believe in the outward trappings of mourning."

"Is there any mourning in your heart?"

Ruth saw there was no help for it. You couldn't fool this man. He could see right into your soul. "I regret his death more than I can say," she said, "but I was no longer in love with him because I no longer trusted him."

"Aye, just so." The inspector's face looked bleaker than ever, which probably meant that he was pleased with himself. "Had ye told him?"

There was the slightest hesitation then Ruth said, "No." Her eyes fell before his frosty gaze and for a moment he was silent. Then he continued, "Ye told Inspector Greer that King came to see ye on the evening of Monday, 19th November, the day before his death, having previously registered at the Ocean Hotel. Did he come to Shellbridge specially to see ye?"

"Yes."

"How long did he intend to stay?"

"He didn't say."

"But no doubt he meant to stay some days? The fact that he registered at the hotel proves that."

"I suppose so."

"Did ye see him at all next day?"

"I never saw him again."

"Did that not surprise ye?"

"It did rather."

"Ye're not being frank with me, Miss Mannering."

"I'm being as frank as I can."

"Or as frank as ye dare?" Ruth was silent, but the inspector pressed on regardless. "When he came to see ye on Monday evening, were ye alone?"

Ruth hesitated. I could see she didn't want to involve me but had no idea how much the inspector knew.

"I was with her," I admitted.

"Ye had met before, of course?"

It was my turn to hesitate. If I answered yes to his question, he'd want to know where and when we had met. If I answered no, he'd want to know what I was doing in Ruth's house the very day I had arrived in Shellbridge. "We hadn't met before," I said. "Miss Mannering is a member of Shellbridge Town Planning Committee and I called on her to canvass for the appointment of Planning Consultant."

I caught Ruth's eye. Evidently she thought that a pretty good one. I caught the inspector's eye, too. He didn't think it a good one at all. "And ye've seen her pretty often since?"

"I was attracted to her and sought her company."

"Aye, just so. Miss Mannering has given us an account of her movements on Tuesday, 20th November, the presumed date of the murder. She said she went to London in the forenoon and there visited, among other places, a firm of Motor Salesmen called Wallace, Hyde & Co. We've checked on that and it seems she purchased a Bentley from them." The inspector paused, savouring his moment. "The engine and chassis number of that Bentley correspond with the Bentley in the drive outside which ye've just told me is yours."

"Smart work, Inspector, but I don't see what it proves."

"It proves to my mind that ye're both covering up something."

He switched to Ruth again. "Miss Mannering, on the day of the murder, a mink coat which proved to be your property was washed up on the beach. I understand your explanation was that ye had tripped over a bollard on the pier and that the coat, which ye had been wearing with your arms outside the sleeves, slipped from your shoulders into the water?"

"Yes."

"Over which bollard did ye trip, Miss?"

"I couldn't tell in the fog."

"There are only three bollards on Shellbridge Pier and they are all set back a good few feet from the edge. If ye had tripped over one and dropped your coat, it would have fallen between the bollard and the edge, not into the water." Ruth looked quickly at me, her eyes flying distress signals, and the inspector said, "Come now, Miss Mannering, don't ye think it's time we had just a wee bit of the truth?"

"The inspector's right, Ruth," I advised. "I think we'll have to tell him. It was like this, Inspector. I came to Shellbridge on Monday the nineteenth, set out to explore the place and found myself on the pier. The fog lifted momentarily and I saw a girl in a mink coat, rather near the edge. I turned back, thinking she might be meeting her boy friend or something then I heard a cry and a splash and realized she'd fallen in. I went in after her, managed, rather luckily, to find her and brought her to safety. Unfortunately, I couldn't rescue the coat too.

"That was why I was at Miss Mannering's house when her fiancé arrived and that is why I am now the proud owner of the Bentley outside. Miss Mannering is very rich and her ideas of a reward are liberal."

"Why didn't ye tell the police the truth when they returned the coat?"

"Because neither Miss Mannering nor I wanted any publicity. She gets too much publicity as it is."

The inspector nodded. "Aye. I can understand that, but there's one thing I canny understand. What was Miss Mannering doing on the pier on a foggy November night?"

Ruth barely hesitated. "It was just because it was a foggy November night that I was there, Inspector. As I expect you know, I compose music. I'm calling my latest, *Symphony for a Foggy Night*, and I was trying to get the atmosphere. It was because I was lost in a particularly tricky musical sequence that I went over the edge."

The inspector looked baffled and I thought that Ruth's brilliant effort had won the day. "And what about the shot that was fired outside this house on Wednesday night when ye were apparently both together? Have ye any explanation of that?"

"I know nothing about that."

"Was anybody found shot?" I asked.

"No."

"Then what are you worrying about?"

"I'm no' the only one in this room that's worrying," said McKellar grimly. "I can see that. Have either of ye ever been to the Mermaid Club?"

"The Mermaid Club!" I repeated, to gain time.

"Do I no' speak distinctly, Mr. Latimer?"

"Most distinctly. I'd put you down as an Aberdonian at a guess."

"Then answer my question, please."

I tried to catch Ruth's eye but she avoided my gaze which was perhaps just as well, for the inspector was watching us with a cold, concentrated vigilance that was wholly unnerving. If I denied all knowledge of the Mermaid Club, he could easily find out that I was lying, for the officials of the Mermaid Club would help the police so long as it was not against their interests to do so.

"I was there once with Miss Mannering," I admitted. I heard Ruth draw in her breath and the inspector gave her a quick look. "When would that have been?" he asked.

"Three nights ago."

"Are ye both members of the Club?"

"No, neither of us is a member."

"Then what took ye there?" He addressed the question, with a sudden out-thrust movement of his head, to Ruth and she replied at once, "I was looking for my fiancé."

"Did ye not know where he lived?"

"Yes, I'd phoned him several times at his flat but got no answer."

"Why were you so anxious to find him?"

"To return his ring. I told you I no longer trusted him. I did not believe the stories he told me about himself and thought I might find out something about him at the Mermaid Club."

"Had ye never been to the Club with him?"

"No, but he had mentioned once or twice that he was a member."

I leaned back in my chair and let Ruth carry on. She seemed to be better at this sort of thing than I, anyway. She met the inspector's probing stare with a stonewall expression that gave nothing away and for a moment I thought he looked baffled again. Then he returned to the attack. "Why did ye take Mr. Latimer with you?"

"I didn't think the Mermaid Club was a place I should visit alone."

"Aye, just so. Had ye no other friends that would have gone with ye? Friends ye've known much longer than ye've known Mr. Latimer?"

"I offered to go with her," I said.

He rounded on me. "Did I ask ye? Let Miss Mannering answer for herself."

"I felt I could trust Mr. Latimer," said Ruth smoothly. "After all, he had saved my life at the risk of his own, and then I didn't think he would take such a gossipy interest in my personal affairs as friends of long standing are apt to do."

"Your friends gossip about ye?"

"Everyone gossips in Shellbridge. It's a comparatively small place, really, and self-centred, especially in winter when there are no holiday-makers to take up attention. I didn't want the dissolution of my engagement to become public property before I was ready to announce it."

"At that time ye had no suspicion that death had already dissolved it?"

"Of course not."

All at once the inspector heaved himself to his feet. In two quick strides he was at Ruth's desk and the next moment the paper-knife that had stabbed Johnny was in his hands. He held it delicately by the point and Ruth wilted before the intensity of his gaze.

"King was stabbed with a thin-bladed knife or dagger," he said. "With something very like this. Has it ever been out of your possession?"

"No." The word was barely audible.

"Ye're sure of that?"

"It lies on that desk all the time," said Ruth, "and if it was missing at any time, I didn't notice it."

"Ye didn't notice it! A young lady like you that's very much in the public eye, that writes music and plays it too, that's a member of the Town Council will get a lot of letters?"

"I suppose I do."

"In fact, there'll be few days when the postman passes your door?"

"Very few."

"So that ye'd be using this knife for opening your letters almost every morning?"

"I don't always use it. If there aren't many letters I just open them with my fingers, sitting here by the fire."

"But the paper-knife was always there if ye wanted it?"

"So far as I'm aware."

"So far as ye're aware! Ye have a staff of servants?"

"My butler, Romney, and his wife and daughter."

"I suppose one of them would notice the absence of the paper-knife?"

"You can ask them."

"I'll do just that, Miss, and meantime I'll borrow this." He slipped the paper-knife into his inside pocket and turned again to me. "Now, sir, perhaps ye'd care to give me an account of your movements on twentieth November?"

"With pleasure. I left my hotel about eleven a.m., had a walk through the main shopping streets of Shellbridge and returned to the hotel for lunch, probably around twelve-thirty. About two-thirty Miss Mannering's chauffeur arrived with the Bentley. I phoned Miss Mannering to thank her but she was out, then I took the Bentley for a run round the outlying parts of the town."

"Ye wouldn't see much in the fog."

"Not much, but I enjoyed making the Bentley's acquaintance. I had never driven such a magnificent car. I was back at the hotel before five and stayed there till seven when I went to the Town Hall, interviewed Shellbridge Planning Committee and was appointed Town Planning Consultant. After that I was in the bar of the Ocean Hotel talking to a man called Leslie Turner till about ten when I came to Miss Mannering's house to thank her for the car."

"How long did ye stay?"

"Not very long. About half an hour, perhaps."

"And then?"

"Back to the hotel and bed."

The inspector rubbed his chin thoughtfully, looking as if he didn't believe a word of it, then he said, "Ye'll be staying in Shellbridge for a bit?"

"At the Ocean Hotel. I won't run away."

"Ye wouldn't run far, Mr. Latimer. And now, Miss Mannering, if I may have a word with your butler?"

"Of course," said Ruth. She took him through to the kitchen, came back and collapsed in a chair, looking very white and tired. I had a cigarette already lighted for her and she took it gratefully. "I feel as if I've been sucked in by a whirlwind," she said.

"Yes," I said. "He's a holy terror, that one, but don't let him get you down. He can't prove anything."

"If only we didn't have to tell all those lies. I hate it."

"I hate it too, Ruth, but that's what happens when you take the wrong course to start with. One lie leads to another until you get so involved that you don't know where you are."

"I don't know where I am now."

"On the right side of the prison gates, which is always something," I said. "Perhaps we should have gone to Mexico. There may still be time."

"Flight would be regarded as an admission of guilt."

"I suppose it would."

Ten minutes later Romney came in. "You can relax," he announced, "the copper's gone."

"Hot stuff, isn't he?" I said.

"He met his match in me, cock," answered Romney, swelling with pride. "See no evil, hear no evil, speak no evil, that's me, I told him, so he just give me a dirty look and went. But he'll be back, the heat's on."

"Thank you, Romney," said Ruth. "You're very loyal."

"I never quarrel with me bread and butter," said Romney with dignity. "Besides, I like it here."

"Well," said Ruth when we were alone again. "No use sitting here waiting for it. Let's go to Woodman's Point. We'll take my little 'M.G.' if you don't mind. It hasn't been out for awhile and a run would do it good."

Ruth's garage stood some distance to the right of the house with a straight run down to the gateway. There were two cars in it, a lordly Rolls of pre-war vintage and a black M.G. sports two-seater. The M.G. started at a touch and as we turned out of the gate Ruth said, "That's queer. When I put the car in last the petrol tank was more than half full and now it's almost empty."

"Has your chauffeur got a girl griend?"

"Blake would never take the car out without my knowledge, neither would Romney, but somebody's had it out."

"It looks quite clean."

"If Blake found it dirty he'd clean it. He would assume that I had been out in it."

I at once thought of the night we had surprised the intruder in Johnny's flat and in my mind I heard again the scrunch of the mis-timed gear change as he made his hurried escape. "Change down to first," I said.

Ruth gave me a puzzled look but obeyed. "Now try to change up to second without putting your clutch out." Again she obeyed and I heard the same horrible scrunch. "Ever hear a sound like that before?" I asked.

"Yes, the night we—Philip! You mean whoever was in Johnny's flat had taken my car?"

"Yes. No wonder we absolved Cousin Peter because his car hadn't been out. He wasn't taking the risk of having his own car spotted near Johnny's flat so he took yours. If we had only come straight back instead of going on to the Mermaid Club we'd have caught him."

"I'll keep my garage locked after this."

"I would if I were you. He might slacken the brakes or something."

Woodman's Point was a narrow promontory at the top of an imposing precipice. A single track run-in led off from the road, sloping rather steeply down to a rickety wooden paling at the edge of the bluff and Ruth swung the M.G. into the run-in, parked it facing the paling with its back to the road and we walked the few yards down to the edge.

The paling creaked as I leaned against it and I drew back hastily. "This paling's dangerous," I said. "Several people leaning on it would be enough to make it go."

"Yes, it doesn't seem very safe. Perhaps you can suggest something else in your Planning Scheme."

"I'd suggest a wall and more parking space. There isn't room for more than one car abreast."

Far below I could see the roofs of Shellbridge, wreathed in a mixture of chimney-smoke and fog. The fog was still thick over the sea but clear enough in the town to afford a reasonable view. Looking down made me a little dizzy at first but after a few moments I got used to it.

Immediately beneath me was a wood from which the cliff rose two hundred feet as sheer as a skyscraper and beyond, the town straggled down to the shore, dwindling to a rash of bunga-loid growths that would have caused the builder to be shot in any civilized country. Almost directly opposite, small and far away, Shellbridge Pier straddled the steel-grey water.

"No one could say it was a beautiful town," I commented.

"All the more scope for you," said Ruth. "How beautiful can you make it?"

"As beautiful as your Town Council will let me. Towns can't be rebuilt for nothing, you know."

"Could you take suitable photographs from here?"

"Yes, I think so."

It was very quiet at Woodman's Point. Occasionally we heard a car go past on the road behind us but there was no other sound. I think it was the stillness that made me look round and what I saw made my heart jump.

Ruth's M.G. was moving silently down the slope towards us, gathering momentum with every yard. There was no one at the wheel and no one in sight and for a moment I was too stunned to move. Then, almost as the car reached us, I clutched Ruth round the waist and made a desperate leap with her to the side. The front mudguard brushed my coat, the car swept on, snapped the flimsy paling like matchwood and toppled over into the abyss.

Ruth clung to me, her face buried in the rough tweed of my coat, her whole body shaking uncontrollably and then, from far below, came the sound of an appalling crash. The echo swelled, died to a whisper and the silence stole back, affrighted. I looked over the edge and saw the car burning with a fierce flame in the dark depths of the wood.

Ruth raised a white face to mine. Her lips were quivering until I kissed them and we stayed locked together for a long time. Tenderly, I stroked her hair and gradually the trembling of her body died away until she was at peace in my arms.

"Darling," I said, and repeated the word because of the joy it gave me. "Darling, you're all right. We're safe."

She said, "Another second and it would have swept us both over the edge. Oh, Philip!"

"Forgive me if I sound critical, my sweet, but next time you park a car on a down slope, it would be a good idea to put the hand-brake on."

"It was on, Philip, and the car was in gear too. It couldn't have moved by itself."

It took several seconds for the implication of her words to sink in and then I remembered being vaguely aware of having

L

heard a car starting up round the bend of the road. Someone must have parked a car just round the bend, walked down to the M.G., released the brake and the gear lever then run back to the parked car and cleared out fast.

"You did make it rather public that we were going to Woodman's Point," I said. I was thinking back over the last few days and in my mind a grim pattern was beginning to emerge.

"Ruth," I exclaimed, "I'm beginning to get it. On Monday last someone tried to kill you in such a way as to make it seem like an accident or suicide. The same person killed Johnny and also tried to kill me because we all knew too much but, in these cases, it didn't matter if it was obviously murder because there was no obvious motive pointing to any particular person.

"Today another attempt was made to kill you and, incidentally, me, in a way that would suggest accident or suicide, therefore whoever is after you daren't murder you openly because the motive would give him or her away."

"You mean my money, don't you?"

"Yes, so it must be Peter or Diana, or Molly Piggott who wants Peter but doesn't want him poor, or Leslie Turner who wants Diana but not undowered."

"Leslie Turner should be teaching in his school just now."

"We can soon find out if he is and if so, that lets him out. We can probably eliminate Molly too, which throws it back on Peter or Diana, jointly or severally."

Ruth shuddered. "It's horrible to think that anyone would— would kill just for money."

"You might think differently if you hadn't got any," I said. "I'm afraid I'm going to be late for Diana's tea-party."

"How you can think of tea-parties——"

"The tea-party may give me a line on Diana," I pointed out, "so let's go."

I didn't speak much during our walk down to the town, for something was niggling at the back of my mind. I had a feeling that there was something I had missed, some incident during the last day or two that would provide me with a clue or a link if only I could remember it, some happening that was odd or out of place. I tried hard but it eluded me, giving me a sense of futility that depressed my spirits.

CHAPTER THIRTEEN

"FALSE WORLD, FAREWELL"

I REACHED Diana's cottage at quarter-past four and went first to the garage. The Armstrong Siddeley was out. The elderly housekeeper showed me into a comfortable living-room where Diana awaited me in an emerald frock that had obviously been made for her by a tailor with ideas—rather low ideas.

"Yes," she said, "Peter's out. I saw you reconnoitring the garage. Are you pleased?"

"Don't I look it?"

"You look like a cat treading very delicately in unknown territory."

"Well, you are unknown territory."

Diana laughed, accepted my apology for being late and dispensed tea with a practised hand. There was a snapshot album on a side-table and I picked it up.

"There are some shocking photographs in that," said Diana, "including one of me with nothing on."

The photograph of Diana with nothing on was the first one in the book. She was lying on her tummy on a pillow and looked about six months' old, but she grew older and less exposed as I turned the pages. There were photographs of Peter, too, at different ages and a worried looking couple who had obviously been their parents.

"I can find you something more interesting than that to look at," said Diana, and left the room. I continued to turn the pages of the album and all at once I came across a photograph that made me sit up.

It showed Peter in the uniform of an army officer. He was sitting cross-legged on a hassock, playing a flute. There was a turban on his head, a silly grin on his face and a cobra twined round his shoulders. There was another cobra at his feet, its long neck raised, its hooded head looking towards him.

Diana came back with a bulky parcel, looked over my shoulder and laughed. "That was taken in India," she said.

"Peter discovered he had a way with snakes. They used to chaff him about it in the mess."

She took the album from my hands, opened the parcel and dumped a bundle of typescript on my knees. "This is Leslie's play," she informed me, "the one you're going to persuade Ruth to finance."

I looked at the title-page. *False World, Farewell,* a play in three acts by Leslie Turner. "Do I have to read it now?" I asked.

"I shall be insulted if you do. Take it home with you and read it tonight."

I laid the play down on the side-table beside the snapshot album and gave Diana a conspiratorial grin. "I'm surprised you didn't invite your fiancé along too," I said.

"Poor Leslie," commented Diana. "He's had class exams today and has to correct the papers after school."

So that was Turner out of it, I thought. He could scarcely have absented himself from the exams to commit murder at Woodman's Point. Diana looked as if she hoped the conversation would take a more intimate turn, so I said hurriedly, "What a charming little cottage you have! As an architect, I'd dearly love to see over it." It was a very ordinary cottage but I wanted badly to have a look at Peter Randall's bedroom.

She seemed quite pleased to show me round and when I had praised the bright kitchen and the tiny dining-room, she led me upstairs to the bedrooms. She was inclined to linger in her own room but I steered her out of it and into Peter's.

It was a small, untidy room, furnished in dark oak with a threadbare carpet. I looked round it with interest and then, glancing through the window, I saw the tree. It grew straight up past the window, a stout branch reaching out almost to the sill.

Diana laughed. "When Peter was a boy he was often sent to bed for being naughty and he used to climb out of the window and get down by that tree."

Not only when he was a boy, I thought. Aloud I said, "How's his cold?"

"There's nothing much wrong with him," sneered Diana, "but if you'd heard him you'd have thought he was going to die. On Monday last he retired to bed in the early afternoon and dared the housekeeper or me to disturb him."

"So you didn't disturb him?"

"We didn't go near him till next morning."

We returned to the living-room and then I heard a car engine and the sound of the garage doors being closed. "Damn Peter!" exclaimed Diana. "I didn't expect him back so soon."

"Where's he been?" I asked.

"Goodness knows. Off on some dark business of his own." She spoke truer words than she knew, I thought, although he certainly hadn't hurried back. I picked up the photograph album, turned to the snap of Peter charming the snakes and was looking at it fixedly when he entered the room.

He stood in the doorway, pulling off his impressive-looking fur-backed driving gauntlets and his eyes fairly popped when they lighted on me. Then he saw the photograph and I knew him at last for the murderer he was.

.   .   .   .   .   .

I closed the album and Peter, watching for my reaction, said carelessly, "I don't suppose you found anything interesting in that."

"Oh, I don't know," I said, "other people's family albums are sometimes quite—illuminating. Your sister's been showing me the cottage."

"Thoughtful of her."

"Yes. She even showed me the tree you used to leave and re-enter your bedroom by. I don't suppose you've had any cause to use that route since boyhood—or have you?"

He knew then that I knew and his face darkened. "My dear sister," he said, as if to himself. "My dear blundering sister." Rage made his hands shake and then he caught sight of Leslie Turner's play and snatched it up. "What's this?" he asked. "*False World, Farewell*—oh, some of Turner's tripe!"

"It isn't tripe," protested Diana.

"Oh yes it is—beastly tripe. I had a look at it yesterday and it ought to be burned. In fact, I'll do my duty to humanity and burn it now." Before we could stop him, he had flung the typescript into the fire and left the room.

With a cry of distress, Diana rushed to the fire-place, raked the burning play on to the hearth and began to beat ineffectively at the flames with her bare hands. I snatched up a cushion, placed it firmly on top of the play and in a few seconds the flames were suffocated.

"Better a scorched cushion than your hands," I said. "Are you burned?"

Diana looked at her hands. "I don't think so; you were so quick." I picked up the blackened typescript. Most of it was still readable but it would need to be retyped and Diana took it from me with a murmur of gratitude. "There's a streak of cruelty in Peter that comes out when he's angry," she said, "though what he's got to be angry about I've no idea. He must have had an unsuccessful day."

"I wouldn't be at all surprised," I commented, remembering Woodman's Point.

I got away soon afterwards, Diana being too much upset over the damaged typescript to resent my departure. There was no sign of Peter Randall but he was probably skulking somewhere in the cottage. While Diana had been occupied with the play I whipped the snake photograph out of the album and I had it now in the inside pocket of my jacket. It was a link in the chain of evidence against Peter that I now hoped to forge.

I was pretty certain that Ruth would be safe now so long as I was alive. I hadn't enough on Peter yet to bring about his arrest but if anything should happen to Ruth I had enough to put the police on the right track. Peter knew that perfectly well and until I was out of the way he would not dare to stage another accident. It meant, of course, that I was next on the spot but I was prepared for that.

I garaged the Bentley and entered the hotel. The bar had just opened and Molly Piggott was behind the counter. I ordered a drink and asked casually how she had spent the day.

"I went to the pictures this afternoon," she informed me.

"Alone?"

"No, with two girl friends."

"What time did you go?"

"About two."

I sipped my drink and pondered. Molly would not have given that account of her movements had it not been true. It would have been too easy to check so she couldn't have been at Woodman's Point that afternoon.

"Where were you last Monday evening between eight and nine?" I asked.

"Here," said Molly, looking surprised.

That would be easy to check, too, I thought and mentally scored Molly off the list of suspects. Peter was in it alone, then, for Diana had noticed nothing significant in the snake photograph and had not hesitated to refer to the tree growing close to his bedroom window. Obviously she was in complete ignorance of what he had been up to and Turner was out of it, too, because he could not have absented himself from his class examinations and besides, he had an alibi for Tuesday night. Henry Crane I had already eliminated and Randall was the only other possibility. Life was not like a detective story, I thought, where the murderer always turned out to be the most unlikely person. Randall had been the most obvious suspect from the start.

"Molly," I said, "how much are you in love with Peter Randall?"

"You're in a very nosy mood tonight, I must say."

"I've a reason for asking." I told her about the Play incident. "Take my advice and chuck him, Molly. A man with a vicious streak like that would never make you happy. Social advancement can be too dearly bought, you know."

Molly nodded. She was a sensible girl and I could see that my words had given her to think. "I shouldn't be surprised if you were right," she said. "There are times when I'm not too sure about Master Peter. He's got a mean streak sure enough."

Someone slapped me on the back and Leslie Turner slid on to the next stool. "Buy me a drink," he demanded. "I've had a foul day with a class of illiterate young fiends the devil himself couldn't educate."

"Where were you on Monday evening between eight and nine?"

"Why?"

"If you can tell me, I'll buy you a drink."

"I was here. On this very stool. Wasn't I, Molly?"

"You're always here. If it wasn't bad for business I'd say you drink too much."

"Anyone else with you?" I asked.

"Patrick Conway, the lawyer, and a couple of other chaps."

I bought Turner his drink, excused myself and, after a meal in the almost empty dining-room, retired to my bedroom and locked the door. Then I sat down and wrote out an account of the case against Peter Randall.

I began with Johnny King. As I saw it, Peter had met Johnny at the Mermaid Club and had hired him to murder Ruth for a share of her estate. Johnny was to make her acquaintance, gain her confidence and then get rid of her, probably in such a way as to suggest an accident, but when Johnny did meet Ruth, he double-crossed Peter. Why kill her for a share of her estate when by marrying her first he could grab the lot?

That was the way Johnny must have reasoned and it had led to his own death. Peter, realizing that Johnny was playing him false, tried himself to stage an accident but, owing to my presence on Shellbridge Pier, the attempt had failed. He must have written the anonymous note and while Diana and the housekeeper believed him sleeping off his cold in bed, he had left his bedroom by his boyhood route and gone to wait for Ruth behind the café on the pier. Ruth had accused Johnny of trying to drown her and next afternoon, while Peter was waiting for Ruth in her drawing-room, he had seen Johnny admiring the new Bentley. No doubt high words had followed and Peter had stabbed Johnny with the paper-knife, bundled him into the boot and slunk off through the fog.

When Blake drove the Bentley to the Ocean Hotel, Peter must have followed in his car to see what would happen. Parked across the road, he had seen me discover the body, followed me when I drove off, watched me bury Johnny and had then dug him out, placed him in his own car and transferred him back to the boot of the Bentley at a suitable opportunity.

Later, he must have watched Ruth and me set out to re-inter Johnny, taken Ruth's car and driven to Johnny's flat to destroy any evidence that might connect him with Johnny and, when we disturbed him there, he had fled via the fire-escape.

By this time he must have been well aware that I knew an attempt had been made on Ruth's life and therefore I would have to go before he could risk a second attempt. As Convenor of the Zoo Committee, he was bound to know of the impending arrival of the fer-de-lance and, as the snapshot witnessed, he had a way with snakes. The fer-de-lance, however, had failed him.

He had known of our visit to Woodman's Point and there he had come within an inch of bringing off a perfect double murder.

Had it come off, it was exceedingly probable that McKellar, suspecting us of Johnny's murder, would have put our deaths down to a suicide pact because we knew he was hard on our heels. Now I had made Peter aware of the fact that I suspected him and the question was, what would he do next?

When I finished the statement, I put it along with the snake photograph, into an envelope on which I wrote, 'To be handed to the police in the event of my death'. Then I enclosed the packet in a second envelope bearing my name and had the manager place it in the hotel safe. I had omitted any reference to Johnny having been in the Bentley and to our having buried him in the sand. The police must never know that Ruth had any part in that but there was enough in the statement to set them on to Master Peter if he should get me before I could get him. For I was under no illusions. From now on it was Peter's life or mine.

I went early to bed with the door locked, window secured and my gun under my pillow and for a long time I lay listening in the darkness, starting at every creak. There was still something at the back of my mind, some unexplained incident that worried me and once more I strove to recall every detail of the past five days. I had overlooked something that might be the key to Peter's guilt but when, at last, I drifted into sleep, no bell had rung.

It was ten next morning before I was down for breakfast and as I poked without appetite at a blackened sausage, Detective-Inspector McKellar arrived, exuding gloom. "Hallo, Inspector," I greeted. "Had your breakfast?"

McKellar looked pointedly at the clock. "Naturally," he growled. He was the type of man who started work at the crack of dawn and was proud of it. "When ye paid your famous visit to the Mermaid Club, did ye meet Tyler Morgan?" he shot at me.

I looked up into two very cold, probing grey eyes.

"Suppose I did," I said, "what about it?"

"He was found on the beach this morning—strangled."

I kept my face straight although my mind was racing. This explained Tyler's recent inactivity and I had no doubt that Peter had killed him. Tyler must have come to Shellbridge partly to blackmail Ruth and partly to blackmail Peter, for he must have known of Peter's connection with Johnny and worked out the significance of their relationship. Well, he seemed to have paid for his greed.

"A lonely spot in which to meet one's end," I commented.

"He wasn't so lonely," said McKellar. "There was another body nearby but it had been in the water and there was no evidence of foul play." So the sea had had enough of Joe, I thought. This could be the way out for me if I could blame Joe's death on Tyler.

"Perhaps he was an acquaintance of Morgan's who strangled him in a quarrel and drowned himself out of remorse."

"Did I say it was a man?"

"A natural assumption on my part," I said. "I didn't think it was a mermaid."

"Aye, just so. If ye'll take my advice ye'll keep away from the Mermaid Club in future."

"I intend to. I'm not partial to mermaids, they're so handicapped. Why do I have to hear the sad story of Tyler Morgan?"

"There's been too many queer happenings since ye came to Shellbridge."

"I'll tell you this, Inspector, there would have been a particularly nasty murder if I hadn't come to Shellbridge."

"What d'ye mean by that?"

"Soon I hope to tell you," I said, "but meantime I lack concrete evidence. Had that paper-knife analysed yet?"

"I'm just waiting for the report." The inspector's tone had a certain grisly relish and I knew that the scientific backroom boys of Scotland Yard would probably find traces of blood. I also knew that if McKellar started questioning people, Molly Piggott would reveal I'd had a fight with Tyler Morgan in the bar. Time was running out and I had accomplished nothing yet.

"If you're still looking for a murderer," I said, "try Peter Randall. Johnny King stood between him and Miss Mannering's money."

"So did Miss Mannering."

"She might not have stood long," I smiled at him. "Use your brains, Inspector. I've given you a straight tip. Go to work on it."

"The activities of Mr. Randall and the other Shellbridge

socialites are not being forgotten," promised McKellar. I met his gaze again and a queer feeling came over me that we understood each other, that McKellar knew very well what he was doing. He had integrity and he had brains. He wasn't out simply to make a case against someone. He was after the real criminal or nobody, and nothing would induce him to rest until he had ferreted out the truth. He would ferret it out too, for I could feel the power radiating from him. It was the power of genius.

"Inspector," I said, "in case anything happens to me, may I place on record now my very great admiration for Scotland Yard?"

He looked at me in silence, his eyes like grey pebbles, then, "Aye, just so," he said, and walked away.

I drove to my office. The fog had vanished overnight, the air was mild and a pale sun played hide and seek among grey clouds. Shellbridge had come to life, the pavements were thronged with shoppers, cars and lorries choked the main street and, out at sea, the smoke from half a dozen trawlers stained the skyline.

The municipal offices had been built with an eye to staff extension and Wilmot had given me two rooms on the second floor of a disused wing. As I passed along the corridor I noticed that the door nearest the staircase stood ajar but thought nothing of it.

Alone in my room I tried to study a street plan of the town but could not concentrate and fell to doodling on my blotting-pad. I had drawn Ruth's face three times before I realized the turn my thoughts had taken and, yielding to impulse, rang her up on the telephone.

When I heard her voice my heart began to beat at racing speed. "Hallo," I said. "Will you marry me?"

"No, Philip."

"Why not?"

"Because you don't want people to say, 'He married money'. You want to be known as 'Philip Latimer, the famous Architect', not just 'Ruth Mannering's husband'."

"Not after Woodman's Point," I said. "My pride's in the dust, Ruth. I want you unconditionally."

"Do you really?"

"There's nothing would give me greater happiness than to be known as Ruth Mannering's husband."

"If the money worries you," said Ruth, "I was thinking of putting part of it into a Trust Fund to help finance the replanning of Shellbridge."

"It doesn't worry me. The only thing that worries me is the fear that you might refuse me."

"You could be a trustee."

"I love you, so stop teasing. I want to marry you and Romney and two million pounds and live happily ever after."

"Then you'd better come round and ask me properly. I won't be proposed to over the telephone."

"I'm on my way."

"I'll be waiting, and Philip——"

"Yes?"

Her voice was so low I could scarcely hear it. "I love you terribly."

I started to whistle as I closed the office door and my foot-steps echoed along the empty corridor, keeping time to the whistling. I had never known such a feeling of happiness, such breathless elation. I was in love for the first time in my life and I felt as irresponsible as a schoolboy off for the holidays. I had no suspicion of danger, no thought of a possible ambush.

At the far end of the corridor a ray of sunlight struck down through the round window that illumined the staircase and a momentary irritation marred my blissful dreaming. I can never refrain from looking at a building with an architect's eye and the round window seemed quite out of place. It should have been oblong, in keeping with the other windows and there was some-thing about the staircase that did not seem right either. It curved too sharply, I thought, and the iron, Adam-style balustrade did not blend with the functional simplicity of a modern office building.

I paused at the top of the staircase and looked down over the balustrade to the terrazzo flooring two storeys below. Yes, the staircase did curve much too sharply, making the well or airspace between too narrow. It was too late to do anything about it now, however, and I was about to turn and descend the stairs when, without warning, two hands grasped my ankles from behind and pulled.

I grabbed wildly at the balustrade but, leaning over as I was, I hadn't the ghost of a chance and the next second I was hurtling head downwards into the airspace. The terrazzo floor seemed to leap towards me and if the architect had designed the staircase properly nothing could have saved me from instant death.

As it was, however, I crashed against the balustrade of the opposite curve, made a frenzied snatch and just managed to get one hand round an iron upright. I could not hold on, however, the momentum of my fall tore my grip away but at least my fall was broken and instead of pitching on my head, I landed heavily on my left shoulder. I heard a bone snap like a stick, a wave of pain swept over me, footsteps clattered down the stairs, ran past me and away and blackness closed over my head like deep waters.

Slowly the waters parted, the blackness receded. I was lying on my left side, my face pressed against cold stone and, when I tried to move, a sudden thunderclap of pain made me cry out. Then I rolled over on to my back and lay looking up at the distant ceiling. I could see the balustrade at the top of the staircase and all at once memory flooded back. I remembered the shock of the hands on my ankles, the terror of the fall, the echo of guilty footsteps running frantically away. In my exaltation over Ruth I had forgotten Peter Randall.

He must have been lurking in the room next the staircase, waiting his opportunity and I had provided him with the finest opportunity a murderer could have.

I sat up, sweating with pain. My collar-bone was broken and at least one rib. It was agony to breathe and my head must have had a knock too, for blood was trickling down my left cheek. I called out but there was no one to hear and then, slowly and painfully, I struggled to my feet.

My whole body must be a mass of bruises and a stab of pain went like fire up my left leg as I put my foot to the ground. The ankle wasn't broken, however, and I was able to walk, after a fashion. I felt the weight of the gun in my right-hand jacket pocket and was glad I hadn't fallen on that side. Groaning at every step, my left arm hanging uselessly at my side, I staggered out to the courtyard. The Bentley was parked nearby and, biting my lips at the pain, I limped towards it. I had to get to Ruth quickly in case Randall had some devilish plan ready to put into effect.

As I reached the Bentley I saw Molly Piggott approaching and when she saw me she quickened her step. "Mr. Latimer! What's happened? Oh, you poor thing!"

"I've had a fall," I explained. "Help me into my car, Molly, and I'll be all right."

She opened the door for me and I collapsed in the driver's seat. "Stay right there," urged Molly, "I was just going to pay Dad's rates and I'll ask the Collector's Office to phone for a doctor."

"I don't want a doctor," I said. "I can drive as far as the hotel." I looked into Molly's troubled, compassionate eyes and all at once, something snapped into place in my mind. I knew now what that unexplained incident was, the incident I had been striving to recall since Woodman's Point. Perhaps the fall had shaken up my brains.

"Molly," I said, "that night I had the fight with Tyler Morgan, you addressed him as Mr. Morgan."

"Well, that's his name, isn't it?"

"Yes, but the point is, Molly, he'd only just come to Shellbridge, so *how did you know it was his name?*"

"I'd met him before at that club he owns in London, the Mermaid Club."

"Who took you to the Mermaid Club?"

"Peter Randall. He's a member. Why——?"

"Never mind," I said. "I must go." So I could prove now that Randall was a member of the Mermaid Club, that he could have met Johnny there. It was the last link.

As I could not use my left hand, I had to let go the wheel to move the gear lever with my right but the Bentley kept reasonably straight while I did so and I managed without much difficulty. The car was exceedingly light to steer and once I had turned off the main street there was no traffic to speak of.

I pulled up at the front of Ruth's house and extricated myself slowly and painfully from the driving-seat. Then I stood for a moment, swaying with weakness. The house seemed to shimmer like a reflection of a house in water and then I heard Ruth playing the piano in her drawing-room. She was playing Mozart's 'C Minor Concerto'—I recognized the dark splendour of the opening movement—and I listened with a surge of relief. She was still safe then. Safe!

The music stopped. Abruptly. In the middle of a bar.

I don't know how I reached the french window at the back but I made it somehow and I don't remember drawing my gun but it was in my hand and the safety-catch was off. The window stood open and Ruth was facing Peter Randall in the middle of the room.

She must have opened the window at his knock for she would not suspect him of evil intentions, there in her own house with Romney in the kitchen. I took a halting step forward, my finger tightening on the trigger and then I heard Randall say, "Leslie's got a new proposition about his Play."

So his visit was an innocent one, after all. I paused outside the window and lowered my gun.

"I've already told Diana I wanted nothing to do with the Play," protested Ruth.

"But listen, Ruth," Peter's voice was persuasive, "Leslie says that if you go over the passages you don't like and mark them, he'll tone them down or cut them out altogether and he's willing to put your name to the play as part author."

"I don't want my name associated with it."

"But your name would be a box-office draw in itself. It would fill the theatre."

"Only on the first night."

"And it's got a smashing title, too, *False World, Farewell* by Ruth Mannering and Leslie Turner. Think how well it would look on the bills. Try it, Ruth. Write it down and see how it looks."

I saw him take a sheet of note-paper from a rack on the desk, lay it flat on the blotting-pad and motion Ruth to sit down. She shrugged her shoulders but obeyed. There was something compelling in his manner. He had a way with people as well as snakes.

"Write the title," he urged, and as Ruth complied, he said, "now write beneath it, Ruth Mannering and Leslie Turner."

"It won't do you any good. I'm not backing the Play."

"Write it, anyway. I bet anything you'll like the look of it."

Ruth began to write and Peter placed his left hand on her shoulder. "Stop there a moment," he said. "Doesn't it look marvellous with just your name alone? I might persuade Leslie to let you appear as sole author."

"It's no use," said Ruth. "I'm not interested. I'd better add the word 'by' hadn't I?" That vanity of hers!

"Just a second before you do that." Peter's right hand moved with the speed of a striking snake and at the same instant I barged into the room and shot him through the head.

Ruth screamed as he fell, then my right arm was round her and her head was on my shoulder. Romney came running from the kitchen and stood staring down at the body. "Steady, darling," I said. "It's all right. Look at his right hand."

Ruth looked. "There's a gun in it."

"Yes," I said grimly. "There's a gun in it. Now look at what he made you write, 'False World, Farewell. Ruth Mannering.' If you'd been found dead with a gun in your hand and that note in front of you, what would the police have thought?"

"A suicide note!"

"Yes, suicide because you had lost your fiancé or because you had killed him. Either motive would do. The cunning swine!"

"Philip, you're hurt! What——?"

"More of Randall's cunning but it didn't come off." I looked at Romney. "Better get the police and a doctor."

"Bit late for a doctor," said Romney. "He's had it all right."

"The doctor's for me, you fool."

"Very good, sir," said Romney.

"You're very respectful all of a sudden."

"If we're going to have you in the family, I'll have to mind me p's and q's."

Romney went out and I sank wearily into a chair. "McKellar will see I'm all right," I said. "He's a good man, that. I told him enough to put him on the track, but I think he had his suspicions of Peter too and it won't come out now about our burying Johnny."

"Philip, another second and I'd have been——"

"Don't think about that," I said. "We have to think of the future now. The danger's past, Ruth. We're safe, we have each other and what else matters?"

She bent to kiss me and in a silence that held nothing of fear we awaited the police.

THE END